T0318609

"Look at me, Lily."

Slowly, she raised her gaze to his, pausing first at his lush mouth, at lips separated to accommodate quickened breathing. Then her gaze reached his eyes, and she saw those banked embers ready to ignite.

"Have you ever been *anyone's* wife?"

The low rumble of his words pulsed in her breasts, then rode low in her belly. Good Lord, but this man did scandalous things to her insides, things she could not put a name to. Longing and desire, and a deep need for him rolled through her like a sudden storm. She shook her head. "No."

In the brief silence that followed, nothing existed but a world about to implode. His chest shuddered, and he released a soft groan as he lowered his mouth.

His lips brushed lightly over hers, and a hot shiver ran through her. "More," she whispered when he paused. "I want more."

He pulled his head back for a moment, his blue eyes smoldering a dark, liquid cobalt. "Oh, Lily, what you do to me."

Also by Kathleen Bittner Roth

Celine
Alanna
Josette
Felice

Lily

Kathleen Bittner Roth

Zebra Books
Kensington Publishing Corp.
www.kensingtonbooks.com

ZEBRA BOOKS are published by

Kensington Publishing Corp.
119 West 40th Street
New York, NY 10018

All Kensington titles, imprints, and distributed lines are available at special quantity discounts for bulk purchases for sales promotion, premiums, fund-raising, educational, or institutional use.

Special book excerpts or customized printings can also be created to fit specific needs. For details, write or phone the office of the Kensington Sales Manager: Kensington Publishing Corp., 119 West 40th Street, New York, NY 10018. Attn. Sales Department. Phone: 1-800-221-2647.

Zebra and the Zebra logo Reg. U.S. Pat. & TM Off.

First Electronic Edition: July 2021
eISBN-13: 978-1-4201-4211-2
eISBN-10: 1-4201-4211-9

First Print Edition: July 2021
ISBN-13: 978-1-4201-5443-6
ISBN-10: 1-4201-5443-5

Printed in the United States of America

To my niece, Dr. Christina Schwindt

Your dedication to your patients, and to the practice of allergy and immunology, makes you the busiest person I know, yet you never fail to take time to read my stories and then sing my praises to the Heavens.

Thank you for being you.

Acknowledgments

A bit of history as to how the Cajuns of southeastern Louisiana came to exist: In 1755, over 18,000 French-speaking Acadians were expelled from their Canadian homeland by British troops for refusing to swear unconditional allegiance to the British Crown. Thousands were killed, innumerable families were torn apart, their property plundered. While a great many of the Acadians were relocated to British colonies, some of them sought refuge in what was then the French colony of Louisiana. These displaced people became the ancestors of our modern-day Cajuns. I am honored to write stories about an independent and proud people with their own French dialect, amazing food, and unique culture.

Although the term Cajun was not formally recognized until 1868, the word had been tossed about for years in various forms by those who either kept shortening the word Acadian or mispronounced it. Since *Lily* is a novel, I've taken the liberty of moving the usage of the word Cajun to 1859, the time period of my story. For the French spoken in my story, I used both a Cajun dictionary, and a bilingual French-Canadian friend as reference, which is why many of the words vary from the formal French language taught in schools.

Many thanks to my wonderful and talented critique partners Tara Kingston, Barbara Bettis, Tess St. John and Averil Reisman. I couldn't ask for keener eyes. Without a doubt, your catches and suggestions made this story so much better.

To the Kensington crew working diligently behind the scenes, you are all beyond wonderful. To my editor, Alicia Condon, there is an inherent grace about you that elevates how I perceive myself as a writer. I thank you for believing in me.

To my agent, Jill Marsal, you've never failed to respond to any questions I might have and offer solutions in a timely manner, despite the huge time difference in our locales.

And thank you, dear reader, for choosing to read my stories. I love hearing from readers. Authors appreciate and need reviews so if you'd care to leave one, I'd be ever so grateful. You can contact me on Facebook, Goodreads, Twitter, or through my website at www.kathleenbittnerroth.com.

Chapter One

"Like hell we'll be taking on passengers!" Clad in nothing but a pair of low-hanging linen trousers, Bastien Thibodeaux barreled down the gangplank, bare feet slapping wood, sweat beading his arms and chest. He landed on the shipping company's dock with such force it trembled. "In case you failed to notice, Monsieur Fellowes, my crew and I are loading bananas and coconuts, not people."

Fellowes, the Englishman he'd hired to replace him as manager of the shipping company, stood before Bastien, unruffled. "A mere two persons—an English gentleman and his wife."

Bastien shoved a hand through his hair and huffed. "Why did you not consult me before booking their passage, *s'il vous plaît?*"

Fellowes shrugged. "Mr. Talbot has urgent business in New Orleans and is eager to be on his way. They arrived from England late yesterday."

Bastien shot Fellowes a hard glare. "They are traveling from England to N'awlins via Jamaica? *Vous n'avez pas trouvé inhabituel cet itinéraire?*"

"Indeed, I did find the route unusual, so naturally, I inquired. According to Talbot, the crucial timing of his aforesaid business matter caused him to take passage on the first available ship. And in case *you* haven't noticed, Mr. Thibodeaux, you are near to shouting. And once again, you've slipped into that lazy Cajun parlance of yours, which I find most irritating."

Bastien cursed under his breath. "You do not have my permission to use the word Cajun, *monsieur britannique.* To you, I speak *français acadien.*"

His accent grew thicker with each degree of irritation. He knew it. He didn't care. "As if I haven't had a bellyful of those *hautains* Englishmen lording it over everything and everyone on this damn island…not you, Fellowes. You be the only decent Brit I've dealt with my five months here."

A corner of Fellowes's mouth twitched. "Mayhap that's because you're the one who hired me?"

"Humph." Despite the man's glib tongue, employing Fellowes had been a brilliant move. Intelligent and well-bred, he interacted easily with the high and mighty controlling the island. Come the morrow, Bastien would sail back to New Orleans and leave the management of the Andrews Shipping Company's Caribbean offices in good hands.

"You know the only reason I sought to captain the *Aria* back home was for the sheer pleasure of seeing the expression on my brother's face when I sail this fine vessel into port. I am of no mind to take on the added responsibility of passengers. Especially a couple of *rigide* Britishers expecting to be catered to. You should've consulted me, damn it."

"And have you turn them down?" Unperturbed, Fellowes stood his ground. "Talbot also mentioned he's an old school chum of the man who founded this shipping company."

"A schoolmate of Monsieur Justin Andrews? *Mon Dieu.* Andrews departed England some forty years ago. How damn old you figure this Talbot to be?"

"Late sixties, perhaps."

Bastien moved to the edge of the dock and peered into turquoise waters so clear, it seemed as if he could reach out and touch the white sandy bottom. A sea bottom that actually lay some thirty feet below the surface. A quick dip would be just the thing to cool off both body and temper. He reached for the top button of his trousers. A school of barracuda, their silver backs flashing in the sun, darted out from beneath the dock. Never mind. He'd take his final swim later, in the isolated cove he favored.

He whistled to his assistant, who was standing near the *Aria*'s stern. At the signal to join him, Henri scampered off the ship, raven hair tangling in the breeze, a wide grin splitting his face. Son of Bastien's no-good cousin, Henri had been the errand boy for their N'awlins shipping offices until this trip. Barely sixteen, he'd taken to seafaring life as if he'd been born a sailor. "You looking forward to heading home?"

"*Oui*," Henri replied. "I had me a mighty good time here, but I have a powerful yearning for some of Maman's filé gumbo, don'cha know."

Bastien chuckled.

Fellowes cleared his throat. "There's something else you should be made aware of before your departure."

Bastien let go a litany of Cajun curses. "What the devil now?"

"Mr. Talbot wishes to board the *Aria* later this evening. Preferably after midnight."

The hair on the back of Bastien's neck stood on end. "Why the odd hour?"

"The gentleman indicated his wife has been ill and has a sensitivity to the sun—"

"*Mon Dieu!* I will not risk bringing a disease-ridden passenger on board." Fellowes shook his head. "Talbot says it's her weak heart, not a sickness."

Some intuitive sense prickled Bastien's gut. "Did you check his papers? Make sure the man is who he says he is?"

"But of course, thorough man that I am."

When Fellowes grew silent, Bastien settled another hard scowl on him. "What you be leaving out?"

"He would like separate lodgings for Mrs. Talbot and him."

"*Sacre bleu.* Next you'll be telling me to bunk with the crew because he wishes the captain's quarters for himself."

The corners of Fellowes's mouth turned up. "Can I offer you a brandy to celebrate your last night here?"

Bastien snorted. "You mean from my own supply?"

Fellowes glanced over Bastien's shoulder. "Looks like your crew's finished loading the fruit. Come, join me. A few good swallows of your fine liquor and you'll get a better night's sleep."

"*Non.* I shall meet with the Talbots before taking to my bed. If it's her heart and nothing infectious, then I will allow them to board. But only because he claims to know the company owner. As it is, I've a mind to set sail early in hopes of leaving them behind."

Fellowes cocked a brow. "You'd leave behind an ill woman? *Tsks tsk, tsk.* I got the impression Talbot doesn't care for Jamaica any more than you do. The heat and all, he said."

"What the devil does he think the weather in N'awlins be like, Northern England?" Bastien turned to leave, then paused to glance over his shoulder at Fellowes. "If I agree to the Talbots' taking passage, then you'd better have a personal maid lined up for the lady. One who speaks English and is willing to travel to N'awlins and back."

Fellowes folded his arms over his chest and smirked. "Already seen to."

"Humph. Come along, Henri. Time for our last swim in this beautiful water since there won't be any bayou swimming back home. Not unless you want those gators making a meal of you." Bastien strolled into the shipping office, donned his shirt, snatched up his shoes, and with Henri by his side, headed for the private beach he preferred.

As they made their way through town in silence, thoughts of Louisiana occupied Bastien's mind. He'd be glad to get back to N'awlins. Five months on this island with the British and their rigid rule over Jamaica had been about four months and one day too long. When he'd offered to act as temporary manager for the island offices, he'd not given thought to how controlling the British might be, or how much he would resent their self-important hierarchy. One would never know slavery had been abolished here years ago, seeing the way those louts treated hired hands.

Bastien and Henri reached the isolated cove with its white sand backed by a stand of palm trees and waist-high ferns. While Henri stripped and hurried into the water, Bastien paused to watch the sun dip to the horizon, sending swaths of orange and pink flying across the waters. His breath caught at the splendor of it all. Despite his constant clashing with those in authority, the beauty of this lush island had turned out to be a soothing tonic for Bastien's thirsty soul. But now, it was more than time to head home.

* * * *

With every bump and rattle of the carriage, pain shot through Lily's head. Despite her efforts to control herself, she moaned aloud.

"Hold steady, dear. We're nearly there. Then all you need do is manage the few steps from the carriage into the shipping company's office while the ship's captain makes a few inquiries as to your health."

"The captain...I...I cannot," Lily managed, barely above a whisper.

"You can, and you must. Soon, you'll be aboard ship and in your own stateroom. Then you can take to your bed for the duration."

It took all the energy she possessed to form words. "Oh, Uncle, I simply do not have the strength."

The arm he held around her shoulders tightened. "Listen carefully to me, Lily. No longer can you call me uncle. What is my new name? Tell me who I am."

All she could manage was a sigh.

"Oh, this simply will not do." He gave her shoulders a shake. "Stay awake, Lily. You must forget your pet name for me. Who am I now? What is my new name?"

At her godfather's words, she sighed. She couldn't think. "Yes...no... Charles..."

"Bloody hell," he muttered. "My name is now Percival Talbot. You must never again speak my given name."

His words echoed through her head in a jumble. No matter how hard she tried, she could not string them together to make any sense.

"Do you hear me?" He shook her again. "Lily, buck up. Your very life could depend on this short interview with the captain."

"Can't think. I...I'll remember when the time comes." She collapsed into the crook of her beloved godfather's arm, wanting desperately to drift away, to not have to think. "Why can we not go to our staterooms direct?"

"The captain is concerned you might have an infectious disease. He insists on examining you before he'll grant us leave to board ship. I told Mr. Fellowes it was your heart making you weak, not some disease that would be of concern to others. Of all the dratted luck. Fellowes claims this Captain Thibodeaux is some kind of Cajun healer out of a bayou in New Orleans. You *must* make it to the shipping office and cooperate, Lily."

The carriage pulled to a stop. One side dipped as the driver scrambled off his perch. Lily was able to make out glimpses of a ship afloat in the harbor. Her blurred vision made it look as though the vessel was wrapped in a gossamer mist. The thought of sailing on turbulent waters yet again sent a wave of nausea washing through her.

The door to the carriage opened and a footman lowered the steps. Her godfather slipped out ahead of her. Leaning back inside, he fitted the hood of her cape over her head, obscuring her face within its folds. Straightening her spine, and with all the strength she could muster, she stepped from the vehicle and into her godfather's arms.

"Good girl," he whispered. As they moved toward the shipping office, he raised his voice. "Shall we, my dear?"

With gas lanterns lighting the way, she kept her head lowered, her hazy vision focused on the wooden planks beneath her feet lest she stumble. As she stepped inside the office, her befogged gaze landed on what appeared to be large, booted feet, then traveled upward, past the tops of leather boots to long legs clad in tight breeches. And from what little she could make out, a trim belly and broad shoulders.

"*Bonsoir*," came a deep and resonant voice.

She jolted. The captain was French? Weren't they supposed to be going to America? Confusion engulfed her once again.

"And a good evening to you, as well, Captain Thibodeaux," her godfather replied.

Heart pounding, Lily kept her head bowed. She'd let Uncle...no...she must forever wipe that word from her mind. In vain, she tried to remember to call him...to call him...what? She'd simply call him husband until—or if—her mental faculties ever fully returned.

"If you wish to make this journey with us, I must insist on examining your wife," said the captain.

Was he truly a Frenchman? What an odd accent. Nonetheless, she found his deep voice with its melodic cadence rather soothing.

The sound of a chair scraping across the wooden floor caught her attention. And then, thank heavens, someone eased her onto its hard seat. Conversation between this captain and her…her husband…ensued, but the words escaped her muddled mind. Someone slid back the hood of her cape, then fingers, gentle but firm, touched beneath her chin, nudging it upward. Eyes closed, she drifted off into sweet oblivion.

"Madame Talbot," came the same lyrical voice. A feathering of breath landed upon her lips. "Open your eyes, *s'il vous plaît.*"

Startled out of her reverie, she did as she was told and found herself staring into the captain's face, fuzzy though it appeared.

"Tell me how well you can see. Can you make out my face?"

How did he know? Had he guessed it was not her heart distressing her? *Oh, dear.*

"A bit," she managed.

Were his eyes really so blue? Was he truly so handsome? Oh, what did she know when everything was such a blur? No man could be so striking. She was tired, so very tired. Her eyelids, excruciatingly heavy, refused to remain open. She held out her gloved hand, desperate to find her godfather's…no…her husband's. She felt his steady grip and relaxed. She needed a moment, just a moment to rest. Leaning her head on his shoulder, her nose and mouth settled against his throat. So comforting. So very comforting.

You smell so good, she thought.

"*Merci.*"

That magical, deep voice rumbled through her. She sat up straight. Had it not been her godfather's hand she'd clutched? His shoulder she'd leaned on? Had she actually spoken aloud? No, she couldn't have. Hallucinating again. She'd only imagined he'd spoken. She went back to leaning on her godfather's shoulder.

"Madame Talbot," came the deep voice.

Fingers, firm but ever so tender, slipped under her chin again and lifted her head away from…oh, Lord, it had been the captain's shoulder she'd leaned into. "Please," she said. "I must rest. It's my heart…"

"Look at me." He tilted her head upward. "I need you to open your eyes one more time. Henri, hold the lantern closer."

She flinched and used her hand to shield her eyes from the painful light.

"Take a breath and exhale, madame, then tell me your name."

She breathed out as he'd instructed. Had he actually sniffed the air? "My name's Lily."

"Your full name."

"She's my wife, Mrs. Percival—"

"I asked her, monsieur." Irritation clouded the captain's words. "Madame, give me your full name, *s'il vous plaît*."

If I please to give you my full name? No, I do not care to please anyone, for nothing gives me pleasure. She sifted through the cobwebs in her mind, found the name in a dusty corner. "Lily…Mrs. Percival Talbot."

"How old are you, Madame Talbot?" While he spoke with that same lyrical accent, his tone had grown stern.

"Five and twenty. What does my age matter?"

"Are you here of your own volition? Has your husband forced you into taking this journey?"

"Now see here," Percival put in.

Panic flooded her being. Her free hand flailed in the air, this time to her left, seeking her godfather's. "Oh, please, do not leave me…Percy."

He grabbed hold of her hand. She clung to the familiar grip, knew it was his hand she held this time around. "He takes care of my every need, sir. Please do not think ill of him." A sob left her throat. "He is all I have in the world."

She felt the pressure of her godfather's hand, a signal to stop talking. *Don't over speak*, he'd warned her. People get suspicious when one talks too much.

The captain grew silent for a long while. At least it seemed a long while, for her mind floated here and there.

"Madame, do you think you have strength enough to make your way onto the ship?"

She managed a nod.

He was silent for another long while. Or maybe not so long. If only time wouldn't escape her so.

"Henri, see to fetching as many oysters as you can to bring aboard before we sail. And pineapples. She'll need pineapples, and ripe bananas. Not the green ones we've stowed away."

"*Oui*, Captain."

Oui? Yes? And the captain pronounces the name *On-ree?* So, this person is French, as well. Fatigue stole what little strength she had left. Oh, she'd think about everything later. The fog took over her brain as sleep overwhelmed her. For the life of her, she couldn't remember where she was or where they were headed, only that she desperately needed a bed.

Strong but exceedingly tender fingers curled beneath her chin once more. With a slight nudge, he raised her head. "Your lips, they are dry and split, madame. With your permission, I would like to tend to them."

"Yes, of course," she managed.

"Henri, open my bag and retrieve the balm I use on cracked lips."

"*Oui.*"

She caught the scent of something sweet yet a little pungent. Then a tender, soothing touch slid across her mouth before thought escaped her altogether.

* * * *

Bastien studied a pale face with cheeks far too rosy and pupils so dilated they obscured the color of her irises. Dull, flaxen-colored hair hung limp about her face and shoulders. More than likely, her locks had once been shiny and soft, framing a now-lifeless face that still held the remnants of remarkable beauty. The young woman was near to dying from the poisons coursing through her veins.

He stood, his thoughts running in circles. He considered the portly, balding man who called himself her husband. Despite his efforts to mask his panic, a muscle twitched in the corner of Talbot's left eye. Had he done this to his wife? Poisoned her? He would seem the likely culprit, yet somehow Bastien doubted it. And Bastien trusted his senses. After all, his very existence had once depended on his ability to read people. But whatever the hell was going on here, he wasn't about to take any chances.

"Monsieur Talbot, have you had occasion to carry your wife any distance of late? I see now that she is too weak to make it aboard ship on her own."

At being told they would be allowed passage, relief flooded the man's countenance. "Indeed. I can manage."

Like hell he could. "With your permission, I should like to be the one to transport her. Since we'd not planned on passengers, the boarding plank was meant for loading cargo only. It is narrow and has no side railings. Also, I know the location of her stateroom. I can take her there directly."

Talbot's head bobbed up and down and the muscle in his eye ceased to tick. "I would be most grateful, sir."

"How long has she been ill?"

"Going on four months, sir."

"Then we need to isolate her, monsieur."

"Why is that when it's her heart?"

"Because three weeks aboard ship from England is too damn long for her to still be carrying this much poison in her."

Talbot sucked in a breath. "I…I don't understand."

"I think you do understand *something*, Monsieur Talbot. If I am not mistaken, which I very much doubt that I am, she is full of both arsenic and belladonna. The last thing I needed was to be transporting passengers, let alone one near death. Under the circumstances, I am not about to refuse the two of you passage. Not when I have a duty to try to save her life. But I'll be damned if you, Monsieur Talbot, will have a moment's access to this woman while she is under my care. You'd better hope to hell she doesn't pass away aboard my ship."

As he carefully lifted Lily into his arms, Bastien gave a nod to Fellowes, who stepped from the corner of the room along with the woman he'd hired as Madame Talbot's personal maid. Speaking in his Cajun tongue, Bastien directed Henri to fetch one of the guards watching over the ship and have him escort Monsieur Talbot to his quarters. Once there, the man was to stand sentry in front of their passenger's locked stateroom door.

Monsieur Talbot was about to become Bastien's prisoner.

Chapter Two

Bastien stood on the aft deck of the fast-moving *Aria*, his eyes on the dazzling rays of the rising sun as they shot into the heavens from behind a low bank of fleecy white clouds.

Henri sidled up alongside him. "*Mon Dieu*, what a sight. We have us the promise of a fine day, *non*?"

"*Oui*," Bastien muttered and fell silent.

As the yellow globe slowly climbed above the clouds where it would spend the day shining down from a clear, blue sky, a subdued Henri spoke again. "Madame Talbot, does she still live?"

Bastien kept his gaze fixed on the horizon and the fast-disappearing clouds. "Last time I checked."

"You are much worried she will not survive, *non*?"

Bastien nodded. "I am trying to reckon some things which make no sense."

"My apologies for approaching you with such cheerfulness when you have much on your mind." Henri shifted from one foot to the other. "I do not wish to displease you."

Bastien stole a glance at Henri's crestfallen face. *Christ.* He cast an arm around his young cousin's shoulder, gave him a quick hug, then released him. "You're doing a fine job, don'cha know. I could not ask for more."

Satisfaction lit Henri's face, removing all signs of dejection. "I am mighty grateful you allowed me to sail with you on this trip."

"Your *maman*, she will be proud." Bastien looked him over, noted the sparse bristles dotting the boy's face, his unkempt hair. "You do not yet have the makings of a beard. You need to shave."

"I didn't have time."

Bastien cocked a brow at him.

Henri flushed. "*Pardonnez-moi.* You be far busier than I am, but you—"

"Found the time." Old memories niggled at Bastien. "You wish to become successful in the world of *les Américains, non*?"

"*Oui.* Like you and René."

"Then, like my brother and me, you must never forget your roots. You must never forget you were born and raised in a bayou shanty. People like us must try harder, work harder, and be smarter than the *Américains* we deal with."

He gave Henri another once-over. "And you must learn to be fastidious about your person. Wear only the finest clothing. Keep your hair clean and neat."

Henri glanced at the top of Bastien's head. "But I wish to wear mine long like René's, not as short as yours."

A corner of Bastien's mouth twitched. "*Mais oui*, it is your choice. However, my brother keeps his trimmed just so, not ragged like yours. Once we reach home, I shall take you to my tailor. Then to Monsieur Dupere's bookstore to collect the right books to give you a decent education."

Bastien removed his superfine jacket, his brocaded vest, and spotless cravat. Carefully folding them, he handed the stack to Henri. "Already the day grows warm. Take these to my stateroom, *s'il vous plaît,* then fetch Monsieur Talbot and bring him to me. Tell the sentry at his door to station himself at Madame Talbot's stateroom."

Henri nodded and trotted off, carefully balancing the clothing in his arms.

"Also bring my bag of medicines," Bastien called as he watched his young cousin hurry away. Wouldn't their relatives be surprised by Henri's transformation. Not only had he been quick to absorb all Bastien had taught him, but gone was the scrawny boy he'd hired five months ago. In his place stood a young man nearly as tall as Bastien's six feet. Rigorous physical labor had turned gangly awkwardness into solid muscularity. Still unaware of the imposing figure he now cut, Henri had yet to notice that the ladies eyed him with a barely disguised hunger—a hunger Bastien knew all too well.

But unlike naïve Henri, Bastien had never been innocent of much of anything. Though he'd risen above what he'd once been, his shadowy past haunted him to this day. Probably always would. At least his growing years hadn't been entirely wasted. Not only had he earned a certain status in the shipping world, he was also known as a fine *traiteur*—a healer—a talent passed down to him from both his *grand-mère* and *maman.* No matter that his mother was a voodoo priestess who walked a questionable line between the Light and darkness, when it came to treating the sick or wounded, she turned no one away. Nor did he. In the end, even she had to admit his gift for intuiting the needs of others transcended hers. Still, he would not be so arrogant as to treat Talbot's wife without seeking his mother's advice upon their arrival in N'awlins—providing his patient survived the journey.

"Ho, there!" Talbot called out as he hurried to Bastien's side. The man wore the same finely tailored clothing as when he'd boarded the *Aria* last night, only now he looked a rumpled mess. If he possessed a hairbrush, he damn well hadn't bothered using it. Clutching the brim of his brown bowler hat in both hands, he turned it in jerky little circles, his mouth taut, his face drained of color.

Bastien regarded the man while purposely taking his sweet time rolling the sleeves of his perfectly starched shirt—two equal and precise turns on each arm.

Talbot's spine straightened and he set his jaw in an obvious move to take command of his emotions. "How does my wife fare this fine morning?"

"Still alive." Something in the way Talbot collected himself signaled class and breeding well above that of a simple businessman. As did his speech. Holding his gaze steady on the man, Bastien finished turning back his sleeves, folded his arms across his chest, and leaned a hip against the ship's railing. "Tell me, Monsieur Talbot, what's become of the poisons you fed your wife? Or did you dispose of any remains before you left your hotel?"

Talbot's head snapped toward Bastien, his eyes flashing. "I tell you the truth, sir. I wish to save her life, not take it."

Bastien lifted a brow. "She had to have been given something during the trip over to Jamaica for her to be in such a state. Had she not, the pupils in her eyes would have returned to normal by now."

Talbot scratched his head, donned his hat, then snatched it off when a stiff breeze threatened to toss it into the sea. "I give you my word, I know nothing of what you speak, only that she was not improving as I thought she should by now. I do not know why."

Bastien continued to study Talbot. "What have you given her to drink and eat?"

"I paid a princely sum to the captain on the voyage from England so Lily…so Mrs. Talbot…could receive proper food and drink from the captain's private stores. Sorry to say, she couldn't keep much down in the way of vittles."

Talbot tugged hard at an ear. "I am befuddled. And so very worried I shall lose her."

"Perhaps the authorities in N'awlins will be able to get to the truth of things, *oui*?"

Talbot hissed out a breath. "No! I mean…what I mean to say is, please do not alert the authorities, Captain. It will go far worse for her than you might imagine if word gets out that she—" He paused to rub at the stubble on his chin. "As I told Mr. Fellowes back in Jamaica, I am an old school chum of the founder of this shipping company. However, there is more to our relationship than mere friendship. There were four of us, close as brothers from a young age. While at Cambridge, we made a blood oath that should any of us ever find ourselves in dire straits, we would seek out the others."

He turned to Bastien. "I am now in those dire straits with regard to Mrs. Talbot, sir. Thus, I am earnestly seeking Justin Andrews to make good our vow."

"What of the third and fourth man?"

Something flickered in Talbot's eyes, only to disappear in a flash. "Whereabouts unknown. Please, I ask you to honor Lily…my wife…by keeping our journey confidential. Rest assured, as soon as Mr. Andrews becomes aware of our dilemma, he will lend us his full support and inform you thusly."

Bastien held Talbot's fretful gaze for a long moment. A sense of unease washed through him. "After all these years, you never found a need to seek out Monsieur Andrews until now?"

Talbot reached into his pocket, retrieved a folded square of cloth, and swiped it across his damp brow. "I did not. I beg of you, deliver me covertly to Justin Andrews. Should he reject my plea, then by all means, turn me over to the authorities."

Bastien had nothing to lose by agreeing to Talbot's plea. Where the devil would the man run off to in the middle of the sea? "If you haven't given her anything harmful, then she should be showing signs of responding to fresh water and broths, yet you claim she worsens."

"Indeed. Can you help her recover?"

"Hopefully." He shrugged. "Unless she's too far gone to be saved."

"Oh, God, don't say that!"

"*Excusez-moi.* I did not mean to upset you." Bastien turned his gaze from Talbot and glanced upward, to the tall masts and spread of canvas, to the extra skysails and moonrakers catching the wind, to the studding sails on the booms extending from the hulls. With all sails set, the sleek clipper had to be doing close to sixteen knots. At this rate, they'd be home in five days.

He hoped to God Madame Talbot would still be alive.

Fatigue caught up with Bastien like a kick in the head. He swiped a hand over his eyes, pinched the bridge of his nose, and turned to the sea. Releasing all thought, he let his mind float free, losing himself in the mesmerizing beauty of the ocean spray frothing green alongside the fast-moving clipper.

How long he stood there before a sudden dawning shot through him, he had no clue.

"Mon Dieu!"

He took off at a run, calling out to Henri. "Get below and collect a good number of coconuts. Have Cook drain the coconuts' milk into a large bowl and take it to Madame Talbot's stateroom along with one of Cook's sea sponges. Tell him to squeeze oil from the coconut, and bring that to me as well. And water. I'll need the tub in my quarters filled with water.

"Rapidement! Quickly!"

Chapter Three

Bastien flung open the door to Madame Talbot's quarters and rushed inside. He found her fast asleep, her skin white as the bed linens she lay upon, her cheeks flushed from the effects of the arsenic. On a chair beside the bed sat the petite, gray-haired woman Fellowes had hired. A Cuban widow, she was free to travel and in need of coin. Aletha—or was her name Altia—hell if he could remember. At least she spoke some English, limited as it was.

"Madame, do you own a pair of gloves?"

Puzzlement swept over the maid's face. "Gloves, señor?"

Not much in the way of English after all, damn it. A sense of desperation gripped him. What the devil would the word for *gloves* be in Spanish? He drew in an exasperated breath. Could the word be close to French? Holding up his hands, he mimicked the act of donning them. "Gloves. *Gants*."

"Ah, *sí, señor.*" She hurried to a small wooden chest in the far corner of the stateroom and dug through the contents. She straightened, waved a white cotton pair, and rushed over to hand them to him. *"Guantes!"*

"Bien. Good. No, you put them on." Once more, he mimicked the act of donning the gloves. Confusion clouded her features. She shrugged her shoulders. The time they were wasting trying to decipher one another's language shredded his patience. *"Merde!"*

The guard stepped into the room. "I am Cuban, Capitán. Perhaps I could translate for you?"

"Merci, thank you. Tell madame—oh, hell—give me the woman's proper name." His jaw clenched as he listened to the back and forth chatter between the guard and the lady's maid.

"She has several last names, Capitán. Very long names, which is typical of us Cubans. She wishes for you to use her Christian name. She is called Allita."

Damn, he'd been wrong on both earlier guesses. "Fine. And your last name is what, *s'il vous plaît*? Choose only one."

Humor flashed through the guard's dark eyes. "It is Rubio, sir."

"*Bien.* Tell Allita she must remove all of Madame Talbot's clothing and deposit it outside the door at once. She is to remove the bed linens as well. And tell her it is important she keep her gloves on throughout. Tell her we will step outside while she completes the task, at which point I shall return with further instructions."

Patience was once again summoned as he listened to Rubio and Allita chatter. She glanced over at Bastien. Her brows creased and her mouth formed a tight slit.

Rubio turned to Bastien. "She wishes to know if the lady carries a disease which could spread to her."

"*Non.* Madame Talbot has been poisoned. I suspect her intimate clothing has been soaked in a toxin which is seeping into her skin. Also, her night rail has probably transferred the deadly substance onto the bed linens, so those need to be removed as well. Tell Allita she is in no danger so long as she wears the gloves. Inform her it is important she move quickly because we've much to do once her task is completed."

Bastien waited for Allita's nod of understanding, then escorted the guard from the room, where he nearly collided with Talbot.

"Your pardon," Talbot said, sidestepping the collision. "I couldn't help overhearing everything. I cannot tell you how grateful I am that it was you and your ship we happened upon. I assure you, I will not be in the way, but I'd like to remain close by so if there's any word—"

"On the contrary, Talbot. Your assistance is required. Not only must your wife drink the coconut milk to help flush the toxin from her body, she must also bathe in it to remove any poisonous residue from her skin and hair. Afterward, she'll need to be scrubbed clean in fresh water. Allita is slight of frame and cannot take on the task alone. It will be necessary for you to assist her and make certain the cleansing process is thorough."

"Bloody hell," Talbot mumbled. Turning his back on Bastien, he stepped to the ship's railing, but not before Bastien caught sight of the man's flushed face.

He moved to stand beside Talbot. "What be the matter, monsieur?"

A sickly shade of gray replaced the flush on Talbot's face. He dragged a hand across his mouth, his mutterings lost in the action.

Anger boiled up from Bastien's gut. His Cajun accent took a deep turn south. "Are you refusing to bathe your deathly ill wife because she will be unclothed, monsieur? What be your concern?"

Talbot gripped the ship's rail so hard his knuckles turned white. "I...I... we keep separate bedchambers. She...she wears a night rail at all times... not unusual in a proper marriage. Not unusual at all."

Bastien clenched and unclenched his fists. It had been a long time since he'd fought an urge to strike a man, but this man's response set up a rhythmic beat through Bastien's fingers. He shoved his hands in his pockets. "You do not wish to come to your wife's aid, monsieur?"

Talbot sucked in a ragged breath. His spine went ramrod straight and color returned to his cheeks. He made a slow turn from the ship's railing and looked down his nose at Bastien. "That is not the way things are, good sir. Not at all. You are the doctor, not I. Shouldn't it be your duty to attend her?"

Bastien's fingers itched. He kept them in his pockets. "I am a *traiteur*, not a licensed doctor. I am trained to heal using natural methods. However, what I am or what I am not has little to do with my request that you assist the lady's maid in washing the poison off your wife's body. This is about preserving your wife's dignity while she undergoes an intimate procedure."

"*Humph.* Whatever you choose to call yourself, surely you must be familiar with patients who present themselves in all manner of dress or undress. Therefore, it would be more efficient if you and the lady's maid tend to my wife. I fear I would be nothing more than a bumbling distraction."

Bastien caught Talbot's gaze and held it.

Talbot's overbearing demeanor faltered. "Can you not see that it is I who am attempting to protect Lily's...Mrs. Talbot's sensibilities?"

A muscle along Bastien's tight jaw twitched. *As I suspected, she is not your wife.* "You, monsieur, have a hell of a lot of explaining to do."

He spun on his heel to return to the stateroom door, now blocked by a pile of clothing and bed linens, which gave him pause. He glanced over his shoulder at Talbot. "Do you wear nightshirts, Monsieur Talbot?"

"Indeed, I do. Why do you ask? Could they also contain—"

"Poison? *Non.* Collect the clean ones you've yet to wear and deliver them to me, *tout de suite.*" He turned to the guard. "Rubio, I need an oiled canvas to spread over Madame Talbot's bed to keep the mattress from getting soaked. You will find one in storage below. *Rapidement.* Quickly."

Bastien kicked aside the pile of fabric and stood in front of the closed door with his hands on his hips while his methodical mind raced ahead, creating a precise order to the proceeding.

Just as Henri approached balancing a large bowl, Talbot rushed from his quarters, nearly colliding with Henri, who managed to quick-step out of Talbot's way without upending the vessel. Coconut milk splashed over the edges.

"*Mon Dieu!*" Bastien snatched the stack of nightshirts from Talbot's hands. "Keep to the ship's rail and do not interfere or I shall be tempted to toss you overboard. Henri, wait here."

The guard hurried back with the folded sail in his arms.

"*Merci,*" Bastien said and knocked on the door. "It is necessary for you to translate for me. To preserve madame's dignity, I will set a chair in a corner to the left of the door. You will back into the room without looking at madame and sit facing the wall. Under no circumstance are you to turn around. You understand, *oui*?"

Rubio nodded. "Yes, sir."

The door opened a crack. Bastien slipped the nightshirts to Allita and motioned to the oiled sail. "Tell her to waken Madame Talbot so the mattress can be covered with the waterproofed sail. Then she is to return madame to the bed and drape one of these nightshirts over her person rather than putting it on her."

While the guard instructed Allita, Bastien retrieved the bowl of coconut milk from Henri. "Gather some of the crew and a few buckets. Fill the bathing tub in my quarters and set out a couple of my Turkish towels for Madame Talbot's use."

"Shall I have the tub brought to her quarters?"

"*Non.* I cannot have the crew traipsing through her room while I tend to her. When we finish here, I will take her to my stateroom. Once the tub is filled, clear the deck of all hands. Oh, and have Cook heat the water."

Henri's eyes widened. "Cook, he already be cursing me, don'cha know."

"Tell him if he doesn't like it, I said he is welcome to swim with the sharks."

Fighting a grin, Henri trotted back to the galley.

Easing open the door, Bastien caught sight of Madame Talbot lying on the bed with one of her husband's voluminous white nightshirts draped over her crosswise. The wide swath of fabric covered her from shoulders to knees. Allita had tucked its long length around madame's body.

Madame Talbot turned her head his way. Her eyes fluttered open. He doubted she saw more than a blurred figure approach the bed. Setting the bowl filled with coconut milk and two sponges on the small bedside table, he turned to find Rubio already seated in the chair with his back to the room, the door closed. Efficient, that one.

"Good morning, Madame Talbot," he said, willing his voice to remain calm, hoping to soothe any anxiety she might be suffering. He leaned over her and gently swept a lock of hair from her cheek, tucking it behind her ear. "Allita and I are here to help you get well, but we'll need your cooperation."

"Thank you," she murmured and reached out for him, trying to form a smile on her lips. "I will do my best so long as you perform your duties with great proficiency."

"Ah, a sense of humor despite all you've been through? I like that, don'cha know." He took her cold, frail hand in his and held it for a long moment, letting the warmth of his flesh flow into hers while he told her what they were about to do to rid her system of the poison.

Soon, he and Allita were working together in a smooth harmony that required few words. They used the universal language of connecting gazes and nods of the head. In the end, he figured Fellowes knew what he'd been about when he'd hired this petite Cuban whirlwind who discreetly bathed the intimate parts of their patient while Bastien tended to the rest of madame's too-thin body.

When they'd completed bathing Madame Talbot, Allita moved to the lady's travel trunk and retrieved a small satchel containing madame's toilette articles.

Bastien shook his head. "Rubio, tell Allita to bring the bag with us to my quarters, but not to touch any of the contents. I suspect the toiletries, right down to her perfume, are likely laced with belladonna. I'll be inspecting them."

His patient, who'd lain still throughout most of the procedure, opened her eyes and stared blankly at him. "You've a most soothing voice," she murmured. "Would you read to me once I am able to remain awake? I truly do enjoy being read to."

Before he could respond, she sighed and her eyes fluttered shut once again. His gaze remained fixed on her. For a brief, extraordinary moment, not only was he able to envision what she would look like once healed, but he seemed to be able to capture her entire essence. In that short, sweet bit of time, a peculiar emotion took hold of him. Slowly, this foreign sensation wound through him, then settled somewhere in the vicinity of his chest.

What the hell just happened?

Blaming it all on fatigue, he leaned over the bed and tucked Talbot's abundant nightshirt about her body, then swept her into his arms and carried her to his quarters and to the bathing tub. He lowered her into the steaming water, then turned away while Allita removed the shirt from madame's body and proceeded to bathe her.

He made his way to the porthole, where he stared at the sea as exhaustion settled in his bones. Who was this woman? What in the world had gone on in her life to send her on the run? Who wanted her dead? He'd bet his life Talbot was not her husband. Nor was Talbot their real name.

Lily.

What a beautiful name for a beautiful woman. He rather hoped this name actually belonged to her. At the realization that he found her lovely despite her condition, yet another peculiar kind of sensation settled in to stay. He stepped away from the porthole and exited the room for a breath of fresh air. He had no business thinking such thoughts.

Whoever this woman was, he had a duty to see to her care.

That was all.

Nothing more.

Chapter Four

A soft breeze blew across Lily's cheek, nudging her awake. She drew in a deep breath. Fresh, salt-sea air moved into her lungs, sharpening her senses.

Where am I?

Too listless to bother to move, she lay on her side with her hands tucked beneath her cheek while her mind and body came slowly into the moment. A wiggle of her toes told her she was in bed with a lightweight blanket atop her. Even the simple act of twitching her feet had taken more effort than she cared to repeat.

Devoid of emotion and lacking any sense of time or place, she felt as if she were being gently rocked back and forth. Opening her eyes, she found herself aboard a ship in what appeared to be a rather small but richly appointed stateroom. Blue skies peeked through an open porthole across from where she lay. A narrow marble-topped table beside the bed held a silver pitcher and cup, three small vials, and a leather-bound book, the title of which she couldn't be bothered trying to make out. A shiny brass surround kept the lot from slipping off the edge should the sea decide to roll about.

How in the world did I get here? And when?

Her muddled mind could not cope with anything more than the here and now. A rustling beyond the foot of the bed caught her attention. She managed to turn over. A tall, broad-shouldered man with dark hair stood with his back to her, his large frame obscuring whatever he was about. Beside him, a petite gray-haired woman held up a small vial. He nodded and she passed it to him. Curious, Lily lay motionless, observing the strangers.

Especially him.

He was certainly a fine figure of a man. At least from what she could see at this angle. A crisp white shirt covered his broad shoulders while snug, tan breeches outlined narrow hips—and a tight bum any man would be proud to claim as his own. She nearly managed a smile at her wicked observation. Her perusal swept down muscular legs to a pair of high-top black leather boots polished to a mirror sheen.

Had she seen those boots before?

Something bleak tugged at the periphery of her consciousness and her head began to buzz.

Indeed, she felt certain she'd seen them—or something akin to them—but it was as if a dense fog in her mind obscured her recollections, including a vague memory of blue eyes. And a deep, soothing voice.

She continued to study him. A physician? The ship's captain? She reckoned he had to be one of the two. What was he up to?

Think, Lily. What is all this?

She struggled to sit. Too weak, she plopped back with a heavy sigh.

The man's head snapped around. "Ah, you are awake." He approached with long, fluid strides.

A shock wave rippled through her entire being and her breath froze. Oh, my, he was a handsome one.

And those eyes.

She was struck by their depth of color, like a deep pool of water. While she'd certainly had many an occasion to observe blue eyes, they'd been much lighter in hue and attached to fair-haired, fair-skinned Brits, not to someone with sun-kissed skin and hair as black as a raven's wing. Lush, dark lashes outlined those captivating eyes. She was reminded of her years in India, where the people used kohl to keep bugs at bay. A thin scar ran from the side of his left eyebrow across to his hairline just above the ear. How had he come by such a wound?

Their gazes locked and the intensity and intelligence of his expression left her speechless. He was a gorgeous man to be sure, beguiling—but also rather frightening. Or was it her unwelcome reaction to him that alarmed her? She had never experienced such an intense response to a member of the male species.

A smile worked one corner of his mouth. "Not only are you awake, but I am pleased to see your pupils have returned to normal, which means your vision has been restored."

The gray-haired woman moved to the opposite side of the bed and made a motion with her hand to her mouth.

Was this person a mute?

He gave the woman a short nod. "Let's help you sit up so Allita can get some nourishment into you."

Leaning over Lily, he swept his arms around her shoulders and gently raised her upper torso off the bed as if she weighed no more than a feather. He held her in place while the gray-haired lady added a stack of pillows behind her. Heat radiating from his body enveloped her, as did his clean, familiar scent, sending her already speeding heart into a furious gallop.

And then it happened.

The curtain of fog lifted. A blinding, painful flash of memory shot to the surface—the months of horror she'd endured, the lies they'd told to gain passage on this ship—it all came back to her. A shudder rolled through her, only to settle in the pit of her stomach in a nauseating ball. Oh, no, she was about to become ill. She swallowed hard against the urge to retch, but a moan escaped her lips.

He tilted his head in puzzlement. Easing her back against the pillows, he took her hand in his. "You look frightened, Madame Talbot. Rest assured, we are not here to cause you harm. Our intention is to see you get well."

She gave a brief nod and breathed slow and easy, forcing herself to relax. "Of course. Are you the captain or a physician?" she managed in a voice barely above a rasping whisper.

The corners of his mouth twitched again and humor danced in his eyes. "Perhaps a little of both for the time being."

The heat of his hand had her itching to pull away and set herself free from the hypnotic effect. That would be rude, wouldn't it? She cleared her throat. "How long have I been here?"

"We've been at sea three days. You don't remember?"

"Bits and pieces. Have I been drugged?" *Pray, not again.*

"*Non.* You collapsed before we got you aboard. You were made comfortable and then you mostly slept. I do not know how you managed to survive the voyage from England to Jamaica in your condition. You, Madame Talbot, possess an impressive constitution."

His lilting accent had thickened, setting yet another odd flurry of sensations tumbling about her insides. She didn't like this internal conflict. She didn't like not being in control. Not at all. Snatching back her hand, she turned on her side and gave him her back.

"I want my husband." Lord, it was revolting enough to have to call her godfather by an entirely new name, but referring to him as her spouse was something she could scarcely bear. Her stomach was threatening to revolt again. "Please, sir, send for Mr. Talbot. I am in desperate need of him."

For a long moment the captain said nothing. Then, he spoke. "It's barely eight in the morning, madame. Monsieur Talbot is breaking his fast, and I do not wish to disturb him at the moment. He's done little these past three days and nights but wear a hole in the deck with his relentless pacing. I only just got him to agree to eat something by threatening to toss him overboard."

She turned back to glare at him. "You'd actually throw him into the sea?"

"*Non.*" He grinned, pulling a wooden chair to the edge of the bed, turning it around, and straddling the seat. He casually draped his arms over the back. "Since I accepted the position of captain on a mere whim, and seeing as how half the skeleton crew is related to me in one way or another, no one took my threat seriously. Even Monsieur Talbot wore the makings of a smile when he headed for the galley."

"What do you mean your command of the ship is based on some capricious notion? And a minimal crew? Good heavens, do you even know how to find the proper port?"

A throaty chuckle rolled up from his belly. "*Oui.* My brother and I are partners in the shipping company that owns this fine cutter. We happen to manage the N'awlins office. We make it our business to know each of our ships in detail. As for the skeleton crew, the sole purpose of this journey was to carry us home after five months in Jamaica. I decided to make use of the empty cargo hold by tossing in some nice fruit. Once we reach port, a certified captain will take over."

A sigh of relief left her throat. "I see."

His voice softened and his accent grew even stronger. "Monsieur Talbot was mighty relieved to know we'd saved your life. However, you must be prepared for a lengthy recovery, which is a subject we shall discuss later. For now, I would ask you to rest easy while we wait for Allita to bring your food. Afterward, I shall fetch your Monsieur Talbot. *Oui?*"

"Yes, of course." She glanced at the book on the bedside table. "Did you read to me?"

"*Oui.* You do not recall asking me to do so?"

"I am remembering now. Vaguely. May I inquire about the book?"

"*Mais oui.*" He fixed his intense gaze on her, as if he were trying to read her mind. "It's *David Copperfield* by—"

"Charles Dickens."

He lifted a brow. "You've read the story before?"

"No. I had no time for frivolous reading."

His brow went up again. "Frivolous?"

Her stomach clenched. *Do not over speak, you fool.* Eager to change the subject, she plucked at her sleeve. "What is this I am wearing? 'Tis not my night rail."

"It is a gift from Monsieur Talbot. Someone saturated your clothing in poison that was making you ill, so I am afraid your husband's nightshirts and your hooded cape are all you have left of your wardrobe until we reach port, where I can see to having your clothing properly cleaned."

He is going to see to it? I think not. She stared at the wooden ceiling as memory after nasty memory flooded her, stirring up yet another round of nausea. She was so angry, she wanted to curse aloud. Well, that wouldn't do.

"No, sir. I do not wish to keep a stitch of what was brought along. In any regard, those clothes were well out of style. Since I am beginning a new life in a new country, I shall order an entire new wardrobe once we reach our destination."

She turned her gaze from the ceiling to the captain. "Do you know of a good dressmaker in New Orleans by any chance?"

Something in those startling blue eyes of his shifted and amusement settled in once again. "*Oui.* The very best in the land, don'cha know."

As he spoke, she watched the movements of his lush mouth. She pressed her fingertips to her own lips. No longer were they dry and cracked, but supple, as his appeared to be. She remembered he'd applied a lovely scented ointment to her lips the night they'd boarded the ship. And perhaps several times over the past few days. Did he routinely apply the same balm to his own generous mouth?

What in heaven's name was she thinking, having intimate thoughts of a near-stranger? Heat crept into her cheeks while a mad urge to laugh at the absurdity of what her life had become nearly took hold of her.

He tilted his head in question. "What has you amused?"

Oh, she didn't dare confess to having such wicked thoughts. "I…well, I never thought to be the kind of woman who'd need saving."

"And why is that?"

When she didn't answer, he leaned forward so far, the back legs of his chair tilted off the floor. "Who did this terrible thing to you, madame? It wasn't your so-called husband was it?"

So-called husband? Heaven help her, he'd seen through their ruse. She frowned, annoyed at herself for sharing entirely too much with this stranger. Her godfather's words reverberated in her head once more. *Do not over speak.*

Collecting herself, she stared at him. Hopefully, her blank expression gave him nothing to use against her. "I have grown quite weary, Captain. I should like to rest."

He studied her for a moment longer. Suddenly those warm, communicative blue eyes of his turned distant and cold, reminding her of who she was and why the reason she'd fled England had to remain a secret.

With a silent nod, he stood, replaced the chair, and headed for the door. He paused to glance over his shoulder. "You are on my ship, madame. And you are headed for my home port where you shall remain for however long Monsieur Talbot chooses to make it your home. Rest assured, you and I are not finished with this conversation."

She watched him leave, watched him shift his body at an angle, just enough to ease his wide shoulders through the door's narrow opening. It was plain he was a unique sort of man. His countenance bore the mark of someone who took exceptional care of himself.

A curious kind of quickening stirred inside her, filling her with puzzlement. She'd met attractive men before, men who'd thought themselves quite the catch, but she'd never had the time for any of them—not with all that had been required of her. So why was this one causing internal chaos?

Her unsettling reaction to him had to be because of her calamitous situation. As soon as they reached New Orleans, she would never set eyes on this man again. Would never give him another thought. And that suited her just fine.

Chapter Five

Checking the navigational sites with his first mate and navigator, Bastien looked up to spy Henri emerging from the galley, gripping a tray of food with both hands. "Is that meant for Madame Talbot?"

"Oui."

"Damn it. Rubio was supposed to do the fetching. Why you be doing his chore when you have your own work to do?"

Henri blew a hank of hair off his face, gave a nod toward the portside of the ship, and responded in his Cajun tongue. "Those two, they not be getting along, so I went."

"Christ." Bastien lit out for madame's stateroom, his booted feet thudding against the wooden deck. Whatever Rubio was saying to Allita, he was clearly agitated. Allita responded by waving her hands about as if she were trying to grab hold of a jumble of angry words floating in the air.

"What the hell's going on?"

Rubio's lips thinned. "She can speak English but refuses."

"What?" Acid caught fire in Bastien's stomach and chewed its way upward. He turned his eyes to a red-faced Allita. "Can this be true?"

She crossed her arms over her bosom, set her jaw, and fixed her eyes on the undulating sea.

Bastien turned to Rubio. "You are certain?"

Rubio nodded. "She speaks with a heavy accent, of which she is much ashamed. No matter how hard she has tried, she cannot rid herself of it. Her false pride is wasting everyone's time."

Allita muttered something in Spanish.

"Enough!" Bastien bellowed.

Allita hiked her chin in the air, squared her shoulders, and turned her gaze on him. He glared back for a long moment. Then he noticed something—despite her show of bravado, the hem of her skirt quivered. *Mon Dieu. She is afraid of me.*

Guilt stabbed him. What the devil had this petite woman been through to cause her to stand before him like a warrior ready for battle? Why, her head barely reached his chest. His foul mood withered to nothing. God in Heaven, no woman should be afraid of what a man might do to her.

Would a little humor ease the tension? He hoped to hell it would. He bent his head to her and willed a smile to replace his frown. "Do you think I would toss you overboard when you are so clever in assisting me with our ailing passenger?"

She tilted her head and studied him with those dark-as-night eyes. "No, señor. I see you are quick to anger. However, you are just as quick to forgive." A cloud passed over her eyes, but was gone in a flash. "Like my son was."

Rubio was right—she did have a heavy accent. *There's a story behind the blunt words she just offered up about her son.* "Like your boy was, you say?"

She gave a short nod. "He was handsome and strong like you. But you can swim like a fish, Capitán. He could not."

She might as well have thrown a bucket of ice water in his face. He stood staring at her for a brief moment while her thickly accented words sank in. "I am sorry for your loss."

She reached over and swatted at Rubio. "He withholds information from you, too, Capitán."

Now it was Rubio's cheeks turning red. "We are family."

"Say that again."

Rubio fidgeted. "Allita is my aunt. Her youngest sister is my mother." A sheepish grin touched his lips. "We are a close family. Close families disagree now and then."

"I'll be damned." Now that Bastien was aware the two were related, he could see the resemblance. Same nose. Same chin. Same teeth. Likely the same streak of stubbornness. The knot of tension in Bastien's gut eased. "Leave it to the ever-resourceful Monsieur Fellowes to hire a lady's maid and guard for Madame Talbot from one household."

Allita turned to her nephew, her eyes glittering with triumph. "Tell him the rest, Rubio."

Rubio fiddled with a button on his jacket. "Señor Fellowes, he is courting my sister. He knew who to look for since we all live together. Even Tía

Allita lives with us. She is the most stubborn and headstrong of us all. We call her Atilla."

Bastien nearly choked on Rubio's words. "Are you saying you compare this slip of a woman to Atilla the Hun?"

Mischief sparkled in Rubio eyes. "*Sí, Capitán.* He was the most fearsome enemy in all the Roman Empire, a man not to be crossed. Tía Allita, she can be like that."

Allita swatted at Rubio again.

He ducked and laughed.

Curiosity got the better of Bastien. "Why did you both agree to make this trip?"

"For the adventure," Allita quipped.

Rubio lifted a brow. "I came along to watch over my daring aunt. Perhaps one day she will tell you of her great adventure with the king of Spain, which was why we left Cuba and ended up in Jamaica."

She gave him another slap on the arm, then without a word, turned and took the food tray from Henri, who'd been silent during the entire confrontation. His eyes were still wide with amazement.

Bastien shot Henri a speaking glance and said in Cajun, "Didn't this get to be an interesting day?"

Henri grinned. "*Oui*, but now I have my work to do before you threaten to toss me overboard." He gave a nod toward Allita. "I shall leave you now, *s'il vous plaît.*"

Tray in hand, Allita nodded back and headed for Lily's stateroom. Bastien reached the door first. Easing it open, he stepped aside to allow the maid past him. No sooner did she enter than she made a hasty retreat, nearly colliding with Bastien.

"What's the problem?" he asked in hushed tones.

Concern stitched her eyebrows together. "The lady is awake, and weeping something terrible."

"Did she see you enter?"

Allita shook her head. "She has her back to the door. Even with the sounds of the wind and the seas, I could hear her. Should we wait awhile before entering?"

Whatever was troubling Madame Talbot, it must have something to do with her poisoning. This sobering turn of events wasn't something he could ignore. Cursing to himself, he bid farewell to a few hours of pleasurable sailing on the foredeck, lifted the tray from Allita, and turned to step inside. "Wait here until I call for you. And close the door behind me, *s'il vous plaît.*"

Once inside, he spied Lily with her back to him, her face buried in her pillow. Muffled sounds of weeping reached his ears. He moved to the opposite side of the bed and stood between her and the narrow cot Allita slept on. Setting down the food tray, he picked up the pristine serviette folded beside the bowl of porridge and tucked it into her curled fingers. He gave her hand what he hoped was a comforting squeeze and stepped back.

She grew still for a long moment, then with a sniff, brought the cloth to her face. "Go away."

"Non."

Another pause and then, "You are quite rude. Please leave me."

She intended to be obstinate, did she? When it came to stubbornness, no one did it better than a Thibodeaux. "Hear me well, Madame Talbot. As the captain of this fine vessel, I am responsible for everything and everyone aboard ship. I am also your *traiteur*—your healer—which means I am committed to helping you regain your health. In all ways. Now tell me why you weep."

More sniffles ensued and a ragged sigh escaped her lips. Then she rolled over onto her back, pushed herself into a sitting position against the stack of pillows, and scrubbed the cloth over her eyes and damp cheeks. Her breathing steadied, her face calmed, and her eyes were dry. Dropping her hands to her lap with the serviette tucked between them, she fixed a steady gaze on him, looking for all the world like a fine and proper lady without a care in the world.

His insides jolted. It couldn't have been easy, re-creating herself like that. At a sudden loss for words, he folded his arms over his chest, met her gaze, and held it while he collected his thoughts. He'd be damned if he'd back down from her stony regard.

Behind their locked gazes an unspoken battle of wills was waged. Who would be the one to break away? Here was a woman with a streak of daring in her soul or she wouldn't be propped up in bed as if she was the one in charge, with her eyes shooting angry arrows at him.

Despite his keen focus, his peripheral vision made note of her smooth white skin, her straight nose, and nicely rounded lips. Even in her weakened state, she was, without a doubt, an uncommonly attractive woman.

A pleasurable sensation heated his chest and wormed its way into his belly. His groin tightened. A shock wave shot through him. Good God, he had no business having a physical reaction to her! He was her caretaker. She was vulnerable. And she was a married woman.

No, she is not! his inner voice cried out. She was English however, and he cared not for their ilk.

A tangle of guilt and confusion gripped him. Locking down his physical reaction to her, he buried it in the same place where he kept all his unwanted emotions.

Breaking eye contact, he gave a nod toward the tray. "If you refuse to tell me what troubles you, then you should at least eat something. I'll collect Allita."

"Is she a mute?" Lily's feminine voice drifted around him like a gentle breeze.

His footsteps faltered a beat, then he proceeded to the door, tossing his words over his shoulder. "*Non.* But Spanish is her first language. Her accent, it is so thick you'll likely have trouble deciphering some of her words."

Lily cleared her throat. "Since I can easily decode yours, I should have no problem with hers."

He paused at the threshold. Had she just...? He glanced back to find a smile working the corners of her mouth. Indeed, those were teasing words. "Ah, so the lady has a sense of humor."

Refusing to acknowledge the warmth trying to invade his chest yet again, he made his way onto the deck. "Allita, come see to Madame Talbot's meal while I see to my duties."

* * * *

Lily peered into the bowl Allita handed her and wrinkled her nose. "What is this disgusting-looking mess?"

"Porridge, coconut milk, mashed bananas, and blackstrap molasses. It's the molasses making it look like mud. *El capitán*, he fixed it himself. Said it would give you strength and put meat on your bones. You are to eat every morsel. Try it. It's tasty."

Lily didn't know why the idea that the captain had personally prepared her food made her throat catch. Then she remembered—Papa used to insist on making porridge whenever she'd taken ill as a child. It had been so long ago, she'd forgotten, but suddenly the memory loomed crystal clear. Against Mama's objections, he'd bundle up his little Lilibet, and carry her to the kitchens, where he'd prop her on a stool, her little feet dangling in midair. While Cook stepped aside, Papa would bustle around the kitchen, whistling a merry tune as he created a soothing concoction. That was, when his legs still worked. She closed her eyes against a sudden sting of tears.

Oh, life took a terrible turn soon afterward, did it not, Papa? And oh, how the direction of my life changed in ways I could never have imagined.

Still, I would not have given up one moment of serving you. We worked so well together, didn't we?

Allita stepped closer. "What's wrong?"

"Nothing." She sniffed away the tears clogging her nose and throat. "Nothing at all. It's just that it's been a very long time since anyone made porridge for me."

She dug her spoon into the thick gruel and shoved a spoonful into her mouth. "Mmmm. This is surprisingly good," she mumbled through her porridge.

A shadow spilled across her bed. She didn't have to look up to know it was *him*. Well, at the least, she could be gracious. He'd saved her life. He'd been nothing but kind. So why did she fear losing control over herself in his presence? Nothing seemed to make sense where this man was concerned.

She shoved another spoonful of food into her mouth.

"*Très bien.* You are eating."

His husky words slid across her skin like a caress. Good heavens. Her imagination had gone wild! She managed a casual nod. "It is quite good, actually. Allita said you prepared it yourself."

His gaze slid to the bowl in her hand, a smile working one corner of his mouth. "*Oui.* A *traiteur* must know which foods help a person to heal quickly."

"Well, thank you." She shoved another spoonful into her mouth, swallowed and handed Allita the bowl. "I'm afraid I cannot eat another—"

"No need." He reached out and took the bowl from her before Allita had time to move forward. "You've done well."

His fingers brushed hers and sent another rush of emotion through her. Their gazes caught. She stared into those mesmerizing blue eyes as if she'd fallen into some bizarre, dizzying trance. Had he felt something, too?

Snatching back her hand, she tried to look away, but her fascination with him kept her eyes fixed on his.

"You are staring at me, Madame Talbot."

Oh, she had to think fast. "Well, since this is a rather small stateroom, and you are a large man, I cannot help but notice you."

He set the unfinished bowl of porridge on the tray ever so carefully. She watched as he lined up everything in precise order, then settled a hip on the edge of her bed. He draped a hand casually across his lap—a clean hand with long fingers displaying evenly clipped and squared off nails. Fascinating.

"You are staring again."

She managed a deep, calming breath. "I paint, Captain. Mostly portraits. I've been known to study people to their distraction. I apologize."

"Really?" He folded his arms across his chest. "Are you any good at it? Painting, that is. Not driving one to distraction."

She shrugged. "So I've been told. With your permission, I should like to paint you one day."

Allita picked up the tray and headed for the door.

"Locate Monsieur Talbot, *s'il vous plaît*. Tell him Madame Talbot is ready to receive him."

If she heard herself called Madame Talbot one more time, Lily thought she'd scream. She waited until Allita was out of sight, then turned back to the captain. "You may call me Lily when in private."

His brows drew together. "You don't care for your name?"

I detest it! She managed a lazy shrug. "It's long and formal, which becomes tedious. After all, you are preparing my food and medicine, so in private, I should think we could do away with formalities."

He moved to the side table. Lifting the lid off a mysterious small pot, he swept his thumb across the top. He rested a hip on the side of the bed once again—only closer this time. Much closer. He leaned over her and brushed a lovely scented balm across her lips. "Or do you want me to dispense with the name because you are not Talbot's wife after all?"

Stunned, she lay still, trying to ignore the slow sweep of his fingers sending a thousand tingles through her. She stared at his luscious mouth as he spoke, his words rumbling through her like an earthquake. Better to not respond at all. She closed her eyes against…against what?

"So you wish to ignore my question, do you?" His hand left her mouth as he leaned close to her ear and whispered, "Madame, if you are Talbot's wife, then I am your pet zebra."

His weight left the bed. At the sound of his retreating footsteps, she opened her eyes and found him across the room with his back to her, measuring some kind of liquid into a glass.

Uncle…Percy rushed in with Allita on his heels. "My word, Lily," he gushed. "You look amazingly like your old self." He grabbed her hand and kissed the back. "How is the most beautiful girl in the world feeling?"

"Much better." She opened her arms to him for a desperately needed reassuring hug, only to glance over her shoulder and spy the captain, with a questioning lift of his brow, mouthing the word, "Girl?"

Oh, dear. *Uncle and I are in need of a talk.* "Might we have a moment to ourselves, Captain?"

The captain smirked. "Not until you have vacated my ship. Since it is a lovely day, why don't we give you some time in the sun?"

Henri rushed into the room and skidded to a stop. "Bastien," he cried out, his breath heaving in and out. "There's a tear in the mainsail."

Lily started. *The captain's name is Bastien?* She ignored Henri's urgent message and let the captain's name roll around on her tongue, let it slowly invade her senses. Bastien. How nice.

He turned to the young man. "Then go mend it."

Henri's already flushed cheeks turned crimson. He visibly gulped. "Me? Up there?"

"You lobbied to be bosun, did you not?"

A wide-eyed Henri stood frozen in place for a moment, then gave Bastien a nod, and turned to leave.

Bastien chuckled. "Set out some chairs on the deck for the Talbots and Allita, then collect a strong needle and a string of hemp. I'll go up with you. Show you how it's done."

Henri blew out a sigh of relief, grinned, and rattled off something in his native tongue as he rushed from the room.

Bastien turned to Allita. "Wrap Madame Talbot's blue cloak around her. I'll carry her to the deck."

He motioned with his head to Percy. "Unless you wish to do the transporting."

"No. No, you'll do best, I'm sure. But is her cloak safe to wear?"

"*Oui.* Your wife had enough layers of clothing to protect this one garment."

Lily was certain the captain…Bastien…had emphasized the word *wife* just to rub it in her face. Oh, to be off this ship.

Allita helped her to sit, draped the cloak around her shoulders and urged her to her feet.

"I don't have shoes?"

"*Non.* Every shoe was doused in poison." Bastien swept her into his arms and carried her the short distance to the deck, where he gently set her down. "You may sit next to her, Monsieur Talbot. Rubio, you are to remain at her side."

Henri rushed toward Bastien, a large needle and heavy thread in hand.

"Off with your boots and shirt," Bastien said to the lad as he motioned for Rubio to help him remove his own tall boots. "Will you? I do not have a boot jack handy."

To Lily's amazement, Bastien's shirt came off next, exposing a physique she'd seen only in her art books. He moved and the ribbons of muscle strapping his abdomen tightened.

And so did the breath in her lungs.

He was a magnificent specimen of a man. He turned and the sun glanced off his skin. Scars. Several scars. How had he come by those?

Uncle made to stand. "Should she...should my wife be privy to—"

"Allita can take her back inside if you do not wish her to see a couple of sailors climb up a mast and stitch together a mainsail. One that will get us to land."

Breathless, Lily watched the young man and the captain scurry up the tall wooden spire until they appeared little more than the size of her thumbs and seemed to float among the clouds.

"You can close your mouth and cease your gawking," Uncle mumbled. He made to stand. "I shall remove you to your stateroom after all."

Rubio shook his head. "You are to remain here until *el capitán* returns. Allita can take her inside."

Lily glared at her godfather. "Oh, for heaven's sake. I have never seen a sailor climb a tall mast. Besides, you know very well that I paint, which is why this scene interests me. I intend to remain right where I sit."

Uncle leaned over and growled in her ear. "Then stop looking at the captain as though he's your next meal."

The blood in her head drained. Anger leaked out of her every pore. "Pray tell, what are you insinuating?" she demanded through her teeth.

He placed a hand over hers and kept his voice low. "I'm no fool, Lily. I know what I see in your eyes whenever you look at him. The last thing we need is to have this charade of ours fall down around us before we reach New Orleans. We need help, Lily. I've kept you safe thus far. We cannot afford for you to become smitten like some schoolgirl over a man who saved your life and whom you'll not see again once we reach land. We've too much at stake."

"Schoolgirl?" Guilt pecked at her dignity. Uncle was right. From the moment her vision had been restored and she'd laid eyes on that man now high up on the mizzenmast, he'd mesmerized her. This wouldn't do. Not at all. She must remember who she was and why they were on the run. Perhaps her stay in New Orleans would turn out to be brief. Then she'd return to Cowdrey Hall. Never again to London. Never to the townhome where the horror had taken place. Never again would she feel safe within its walls.

The thought of returning to Yorkshire and to the dismal moors near Haworth chilled her to the bone. She'd live alone once she returned. With only the servants to keep her company. Without her dear Papa. Tears stung her eyes.

"Lily?"

Blinking, she waved a dismissing hand at her godfather. "I'm fine. Truly I am."

She went back to watching the captain and his bosun. Of all the men who'd crossed her path as they sought entry into Papa's study—and there had been a great number over the years—none had come close to affecting her the way the captain had. She took a deep breath of sea air. Her head cleared. She had never come so close to infatuation before. Silly, that. She should be grateful to Uncle for having recognized and put an end to such foolishness.

The mending of the sail completed, the captain and his bosun worked their way down the mainmast. Bastien. She rather liked his name. She also liked the way he moved with the agile grace of a sleek panther. But she still wanted to paint his portrait. Would love to try to capture his many enigmatic expressions. She'd take his painted image back to England. Hang it on the wall in the privacy of her bedchamber for no one else to see.

She smiled inside. After all, a woman could have her dreams, couldn't she?

Chapter Six

The sleek clipper *Aria* sailed into the New Orleans harbor and headed for the shipping company docks with Bastien at the helm. Squinting against the hard sparkle of the morning sun dancing off the water, he caught sight of several figures milling about, one of which was his brother. Alongside René stood his wife, Felice. The brown object running in circles around them had to be Miz Sassy, the mongrel René treated like a child born of his own blood.

A gust of wind grabbed the sails and the ship pitched.

"Ho there," the first mate called out. "Wind's picked up a bit."

Bastien wrestled the wheel, setting the vessel aright. "Christ. Didn't see that one coming."

"Water's got a bit choppy of a sudden," cautioned the first mate.

Damn it, sailing the clipper smoothly into the tight slip directly opposite the shipping office should've been the highlight of Bastien's journey home. God knew he'd practiced the tricky maneuver enough times back in Jamaica. But he was not fool enough to take chances.

"I'm too damned distracted to risk making a mistake." Cursing under his breath, he turned the task over to his first mate and stepped aside.

"Have Talbot report to me *tout de suite*," he growled at Henri.

Henri's shoulders jerked.

"Pardon," Bastien responded and slipped into his native tongue. "I didn't mean to sound so gruff. This should've been a high-spirited journey, not one beset by tending two passengers day and night."

"At least you'll be rid of them once we reach port," Henri responded in kind.

A measure of guilt mixed with his sense of duty as a *traiteur.* "Talbot refuses to stay in a hotel. Instead, he inquired about leasing a private residence. Where the devil am I supposed to locate one within an hour of reaching port?"

Henri shrugged. "I could ask the Kennedys, who run our company boarding house. They seem to know everything going on in town."

Bastien kept his eyes on the looming dock and his kin. "Madame Talbot is still in no condition…never mind. Go find Talbot."

"Aye-aye, Cap'n." Henri hurried off in the direction of the staterooms.

A flash of color caught Bastien's eye. Lily moved to the ship's railing, her pale blue cape covering Talbot's nightshirt. Talbot came into view beside her. She shook her head in response to whatever he'd said.

A muscle twitched in Bastien's jaw. Where the devil was Rubio? Bastien didn't care to have Talbot so close to her with no one on guard. Watching her as she managed to slowly make her way to the railing on her own, he knew what he had to do. Must do. Even though her appetite had returned, there was no getting around the fact that her illness would beleaguer her for some time.

Unsurprising to Bastien, she'd begun experiencing severe headaches, a condition he figured might last for several weeks or months. To top it off, Allita made mention that Lily had begun having nightmares. Lingering hallucinations were another side effect of the poison remaining in her system.

In short, Lily still required his attention. The certainty of where she belonged while she healed settled in like a rock sinking to the pit of his stomach—there was only one place to board his passengers that made sense—Le Blanc House. Once his sister Josette's private residence before her marriage, the Garden District mansion now belonged to the shipping company—for the time being, at least.

His cousin Vivienne managed the mansion while another cousin, shy Régine, ruled over the kitchen like a chef supreme. A seasoned cook privy to fabulous back gardens filled with fresh fruits and vegetables, she'd see to it Lily received the best in the way of sustenance.

Le Blanc House was also where he lived.

Should Talbot indeed turn out to be a close friend of Justin Andrews's, the patriarch would insist on the couple remaining in residence. Truth be told, what better place to situate Madame Talbot since he'd need to tend her on a daily basis.

Talbot scurried to Bastien's side. "You called for me?"

Bastien nodded. "Allita informed me that Madame Talbot has begun having night terrors. She is also talking in her sleep, some babble about being helpless to save her father, and something about jewels. What do you know of this?"

Talbot's cheeks flushed. He snatched his hat off his head and, gripping it by the brim, spun it around and around. "I surely do thank you for allowing us passage aboard your ship and for the care you've taken in treating my wife. Do you know when I might be able to contact Justin Andrews?"

Bastien decided to ignore the man's sidestepping his question. For now, anyway. "If he's upriver on his plantation, we'll have to send someone for him. Could take a couple of days to get him back here, don'cha know. On the other hand, if he's in residence in his townhome, perhaps he'll see you *tout de suite*."

"If it turns out to be a journey upriver, might I accompany whomever is to call on him?"

"*Non.* That would be Henri's task. I'll check with Monsieur Andrews's daughter, who happens to be dockside awaiting our arrival. She is wed to my brother, the company's senior manager. If her father is not in town, then Henri will go directly to Carlton Oaks to collect him. Since Madame Talbot should not be traveling, you will wait here with her."

Talbot pinched the bridge of his nose, then stared across the water. "Did you happen to think of a residence we might lease?"

"*Non.* You will reside at Le Blanc House. It is a company-owned estate where your wife will have the privacy she needs, the best cook in the city, and fresh food and healing herbs from the extensive gardens."

He turned to look at Talbot. "It is also where I reside. She will still need tending to."

Talbot paled. "But...but we cannot...it would not be proper for Lily to share...sir, you are a bachelor. It is one thing to be aboard ship, but in your home..."

Bastien paused a few beats, knowing full well Talbot would be flustered at what he was about to present to him. What the hell, he couldn't resist goading the man. A corner of his mouth twitched. "It would not be improper for a married woman with a husband to protect her to reside at Le Blanc House. The bedchamber that would be yours is large, with a separate sitting room, and a balcony overlooking the gardens. I can assure you, the two of you will be quite comfortable in one of our palatial suites."

Talbot's cheeks did not wear the color purple well.

"If you'll excuse me," Bastien said. "We are about to dock and I must speak with my first mate. Please ask Allita to prepare your wife to disembark. If you feel you cannot help her down the narrow gangplank, then wait until I have completed my duties and I shall do it."

"Yes, yes. Of course. I'll see if Lily...Mrs. Talbot is able to manage on her own."

"*Non*, Monsieur Talbot. It will be either you or myself who will tend to her. You decide." Bastien suppressed a snigger as he watched the man hurry back to his wife—or whatever she was to him. He returned to the helm, and taking his place beside the first mate at the wheel, he signaled for Henri once again.

If enthusiasm could drive the ship, then Henri's exuberance would be all they'd need to sail her into port. His long legs made short work of the distance between him and Bastien. "Can I have permission to stand at attention on the other side of your first mate while we dock?"

"*Oui.* You've done a fine job on board but before you race home to your *maman*, I've a few errands for you."

Henri nodded.

"You will be the first to disembark. Ask Felice if her father is in town or upriver and give me a thumbs-up if he's here. If he's at Carlton Oaks, you'll need to fetch him."

A cloud passed over Henri's eyes, then dissipated.

As much as the lad had matured in their five-month absence, Bastien knew he'd be eager to reunite with his mother. "Then tell Donal to bring the carriage around to the docks and transport the Talbots to Le Blanc House. Tell him to swing by the company boarding house on the way and let the Kennedys know the ship is in. Inform them they'll have a full house tonight. Next, grab a pirogue and collect my mother."

Henri turned pale. "But when do I—"

"See your *maman*? You can visit her for an hour before you head upriver to collect Justin Andrews. We're about to dock, so look sharp, now. A bosun who stands alongside his captain and first mate does so with his spine straight and chin up."

Henri snapped to attention, his countenance aglow with anticipation. "A long visit with Maman will have to wait. I have important duties to perform, don'cha know."

Felice waved at them, and Bastien's brother, locking gazes with him, gave a short nod of welcome. He knew that look. Had lived with it all his life. René was mighty glad Bastien had returned.

Something warm blossomed in his chest. He returned the nod, then focused on the lines being tossed to the onshore crew, felt the bump of the ship against the dock as they moored the clipper. He grinned when a loud cheer went up aboard ship.

"Off you go to attend to your errands, Henri." The lad leapt off the five short steps to the top deck and, once the gangplank was lowered, he scampered down and headed straight to Felice.

Bastien left the helm and strode to where Lily, Talbot, Allita, and Rubio stood.

Despite the heat, Lily glanced at René and Felice, who stood watching them, and eased the hood of her cape over her head, as if trying to disappear. She turned to Bastien, concern etching her lovely features.

"What be the matter, madame?"

"Sir, I have no shoes."

Bastien chuckled. "Madame, my brother and I grew up shoeless. You will fit right in."

Her brows arched. "You were poor?"

If she only knew the half of what growing up in a bayou shanty with a voodoo priestess for a mother was like. "Being poor had nothing to do with not owning shoes. My *maman* did not believe in wearing them. She is convinced we draw energy from the earth through the soles of our feet."

"I find her reasoning rather interesting." Lily eyed him with undisguised curiosity. "Did you outgrow the practice or are you still known to indulge?"

Stifling a grin, he said, "Given the opportunity, I still prefer the feel of the earth to hard leather."

He turned to address Talbot, Allita, and Rubio. "I shall transport Madame Talbot to the carriage. Follow along behind me, *s'il vous plaît*."

Sweeping her up in his arms, he held her close and headed for the gangplank. "Relax, Madame Talbot."

She set her cheek against his chest and slid an arm over his shoulder. "'Tis Lily," she murmured. "Call me Lily."

As her fingers trailed through the hair at his nape, he tried to ignore the warm rush across his skin. He slid his gaze to her face. Her eyes were closed. Shoving aside his unwanted reaction to her touch, he strode down the gangplank.

He nearly laughed as both René and Felice moved to the end of the walkway, their arms crossed over their chests, curiosity obvious in their deportment. At the sight of their undisguised nosiness, mischief got the best of him.

"*Bonjour*, brother. *Bonjour*, Felice," he quipped as he swept by them. "This woman in my arms is Madame Talbot. Behind us is her husband

and behind him are two feisty Cubans. Meet Allita and her nephew, Rubio. Their carriage awaits, so *pardonnez-moi*."

"You'll like my brother's wife," he said softly to Lily as he carried her to the waiting carriage. "She'll make a good friend and provide you with endless chatter."

Gently, he set Lily onto the rear seat of the open carriage and waited while Talbot settled in beside her with a grunt. Allita and Rubio climbed up front with the driver.

"Donal," Bastien said to Felice's nephew, who'd replaced Henri as the company errand boy. "When you deliver all four of these fine people to Le Blanc House, inform Vivienne that Madame Talbot is to have the largest suite and a bed brought in for Allita, her lady's maid."

"No," Lily responded. "I wish to be alone."

He raised a brow. He'd bet she didn't want Allita overhearing should Lily continue to talk in her sleep. "You do not wish for Allita to see to your needs?"

"Could she be installed in a nearby room where I might ring for her?"

"*Oui*. There is a suite with an adjoining room. Would that suit you?"

Lily nodded while Allita scowled and sent a speaking glance to Bastien. Rubio squirmed in his seat. Where Allita went, Rubio followed. After all, it was his family duty to look after his aunt. And Lily had made it clear two days ago that she wanted only Allita tending to her.

Bastien was of a mind to make Rubio and Talbot share a room. Oh, hell. There were plenty available. "The two of you are to remain with Madame Talbot."

Bastien nodded to Donal to proceed. With a click of his tongue, the lad set the pair of horses in a trot down the street.

Bastien made his way back to René and Felice. "Where are our two other workers?"

"They are at sea inspecting a new ship," René responded. "They are due to return on the morrow." He gave a nod to the disappearing carriage. "Would you mind telling us what all that was about?"

Bastien snorted. "The sun is high. I am going inside. Once I am out of this blasted heat, I will explain."

"By the way," René said, "since Felice's father is due in town sometime in the next day or two, we told Henri there was no need to go for him."

"*Merci*." Bastien stepped to the office door and halted. His once tidy desk was strewn with papers while Midnight, the company cat, lounged atop them, tail twitching and yellow eyes staring at him.

"What have you done to my desk?" He cursed under his breath. "Off with you, *minou*. Scat!"

"His name is Midnight and you well know it," Felice said. "Stop calling him *cat*."

After a haughty glance at Bastien, Midnight made a silent jump to the floor and strolled across the room to where a dog lay with its chin resting on its crossed paws, only its eyes moving. The hound didn't so much as twitch when the cat curled up against it.

Felice crossed her arms and tapped a foot. "Now then. Do tell us who those passengers are."

Bastien proceeded to explain the events of the past ten days—a journey that, due to a loss of wind, had taken ten days to complete instead of six. When he finished what he realized seemed a rather bizarre tale, Felice quickly gathered up her reticule.

René frowned. "What are you up to, *chère*?"

Her eyes sparkled with undisguised eagerness. "Why, the woman has no clothes or shoes. Therefore, I am off to collect Madame Charmontès, who will undoubtedly have a few gowns ready to adjust to Madame Talbot's figure. I'll pick up some shoes in different sizes from the shoemaker as well and—"

"And rush right over to Le Blanc House to stick your nose into my business," Bastien said.

René laughed. "Better yours than mine, since I am obviously about to conjure up payroll for your crew in my wife's absence and then hie off to the bank to collect it."

He walked over and pressed a kiss to his wife's cheek. "Do tell Régine to expect us for dinner. I wouldn't miss any of this for the world."

"Christ," Bastien muttered. "In case you've forgotten, *mon frère*, I just spent ten days commanding a ship while tending to a seriously ill passenger. Since I won't be leaving here until the cargo is unloaded and every sailor has been paid, I have no plan to do anything tonight other than seek my bed. Another night, *s'il vous plaît*."

"As you wish." Felice patted him on the shoulder and flew down the street.

René stuffed his hands into his pockets, rocked back on his heels and grinned at Bastien.

Bastien scowled. "What?"

"Something tells me there is more to this story than you are telling. Far more."

Chapter Seven

With a click of his tongue, the driver urged the two horses forward, but Lily gave in to temptation and glanced back at the three figures clustered together on the shipping dock. Was it the way he was standing, or could Bastien be a bit taller and broader across the shoulders than his brother? In any case, except for the stark contrast in eye color, there was no mistaking the strong familial resemblance. While René wore his hair long enough to brush his collar, and Bastien kept his shorter, the color was the same—black as a raven's wing and just as shiny. At the thought of having swept her fingers through Bastien's thick, wavy locks, her fingers tingled.

The willowy, dark-haired beauty standing alongside them was the brother's wife. Miss Felice, as Henri had called her. As if she sensed Lily's eyes on her, Felice turned her head and stared straight at Lily, her penetrating gaze closing the distance between them.

"Do turn around," Uncle snapped. "It is unseemly to be gawking."

Lily did as he ordered, not out of obedience to her uncle's wishes but to allay the sudden emotion enveloping her. She closed her eyes and took in a deep breath, as if doing so would displace the sense of forlornness that had overcome her. Feeling strangely incomplete now that the connection between Bastien and her had been broken, she settled low in the carriage, as if hoping the world and all her problems might disappear. She took to studying her surroundings as the clip-clop of the horses' hooves drew them closer to their destination, and farther from the one person she hadn't realized she'd become dependent upon. Silly, that.

Sweeping aside the pervasive cloud of gloom surrounding her, she inquired of the driver about where they were headed.

"I've orders to take you to Le Blanc House," the red-haired lad announced over his shoulder. His wide grin exposed a gap between his two front teeth. "I expect you'll be liking the place and the people in it. Henri took a shortcut on foot so he'll beat us there and inform Miss Régine and Miss Vivienne to be expecting you."

"Life in New Orleans must be rather informal if the ladies are being referred to as miss so-and-so."

Donal shrugged. "You're in the South now, ma'am. We're mighty respectful of our ladies hereabouts. Although some reckon it's too hot to bother with long titles, so we keep it to *miss*."

"How interesting. As a married woman, would I be called the same or something different?"

"With yer permission, ma'am, you'd be called miss so-and-so as well. Or ma'am. Dependin'."

Hmmm. Lily decided she might like the idea. "Depending on what, might I ask?"

"On yer preference. Also, dependin' on the occasion and what people you happen to be around, ma'am."

His sweet way with words brought a smile to her lips. "Then please, call me Miss Lily."

Uncle scowled at her and gave a stern shake of his head.

Raising a rebellious brow, she ignored him. "Would my lady's maid also be called Miss Allita?"

"Yes, ma'am."

Allita glanced over her shoulder and beamed at Lily.

Rubio rolled his eyes.

"Forgive my curiosity," Lily said. "Since everyone I've met here and aboard ship seems connected in one way or another, might you somehow be part of this clan, as well?"

"Yes, ma'am. I am proud to report that Michel Andrews is my pa. He married my mum, then took all six of her kids in and made us his own. He's brother to Miss Felice. Used to run the shipping office like René and Bastien do now, but since he got elected mayor, he can't be doing that no more. And here we are."

Donal pulled the carriage to a stop in front of a grand mansion that took up an entire city block. Though the air was heavy with moisture and a bead of perspiration trickled down her spine, her surroundings felt like a breath of fresh air. The mansion's size alone rivaled anything back home in the Mayfair district. Pristine white and surrounded by a deep, columned porch, the house was set back on a wide lawn amid lush azaleas, oaks, and magnolia trees.

"Is this a private home?"

"This is Le Blanc House, ma'am. Belongs to the shipping company. It's a long story. Miss Vivienne will tell you all about it if'n you care to inquire."

A set of double doors swung open. Out stepped a diminutive dark-haired woman dressed in a pale gray gown, its sleeves and collar trimmed in crisp white. She gave Donal a nod.

"That would be Miss Vivienne, cousin to René and Bastien. Don't pay no attention to how stern she looks. Won't mean a thing once you get to know her." Donal sprang from the carriage, freed the step-down, and held a hand out for Lily. "If'n you please, ma'am."

A grunt and a groan brought Lily's uncle to the ground. Rubio assisted his aunt's exit, and together they walked behind Lily and Uncle down the long walkway and up the stairs to where Miss Vivienne stood.

Introductions completed, Vivienne said, "I'll show you to your rooms directly."

Spine ramrod straight, she guided them through a wide entry resplendent with gold-framed artwork hung against silk moiré walls of lovely emerald green. Chandeliers hung from the high ceiling. Every side table and whatnot sitting atop it was of fine quality. Lily hadn't known what to expect—hadn't thought about where they'd be staying, actually. Thus far, it was plain to see, Le Blanc House, its environs, and everything within it had been cut from the finest cloth.

Vivienne led them to a wide staircase, then paused a moment to glance at Rubio.

"He's nephew to my lady's maid," Lily said. "He is to remain near her by order of his family."

"Ah, yes," Vivienne said to Rubio. "Henri told me you are to be considered a guest and not in service."

Rubio said nothing, but Lily swore he looked relieved. No doubt he'd have enough on his hands watching over his spry aunt.

Vivienne motioned for them to follow her up the stairs. "I'll give you a tour of Le Blanc House later, if you wish. Régine, my cousin, has prepared a nourishing luncheon for each of you to take in your room."

She turned to Lily. "Afterward, I shall prepare your restorative bath. That is, unless you'd rather rest first. However, Henri has gone to fetch my aunt who is also a *traiteur*—a healer—and I am told Miss Felice is busy visiting the dressmaker for you. Since they should all arrive within the hour, I do recommend the bath, *tout de suite*."

Vivienne spoke with the same lilting accent as Bastien and Henri. Lily found the sound oddly soothing. "I must admit, even though we broke our fast with a lovely meal aboard ship, I am famished yet again. I've had no appetite for a long while, but now that it has returned, it has done so with a vengeance."

Lily grinned at Vivienne. "I should be embarrassed, but I am not."

Vivienne nodded in return. "Between Bastien's care and Régine's cooking, we'll have you looking like a bright ray of sunshine in no time."

Good heavens. How much had Vivienne been told? Nonetheless, at the sound of Bastien's name, a flicker of that sunshine the woman had mentioned glimmered in Lily. "Will he be coming here to treat me?"

A curious expression crossed the woman's face. "*Mais oui*. Every day, don'cha know."

A huffing and puffing Donal appeared at the top of the stairs loaded down with luggage. Rubio rushed to his aid.

"Show the others to their rooms, *s'il vous plaît*," Vivienne said to Donal. "Then join Régine in the kitchen. She's made étoufée, and I think she also has a little treat for you."

Donal grinned. "Beignets?"

"I would not spoil the surprise." Vivienne led Lily into a large suite lavishly decorated in pale peach and white, with touches of green the color of spring leaves. Lily glanced up at the painted ceiling filled with winged angels darting about in a heavenly sky of blues, oranges, and grays.

"Oh, my. Perhaps I would like to lie down after eating. I could feast my eyes on this lovely scene all the day long. In fact, at the moment, I could be held prisoner here to the end of my days and never once object."

A corner of Vivienne's mouth twitched. "You haven't seen the gardens yet."

* * * *

Lily awoke to a light rapping and the sound of her door opening. Stark fear shot through her. Scrambling off the bed, she spied Vivienne at the threshold and remembered where she was. She breathed a sigh of relief. No need to be afraid. Not in this house. Nonetheless, she made note to ask about a key to the lock. Just as a precaution.

Vivienne stepped into the room. "Pardon. I did not mean to disturb you."

"Pay no attention. I fell asleep and for a moment, I forgot where I was." She pushed a hank of hair off her face and paused when a woman stepped into the room behind Vivienne. She was dark-haired as well, and bore the same fine features Lily had noted in these bayou French. But this beautiful woman gave her pause. Impossible for Lily to guess the stranger's age. She appeared ageless and had an air of importance about her. Being of noble blood herself, Lily was well acquainted with royalty. She'd never been intimidated by any of them. But this person, simply by entering the room, changed the very energy within its walls. Who *was* she?

"This is Mademoiselle Odalie Thibodeaux. She is my aunt, as well as Bastien's mother," said Vivienne. "She is a *traiteur* and here to help heal you."

"I should have taken a bath first, but I fell asleep. I am sorry."

Odalie Thibodeaux moved to where Lily stood and took up a handful of Lily's hair. "We must do something to restore your hair, *tout de suite*."

"Quickly, you say? It's more like straw than hair."

Five women hurried into the room, one of whom Lily recognized as Felice.

"We met dockside," Felice said. "I've brought along Madame Charmontès and her assistants. She is the most fabulous dressmaker in all the world."

"*Oui*," the little woman said. With a nod, in filed her workers, who immediately began spreading garments over the bed.

"To the bathing room," Odalie announced and exited the room.

Madame Charmontès scowled at Odalie's back and slammed the door behind her. "I must first take measurements." She wiggled dismissive fingers at the nightshirt Lily wore. "Off with that…that thing you are wearing so I can take your measurements."

Once the dressmaker had finished painstakingly noting Lily's every dimension, Vivienne motioned to Lily. "Follow me."

In moments, Lily found herself sinking into a large tub filled with steaming water hinting of lavender and with rose petals floating on top. She'd never once considered lighting candles in a bathing room in broad daylight, but who was she to complain?

Gracious, was it because she'd lacked a mother and served as her father's secretary that she'd never taken the time to pamper herself? Well, it was about time to do so in these heavenly surroundings.

Despite being surrounded by women who were serving her with obvious kindness, and despite the presence of her uncle just down the hall, Lily still felt a void somewhere in the vicinity of her chest.

Whatever it was, it wasn't caused by the grief of losing her father—those emotions were still buried deep in her broken heart and likely would remain so for the rest of her life.

With Allita standing sentry, Bastien's cousin scrubbed Lily's skin until it shone, washed her hair in a strange mixture of blackstrap molasses and vinegar under the direction of Bastien's mother.

Lily could not recall ever having been intimidated by anyone—not even the prime minister when he'd come to call on Papa. She'd felt respectful and honored to be in his presence, to be sure, but intimidated? Never. This woman's dark piercing eyes seemed to see right through Lily. Vivienne, however, did her bidding without seeming to be disturbed at all by the woman's stern demeanor.

Even the air around Odalie Thibodeaux seemed to shimmer in a way Lily found disturbing and puzzling. Something about the woman made Lily yearn to return to the privacy of her rooms, free from those steely dark eyes.

What had life been like growing up with a mother like her? Perhaps being raised by such a woman had something to do with the unique aura surrounding Bastien.

At the thought of him, she became once again aware of the void in her. Could his absence be the cause of the feeling? Had she grown too comfortable around him in those ten days aboard ship? Well, seven, if she subtracted the three days when she'd been unconscious. No, she'd had a vague sense of him even as they'd boarded ship that first night. His scent. His deep, lilting voice with that resonant accent she'd grown accustomed to. Those blue eyes that could look right into the depths of her being.

She wondered if he was still at the shipping company offices. Or was he now in his home? She wondered where he lived, what sort of setting he might occupy.

Wrapped in a robe provided by Vivienne, Lily relaxed while Allita brushed her towel-damp hair, and Bastien's mother did something heavenly to her feet and lower legs. Whatever she was about, her actions were more than simply applying a soothing lotion that made Lily's skin tingle. It seemed as though each stroke of the woman's strong but gentle fingers energized her.

The deep pressure of the woman's thumb running along the bottom of Lily's feet nearly caused her to moan aloud. "Whatever you are doing, it feels marvelous."

"You nearly had the life force sucked from your bones," Bastien's mother said. "You'll be feeling more alive as the days stack one upon the other."

"Bastien said he and his siblings grew up without shoes. Should I adopt the same practice? Would it help me to heal faster?"

His mother paused with Lily's foot in her hand and studied her for a long moment. It felt as though Lily's very soul was being scrutinized. Despite all the woman was doing to help her, Lily wanted to rush to her room and hide away.

"*Oui*. Keeping your feet bare would draw the earth's healing forces into you, but it is your decision. Madame Charmontès has brought several pairs of shoes for you to wear." She paused a beat. "Or not to wear, as you so choose. In any event, it would be wise to spend time in the gardens."

She set Lily's foot down, stood, and moved toward the door. "I am finished. I shall spend some time in the garden myself."

"Come along back to your suite," Vivienne said to Lily. She glanced at Allita. "We can help her into her clothing and then perhaps both of you would like to tour Le Blanc House?"

As they left the large bathing chamber and headed for Lily's suite, she noted the fine furnishings lining this wide, second-level corridor. The damask wallpaper on this level was a soft yellow, the candelabras and chandeliers as lovely as what she'd passed on the lower floor. "I look forward to taking a tour. Thank you. If the exterior and this floor are any indication of what lies below, Le Blanc House indeed rivals my home in England."

A shudder went through her. Never again would she so much as set foot in their London home. The shock of the night her uncle had swept her away rushed through her. Lord, if she ever returned to England, it would be to Cowdrey Hall, up north. She'd live a reclusive life there, safe from people like Julian Stanhope.

Allita touched Lily's arm. "Are you all right, madame?"

Lily shook off the dross of bad memories and hastened to her room. "I am fine. I look forward to some new clothing." She managed a small smile directed at both Allita and Vivienne, and tried for a bit of humor. "I've grown quite tired of wearing Mr. Talbot's nightshirts."

Vivienne took her other arm and halted her. "You're headed to the wrong room, madame. Yours is right next door."

"Oh, forgive me." She made to turn and then paused to take in the door at the end of the hallway. A large brass lion's head was affixed to the carved panel.

"Is that also a bedchamber?"

"*Oui*," Vivienne said.

"Forgive me if I am being too inquisitive, but why is there a knocker attached to a bedchamber door?"

Vivienne's mouth twitched. "This is Bastien's suite. He has been known to sleep like the dead, so when we need to wake him, we give the lion a good rapping."

A buzz shot through Lily's head. "His suite? Does he sleep here on occasion?"

Puzzlement carved a line between Vivienne's brows. "*Non*, madame. Bastien lives here."

And just like that, the void inside Lily disappeared. A warm glow started in the center of her chest and radiated outward. She glanced away from Vivienne, lest the woman see how her words had heated Lily's cheeks. "Is this the reason he wanted Mr. Talbot and me to board here, so he could continue to treat me?"

"In part," Vivienne responded. "Apparently, your husband and Monsieur Andrews the elder are acquaintances. Therefore, he would want you here, as well." She opened the door to Lily's suite and ushered her inside.

Madame Charmontès, a tiny French woman who appeared older than Methuselah, awaited with several day gowns laid out on the bed. Miss Felice sat in a chair, her sparkling eyes studying Lily.

"Which would you like to wear today?" Madame Charmontès asked. "My seamstresses have temporarily tailored them all to your figure, but they've also created seams-within-seams, so as you fill out, we can ease out each seam as needed."

Lily looked over the garments. "They are all quite lovely, but which one would be the coolest? I fear I am not used to this sultry weather."

"You must be thirsty," Felice said.

"Indeed," Lily responded.

Madame Charmontès clapped her hands at Allita. "Quickly, go to the kitchen and fetch some iced lemonade for our dear lady."

Allita showed her palms in a helpless display. "I know not where the kitchens are."

"Come along," Vivienne said. "I will take you to meet my cousin Régine, our cook. After we deliver the iced drinks to everyone, I shall take you on the tour I promised."

"Indeed. I am curious to see the rest of your home," Lily said.

"And the gardens," Vivienne responded. "Bastien's sister designed the gardens years ago, but seeing as how she now lives in England, he oversees them."

"Bastien…I mean Mr. Thibodeaux…manages the gardens?"

"*Oui.* He has been known to dig in the soil, but mostly he manages the gardeners who take care of everything. Growing healing herbs and fresh food here is important to him. And please, feel free to call him Bastien in our home. We are all related, and quite informal, despite our elegant surroundings."

"Then I'd much prefer it if you were to call me Lily." *I cannot tell you how I loathe the name Talbot.*

"Which shoes?" Madame Charmontès asked, indicating several pairs of slippers and a good leather half-boot.

Her thoughts never far from Bastien, Lily felt a tickle of rebellion. "Thank you, but I've decided to forego shoes altogether."

Felice laughed.

"Humph." Madame Charmontès fisted her hands on her hips. "That voodoo witch convinced you, did she?"

"What do you mean, voodoo witch?"

"Ah, no one has told you?"

Lily shook her head.

"The Thibodeaux siblings have all turned out quite well despite their rough beginnings, and despite having been raised by a voodoo priestess who can be quite dangerous if she's a mind to be. Watch out for her."

Chapter Eight

By the time Bastien reached Le Blanc House, the sun had long ago surrendered to a bright yellow moon that bathed the night in a luminescent glow. Ignoring the muggy air, he'd walked the couple miles home, his thoughts never wandering far from Lily. How had she fared in her strange surroundings?

Vivienne met him at the bottom of the stairs leading to the upper floor. "Régine made étouffée."

"*Merci*, but Henri's *maman* delivered jambalaya and cornbread to the office." He managed a small grin. "Her son's favorite, don'cha know. How did things go here today?"

"Rather splendidly, actually."

He loosened his cravat and unbuttoned his waistcoat while they chatted. "*Bien.* Did she eat the étouffée?"

Vivienne's lips twitched. "Twice. Followed by several beignets."

His cousin never smiled. A little twitch to her mouth was as good as outright laughter from anyone else.

"What has you so amused?"

"By *she*, I take it you mean Miss Lily."

Christ. Are my thoughts so transparent? "Had she no objection to our local spices pricking her…ahem…delicate English tongue?"

"*Au contraire.* Were you aware she was born in India and raised there until her seventh year?"

"I did not know this. One more thing revealed about our mysterious lady."

"She said she was weaned on their hot and spicy food."

"Hmm." He'd expected a woman of her obvious breeding to look down her nose at hardy Cajun fare. "How are the others in her entourage faring?"

Vivienne's lips twitched again. "Well settled in their assigned quarters. They also found our delicious Cajun food to their liking. Monsieur Talbot demonstrated a good appetite, as did those two Cubans. However, I suspect when Rubio wandered into the kitchen, he found the cook even more to his liking than her abilities at a stove."

"Really?" Bastien hiked a brow. "Régine didn't run him off with a kitchen knife?"

"*Non.*" Vivienne clasped her hands together, straightened her spine and lifted her chin. "Not only did our cousin allow a strange man to occupy the same space as her, she seemed to trust him enough to let herself enjoy his presence."

Could Vivienne be envious? *Merde.* "I had him figured for a good and loyal man, but isn't this a pleasant surprise?"

When his cousin's lips thinned and she failed to respond, he decided changing the subject might be a good idea. "What of Lily's...Madame Talbot's healing treatments and clothing?"

"As you would expect on both accounts." Vivienne visibly relaxed. Another twitch to her mouth. "Felice was in the thick of things, and having a gay time of it."

Bastien chuckled. "No surprise there. Henri said Madam Charmontès and Felice were already here by the time he delivered Maman. Is my mother still here, by the way?"

"She has taken to her bed like everyone else." The humor left her eyes and her brow creased. "Everyone except Miss Lily, that is."

He frowned. "Where is she?"

"At the moment, in the gardens taking in the magic of the fireflies. They are especially thick this evening."

Bastien took note of his cousin's sudden reserve. "What is it you are not telling me? Did Maman not take well to treating an Englishwoman?"

Vivienne shook her head. "Unlike you, she no longer disdains the English. Allita has another concern, however. Perhaps you should seek her out."

Bastien took the stairs two at a time. He didn't have to look far to find Allita—she was in the corridor, pacing and twisting her hands together.

"What's wrong?"

"Oh, señor. I am most concerned about Lily...pardon...she insists we call her Lily. She asked Miss Vivienne for a key to the lock on her bedchamber door. Miss Vivienne said she would have to hunt one down because no one bothers locking anything except the exterior locks. This seemed to disturb Lily, but she went into her room to lie down anyway. I settled into my quarters for a nap. Not long after, I heard cries coming from her room.

I reckoned she was having another bad dream or hallucination, so I went to her. When I tried the door between us, it would not open. I rapped and rapped on the panel. When she finally responded, I could hear her moving something aside to let me in. Right off, I saw she had a chair wedged under the latch on the entry door to her chamber."

What the devil? "Did she do this kind of thing while aboard ship?"

"Never. Back then, I was with her at all times and Rubio was guarding us, so she seemed to feel secure. I do not think her insisting on a room to herself is such a good idea. Perhaps it would be best if she shared her husband's quarters."

God, no. Bastien scrubbed a hand across the back of his neck and let go a heavy breath. "I'll go in search of her."

"She's wandering around in the garden wearing nothing but a thin night rail, señor. Shall I go with you?"

"No need. You may turn in for the night." He nodded toward the door behind Allita. "Is this her suite?"

"Sí."

He stepped inside and saw that the windows were open, the curtains swelling with wind. Lightning pulsed in the distant clouds. There'd be a storm hitting soon. Very soon. He closed the windows, grabbed a lightweight throw at the end of her bed, and started for the door. He paused long enough to remove his cravat, jacket, and waistcoat. Rather than waste time taking them to his quarters, he draped them over a chair nearest the exit, intending to collect them later.

* * * *

Lily felt Bastien's presence before she saw him. Her heart skipped a beat and her throat caught. She swallowed hard against the constriction. Why in heaven did she find it difficult to breathe around him of late? She remained where she was, intending to wait for him to locate her in this back part of the garden, but as the wind kicked up, the treetops filled with moving shadows that seemed to battle one another. Despite the heavy air, she shivered. "I'm back here," she called out. "On the swinging bench in the far corner of the garden."

He stepped from the shadows and paused. His gaze traveled from her head to her bare toes and back up again. "Moonlight becomes you, *chère*."

The husky, mellow sound of his voice floated in the darkness, soothing her. Was that an endearment he'd just used? "It certainly is a bold moon. It shines like a spotlight on you."

"Not for long." He settled a lightweight throw over her lap, then eased onto the other end of the bench.

"Why is that?"

"Storms sweep in from the Gulf on the devil's schedule. This one will be upon us in no time." He wedged himself into the corner, stretched out his long legs, and draped an arm across the back of the bench, his hand mere inches from where she sat. Reaching over, he caught up a lock of her hair and held it between his fingertips. "I see my *maman* did her magic and brought your hair back to life. It's lovely now."

It wasn't his action that startled Lily. It was the fleeting expression on his face that nearly sucked the air from her lungs. "You couldn't have done the same aboard ship?"

"I didn't have the right potions."

His lilting words slid over her like warm honey. "I don't think your mother cares much for me."

He let go a soft snort. "She doesn't care much for anyone. Not even her children."

"What an odd remark. Would you care to elaborate?"

"*Non*." He gave a nod at her hand. "What do you have there?"

She opened her fist to him. "It's the small pot of lip balm you gave me. I'm as fond of the scent as its healing properties."

Leaning over, he relieved her of the container. The brush of his fingers across her palm swept right through her and lit a small flame in her belly. The heat reached her cheeks.

He paused. His gaze moved across her face as if he were looking for something. Without a word, he lifted the lid off the tin, gathered a bit of the ointment on his thumb and slowly swept it across her bottom lip.

Startled, she sucked in a quick breath. "Oh."

He repeated the action on her upper lip. It was as though the tips of a thousand feathers shimmered over her mouth and coursed through her body, catching her off guard.

Those thick lashes still framed amazing blue eyes, but in them, she caught something she hadn't seen before. There shone within a light that spoke of…what? Of desire? She must be wrong. He was merely trying to help her. A rogue thought slid sideways into her mind—how well acquainted with passion this man must be.

Heavens, what a forbidden thought.

He set the tin back into her hand, closed her fingers over it and leaned back. "Did you enjoy the fireflies dancing about this evening?"

"Enormously." She glanced around. "What's happened to them?"

"It's the storm about to arrive. They've gone into hiding. Do you not have them in England?"

"We have glowworms." She stared at his lips and wondered what it would be like to kiss them. "I do not know if they are the same or not. In any case, they inhabit Southern England and I've not been there."

He settled a shoulder deeper into the corner and studied her. "Allita said you had another nasty dream. Tell me about it."

Please don't ask. Her spirits plummeted. She blinked her eyes against a sudden sting of tears. "It was nothing."

He raised a brow, as if challenging her response. "You also inquired about a key to the lock on your door. What of that, Lily? Did someone attack you in the past?"

At the mere mention of the key, she shivered in response to the fear and shadows stirring inside her.

"I was poisoned, Bastien. After such a daunting experience, I'd think any woman would be on her guard."

Anxious to change the subject, she glanced up at the trees whipping in the wind. "I suppose now is a good time to get inside, before the rains come, don't you think?"

His eyes searched her face again. "If you wish."

A part of her wanted to run away from this conversation, which was getting too close to the heart of her fears, while another part of her wanted to remain right where she was—near him. Her gaze traced the gentle curve of his mouth. An urge to set her lips to his grabbed hold of her. Never before had she wanted to be close to a man. Never before had she experienced a desire to touch and be touched.

The electrifying realization made her heart stammer. Her mouth turned dry as cotton. Such a thing was simply out of the question. She knew what she could do, however. She'd find a way to convince him to allow her to paint him. She could reproduce every emotion she'd seen flit across his face. The urge to capture his image, and to keep it forever, provoked an uncommonly wild streak in her. Slipping the top off the tin of balm, and mimicking his previous administrations, she ran her thumb over the scented ointment.

He watched her movements, saying nothing.

Leaning his way, she swept her thumb across his bottom lip, duplicating his action.

He sucked in a breath.

Just as she had done.

The blue of his eyes deepened and there it was—the precious expression she'd seen once before. A burst of energy coursed through her, demanding an outlet. "I should like to paint you."

Another emotion flitted over his countenance. Amusement? He studied her through heavy-lidded eyes.

"I fear my talents are somewhat limited, but would you allow me the pleasure of attempting to capture you on canvas?"

He bent his arm, and leaning the side of his head against his fingertips, studied her for a long while. When he spoke, his words came as a husky rasp. "When?"

"On the morrow?" Heaven help her, the fireflies must've landed in her stomach and decided to flit about. "I've only charcoals on hand, but I sketch first with them anyway, so no matter."

"I'll have paints brought in."

The slam of a door followed by a loud crashing about in the garden startled her. A lantern light flickered through the leaves.

"Lily, where the devil are you?"

Good heavens. Lily swept a hand across her brow. "Here, in the back. I can see your lantern swinging, so I know you are on the right path."

Her uncle appeared. His eyes, filled with fury, swept from her to Bastien and back again. "What the bloody hell are you doing out here? In your night rail, no less. This is indecent. Come along this minute."

Bastien looked at her uncle, then back at her. She noted Bastien's clamped jaw and set face. Then he crossed his arms over his chest, his bearing suddenly nonchalant. "She's done nothing wrong, monsieur."

"Nothing wrong? She's out here with a man and in her bloody nightclothes, for God's sake."

Lily stole another glance at Bastien. He seemed perfectly at ease, yet somehow dangerous. She sensed a coiled strength within him and held her breath, waiting for what might occur next. She had no desire to do her uncle's bidding and was about to tell him so.

Bastien used his heel to start the swing moving again. "Unless you've forgotten, the entire time I treated Madame Talbot aboard ship, she wore nothing but your nightshirt, which was far more revealing than what she now wears."

Anger leaked out of her uncle like a sieve. "She's not aboard ship now. Since your mother is capable of tending to Madame Talbot, we shall require your services no longer. And by the by, what the devil is your clothing doing in my wife's room? You've a lot to explain, both of you. Now come along, Lily."

A muscle jumped in Bastien's jawline. "My mother is here as a consultant only. I called on her as a courtesy, and out of respect." He turned to Lily. "I believe it should be the lady who chooses her *traiteur*. Lily?"

"Don't be ridiculous." Her uncle held out his hand to her. "Come along."

Good Lord, her uncle was telling her that she could not make her own decisions. She could feel herself beginning to fall apart inside. All at once, she became so angry it hurt, and her words spilled out unthinkingly. "After all I have been through and survived, I would think you'd want me to make up my own mind about who I would like to attend me. Furthermore, as a responsible adult, I shall decide when to come in out of the rain. Which I will do when the first raindrops fall on me and not before. Do not make a scene. Please leave."

Mouth agape and cheeks flaming, her uncle stared at both of them for a long moment. "You are as stubborn as your father."

"Indeed, and I thank you for noticing. Good night—" She clamped shut her mouth. Good Lord, she'd nearly called him Uncle. Her hand slid to her throat. "Good night, Percy."

He stiffened and a soft noise left his throat. Had he also realized her near mistake?

"We shall speak in the morning, Lily." He turned on his heel and disappeared around a bend in the path, the flickering light of his lantern vanishing along with him.

She turned to Bastien and paused when she spied yet another emotion she could not name, leaving her suddenly defensive. "Have I made a terrible fool of myself?"

He said nothing for a long while, but those eyes of his fairly glittered. "I would like to ask you a question, Lily."

She let out a deep sigh. "If it has anything to do with my being poisoned, the answer is no."

"It does not. Actually, mine is a rather selfish question. One I shouldn't ask, but temptation just got the better of me."

"Really? Now you have me curious. You may ask. However, I do not guarantee an answer."

He leaned toward her and studied her with a strange expression she made a mental note to capture on canvas.

"Your question?" she asked.

"Are you or have you ever been anyone's wife, Lily?"

He knows.

The part of her that wanted to free her soul with a confession battled with the part that feared she might fall apart completely and never find the strength to bring herself back from the brink.

Springing to her feet, she tossed the throw over her shoulders and declared, "The first raindrop has touched my cheek. Therefore, I shall remove myself to my rooms. Good evening, sir."

She'd only taken a few steps when she realized there was no longer a moon and it was dark as pitch. "Blast it all," she muttered.

A chuckle came from behind her as Bastien swept her up in his arms, carried her to the house, and started up the stairs.

"I can manage on my own now," she said. "Set me down."

"You've mud on your feet. You'll leave tracks." He carried her up the steps and into her room. Then he set her down, backed her up against the wall, and slapped his palms against the wall on either side of her, caging her in.

Was he about to kiss her? She doubted she could say no. He was so close she could see the thin black striations in the blue of his eyes.

"What do you want?" she murmured.

"Who are you? What is your real name? And why are you in hiding?"

"My name is Lily."

"Oh, I believe your Christian name to be true, but is your surname Talbot? Do you and monsieur even share the same name?"

A flash of lightning lit the sky, followed by a boom of thunder that shook the house. It might as well have been her heart exploding. "I don't know what you mean."

Stepping away from her, he moved to make his exit. "If you still wish for me to sit for a portrait, I'll see you at ten in the library."

He crossed the threshold, only to pause and lean back far enough to catch her gaze. "By the way, you nearly called Talbot by a different name back there in the garden. You are getting careless, *chère*."

Chapter Nine

Sketching a charcoal of Bastien had been a grand idea originally. She'd thought the exercise a clever way of openly studying him without getting caught staring. But blast it all, the tables had turned. Now it was Bastien who settled his intense gaze on her, and there wasn't a thing she could do about it. To make matters worse, he'd switched the venue from the library to the garden, where their activity had attracted a small crowd.

Vivienne, Rubio, and Allita strolled about the garden chatting with each other whilst stealing glances at the canvas as they wandered by. Even shy Régine popped outside for an occasional glimpse. Felice, on the other hand, made no excuse for the curiosity consuming her. She'd shown up early, ostensibly to check on Lily's well-being, and here she remained. Her attention seemed more focused on Bastien than on Lily's undertaking. While Lily found her audience exceedingly distracting, Bastien seemed to find the entire affair amusing.

The toad.

Much to Lily's disappointment, Bastien arrived for his sitting dressed in charcoal trousers, a superfine jacket, gold waistcoat, and snowy cravat. She could say nothing, of course, but privately she'd hoped to see the same dashing attire as he'd worn aboard ship—there was something to be said about a man dressed in tall boots and fawn-colored britches that clung to him like a second skin.

He'd insisted on selecting the location—a cushioned bench nestled amid a dazzling display of flowers, which made for a spectacular backdrop. However, the wrought-iron affair was a bit short for him. He'd merely shrugged, flung one long leg over the armrest, and leaned an elbow against the other. He lounged about casually sipping iced lemonade, his penetrating gaze fixed on her.

"I can't get your mouth right if you insist on holding a glass to your lips."

He flashed her a heart-stopping smile, guzzled the remaining liquid, and set down the glass on one of the stone pavers beside the bench. The man was nothing short of gorgeous. Something deep inside her ached. She turned her focus back to her work, determined to think of him only as a male model. She needed to conclude this spectacle.

She sketched furiously, trying to capture the moods shifting over Bastien's features. She'd committed to memory a certain imperceptible something that passed through him every now and then. She wanted it in the largest sketch, intended to study it when it was completed. Besides, she wanted to know just what it took to cause that look to flash across his features.

Bastien's mother stepped into the garden, folded her hands in front of her, and slowly took in the scene. Lily's hand faltered. It took everything she had to maintain her deportment. She dared not take in so much as a fortifying breath lest her unease be revealed. Using her thumb, she furtively erased the smudge the woman's entry had provoked and continued sketching.

Odalie moved to stand behind Lily and said nothing for a long while. And then she murmured something unintelligible under her breath.

Lily paused with the piece of charcoal in her hand and turned at the waist. "I beg your pardon. Did you say something?"

His mother looked startled for a moment, as if she hadn't meant to speak. "Do you mind if I continue to observe? I know how sensitive artists can be when they work."

"Not at all," Lily responded while wishing she'd had the courage to say she did indeed mind.

Odalie raised a brow and studied the portrait through eyes as cold and dark as a deep well. "What a clever idea."

Bastien stared intently at his mother's open hand splayed across her stomach. When his mother seemed to realize where his gaze fell, her hand dropped away. Lily decided it must be an unconscious gesture when struck by a strong emotion.

"After my comment about your cleverness," his mother said, "I am sure Bastien fairly itches to see what you are about."

He picked up his glass, fished around for the remaining piece of ice, and popped it into his mouth. "You did that on purpose."

Lily turned back to her work of fashioning a montage of sorts. In the center she'd created an oval-shaped portrait of Bastien sprawled on the bench in full repose. A cluster of cameos from the shoulders up circled the central figure. Each image captured a different mood she'd seen flit across his countenance at one time or another. All except one. She'd only seen the one expression fleetingly, but the look was charged with something so powerful her mind scattered whenever he directed it her way. That was the image she'd committed to memory and hoped to accurately portray on his face in the large, central oval.

His mother left Lily and moved to where Bastien lounged. She ran her fingers through one side of his hair, gently combing a few strands into place.

He gave a jerk of his head, deflecting her hand from his person.

"Merely tucking in a few strands for the artist." A faint smile touched the corners of her mouth. "You are such a pleasant sort. I expect most believe you to be a man who never utters a cross word to his *maman*."

At his mother's innuendo, a slow look of mischief spread over Bastien's countenance. Only he could know what his mother's true meaning was.

"Enough, Maman. Time to take yourself elsewhere." He settled his gaze on Lily once again.

She glanced up and caught Bastien's mother studying her with a thoughtful look on her face. "I am an amateur at best. Forgive me if I do not do your son justice. I'm simply passing time with a bit of a frivolous entertainment."

"On the contrary. I'd say you've captured my son quite...perfectly. Claiming to be an amateur does *you* the injustice. Do take care of that sketch, for it looks like rain. You wouldn't want it spoilt. Perhaps you will one day decide to transfer it to something more permanent than charcoal. Do you paint in oils?"

"It's my preference, actually." Lily paused in her sketching to give Bastien's mother her full attention. "Blue," she said thoughtfully. "It would indeed take oils to catch the remarkable blue of his eyes."

"What a fine goal." The woman cast Lily an odd look, then left her son's side to return to Lily's.

Oh, how Lily fought the urge to squirm.

Odalie examined the portrait again, her gaze fixed on the central drawing. "Just as I thought," she murmured. Without another word, Bastien's disarming voodoo priestess mother exited the garden.

She knows I'm attracted to him.

Lily's throat felt suddenly parched. She tossed her charcoals into the box, gave her hand a quick swipe on a towel, and lifting the drawing from the board, turned to make her exit. "If you'll excuse me."

"Whoa," Bastien called out, swinging his legs off the bench and rising. "Where are you off to in such a rush?"

"To my bedchamber for a rest." She headed for the door, her heart in her throat.

Bastien followed behind her. "You intend to scurry off without so much as showing me why I have been straining to sit in one place for so long?"

Lily paused. "You've hardly been straining yourself."

"Give me one good reason why you're making such a hasty exit."

"I'll give you two." She lifted her chin in defiance. "One, it is about to rain, and didn't your mother say I ought to save this wretched piece? And two, I am rushing off to my room, as you so crassly put it, to complete the sketch before my memory fails me. You'll see it when I am finished. Not before."

She hurried off with Allita scurrying along in her wake.

"What's gotten into you?" he called out.

"The coming rain," she called back over her shoulder.

One would've thought the others gathered in the garden were at a cricket match the way their heads bobbed back and forth between Bastien and Lily. Oh, there was going to be gossip at the dinner table tonight.

"Get back here, Lily…er…Madame Talbot. That portrait is mine."

"I'm the person who sketched it, so 'tis mine actually." She hurried up the stairs, eager to complete the piece while her memory was still fresh.

A flash of lightning followed by an immediate crack of deafening thunder sent a squealing Allita scurrying into Lily's suite behind her. Lily shut the door and turned to Allita. "Don't let anyone in. I don't care if it's the blasted devil on horseback."

She glanced out the window at the darkened sky and frowned. "I am already tired of these blasted storms thundering in off the Gulf."

Allita nodded in agreement. "Vivienne said in these parts squalls can come out of nowhere and hit so fast and hard, there's no time to close the stable doors."

Lily pursed her lips against a smile. "Hmm. I'll remain in my rooms for the remainder of the day, including dinner. You're dismissed to go about your own business."

"Didn't you just tell me to guard the door?"

Lily waved her off. "Indeed, but it was silly of me. I'm perfectly capable of managing on my own."

"I don't mind waiting here with you until the storm blows over. That is, if you don't mind."

Was Allita, who seemed to fear not much of anything, afraid of thunderstorms? Oh, dear. "Actually, I could use the company. Providing you won't be prone to chatter."

"No, ma'am."

Lily went to work, briskly copying the portrait before her. She'd give Bastien the copy and keep the original as a master. She'd reproduce it yet again in oils when she took leave of Le Blanc House. As the room darkened even further, the sky opened, spilling out a torrent of rain so fast the ground couldn't swallow it up. Small ponds began to dot the deep-set front yard and turn the street to a river.

"Light some candles, will you, Allita? You can leave the doors open between our rooms if you like."

"*Gracias*." A relieved-looking Allita hurried about lighting candles. "Like you, I do not care for fierce storms. Not at all. Since it is near the noon hour, would you like me to check with Régine and see what she has planned for a meal?"

"Thank you, yes. And perhaps some tea for the two of us while we wait?"

Allita turned to Lily, a look of surprise on her face. "Begging your pardon, but you would like to share a cup of tea with me?"

Lily set down the charcoal. "The storm truly upsets you, doesn't it?"

The woman nodded.

She took Allita by the shoulders and stood eye to eye with her. "Fetch the tea and bring some biscuits if Régine has any about. Look here—" Lily rapped softly on the door three times. "This is our signal so I'll know it's you."

"Oh, I understand." Allita's eyes twinkled. "You don't want señor running in here after you."

Lily merely shrugged.

"It'll be the portrait you're not wanting him to have, isn't it? Señor Bastien wants it, and seems to me he's used to getting what he wants." Allita opened the door, looked both ways, and then scurried down the hall.

Lily shut the door behind her and went back to her drawing. She was expecting the sharp rapping on her door that came a few minutes later. "Go away," she called out.

"I'm coming in," Bastien said.

"You cannot. I am not dressed," she shouted and slipped the drawing under the bed.

The door swung open. Bastien folded his arms across his chest and leaned a shoulder against the doorframe. His lazy gaze slid the length of her body. "You look plenty clothed to me, *chère*."

Her chest shuddered on an intake of breath. Lord, this playfulness he'd been exhibiting all morning might be more dangerous to her equilibrium than the comfort he'd extended to her last evening. "I'd invite you in, but I see you are already here."

"*Non.* I am merely standing in the doorway. You may extend the invitation, *s'il vous plaît.*"

"What do you want? I told you I needed to complete the charcoal in private. All those people wandering around out there, and especially your mother, became too much of a distraction."

She swept her hand toward the window. "And as you can see, the weather has not cooperated."

"That's not why I'm here. Henri has come to relay a message that Monsieur Justin Andrews arrived from upriver. He's at his townhouse and will venture here once the weather clears."

A chill ran through her. What would happen when Mr. Andrews met up with her uncle? She turned her back on Bastien lest he see her quivering hands. "Thank you. Please leave and close the door behind you."

Instead of retreating, he marched across the room and came up behind her, his essence surrounding her like a great, warm cloak. "What be the matter, *chère*?"

She shook her head, "Nothing. I am merely anxious to greet my…my husband's old friend and take care of some matters that are of no concern to you."

He grew silent but moved even closer, until the heat of his body seeped through the very clothing on her back and permeated her skin. Too stunned to move, she closed her eyes. It was as if his lifeblood pulsed through her.

"I don't believe you," he murmured, his voice deep and throaty. Leaning even closer, he reached around and took her clenched hand in his. Easing it open, he slid a large key into her palm. "It fits your bedchamber door."

She stared at the key, her mind a blank as every nerve in her body reacted to being virtually held in his arms, to his breath ghosting across her cheek.

Then he dropped his hand from hers, walked away, and opened the bedchamber door. "I'll fetch Monsieur Talbot for you, and then I'm off to the shipping office for the remainder of the day."

Male voices echoed down the corridor; then her uncle hurried into the room and closed the door behind him.

She turned from the window, her knees shaking. "I am so sorry for the things I said last night, Uncle. I do not know what came over me."

"No need to apologize, seeing as how I am the one who was rude. I worry overmuch about you, my dear. But now that we are to meet up with my old associate Mr. Andrews, I'm certain he will come to our aid."

Fear washed over her, fresh and new. "What if he sends inquiries to London and learns I am wanted?"

Her uncle waved a hand in dismissal. "Hush, Lily. You cannot allow such thoughts to enter your head."

"But what if he does investigate and believes the authorities, then what?"

"Everything will be sorted out once we locate Molly. Come now, let's make our way to the library and await my friend."

Allita met them coming up the stairs. She carried a tray with tea and an array of sweet confections.

Lily paused mid-step. "Oh, dear."

Allita looked from Uncle to Lily and gave her a smile. "It will be fine, Miss Lily. The storm has passed and my nephew likes tea."

"You've a kind heart," Lily said and continued down the stairs. "With the storm over, we can anticipate Mr. Andrews's imminent arrival, can we not?"

"Indeed." Uncle escorted her to the library, where Lily, spine stiff, sat in a brown leather chair while her uncle paced in front of a darkened fireplace. They waited mere moments before voices sounded beyond the door. Lily sucked in a breath, and her hand went to her chest as if doing so might slow her racing heartbeat.

The door opened and a tall, gray-haired man rushed in. He stumbled to a halt. "Charles? Charles Langdon?"

"'Tis I," her uncle said.

"Good God," Andrews said. "Except for that paunch and gray hair, you've not changed a bit. What brings you here?"

Uncle spread a hand, palm up, toward Lily. "Meet my godchild, Lady Liliana Stanhope. Lily, meet Justin Andrews, my dear friend, and a member of our old fearsome foursome."

"Stanhope…Stanhope," Justin repeated. "Any relation to our cohort James Stanhope, Earl of Cowdrey?"

"Indeed," Uncle responded before she could so much as open her mouth to speak. "She is Lord Cowdrey's daughter, but I'm afraid the good man is no longer with us."

Justin frowned. "Recently?"

Lily could only manage a brief nod.

"I'm sorry to hear that. My condolences." Mr. Andrews took a moment to study her through intelligent eyes that gave away nothing of what he might be thinking. Then he turned back to her godfather. "While it is well and good to see you, I thought I was to meet up with Percival Talbot. Where is the old chap?"

Uncle closed his eyes and pinched the bridge of his nose. "Dead as well, I'm afraid."

Chapter Ten

"Easy boy," Bastien crooned as he tried once more to mount the horse. The snorting beast danced sideways and kicked out. Cursing under his breath, Bastien tossed the reins to the Le Blanc House stable hand. "Never mind, I'll walk to work."

Henri eased his horse back into its stall and rushed to catch up with Bastien. "Why didn't you make that contrary beast mind you?"

Bastien shook his head. "Forcing an animal to do my bidding doesn't sit well with me."

"It can't be good to let them have their way. They can turn stubborn."

"Horses have their reasons for not wanting to be ridden. Sometimes it's smart to give them their head."

"Why didn't you take a different one?"

"Wouldn't be right. The one I tried to ride sensed my foul mood and wanted nothing to do with me, so why would another be any different? Horses are keen to sense the disposition of the rider. There's respect and there's trust, Henri. If we don't give it, we won't get it back. You should know that by now."

"What got you outa sorts, anyway? Was it because Vivienne took the rig to market when you be needin' it?"

"*Non.* The carriage belongs to Le Blanc House. She has every right to it." Bastien knew damn well what was wrong with him, but he sure as hell wasn't about to discuss his predicament with anyone, let alone a green sixteen-year-old.

Henri swiped at his brow. "Whew. This be some kind of heat, *non*?"

"Did I say you had to walk?" A bead of perspiration trickled down Bastien's spine. He raked his fingers through his hair, and his hand came away slick with sweat.

"Christ," he muttered. Enough of being inconvenienced. Enough of taking whatever mode of transportation happened to be at hand. It was about time he purchased a horse and vehicle of his own. Especially now that he'd decided to settle into a more permanent living situation.

He glanced at Henri, who was trying valiantly to keep up with Bastien's fast pace. Perspiration ringed the lad's collar, and his cheeks were flushed. Blast it all, Henri needed decent transportation, as well.

"Go on with you, Henri. Take yourself over to Monsieur Fontenot's place. Inform him I'll be stopping in to see him at half past five today. Tell him to have his catalogs ready for my inspection."

Henri stumbled, corrected himself, then did a quick double step to match the rhythm of Bastien's feet pounding the wooden boardwalk. "You buying yourself a rig?"

"*Oui.*"

Henri grinned. "Ain't that something."

"*Isn't* that something. Let Fontenot know I'll be wanting the finest buggy made. One of those sleek two-seaters. Smart and fast, with fine leather seats, good suspension, and a top I can roll down in decent weather. Then trot over to Monsieur Marvin Hardin's and have him find me the best seventeen-hand horse in the country. Needs to be an agile, even-tempered gelding. One that works well either under saddle or pulling a carriage. Tell him to look for a chestnut bay with a lush black mane and tail. And four white stockings, if possible."

"Whew. That be a mighty tall order. Could take a while, don'cha know."

"*Oui.* Also, if you've taken a fancy to any horse at the Le Blanc House stables, let me know and I'll negotiate for you."

This time Henri stumbled over his own feet. He halted. "I don't have the coin—"

"You're my personal assistant now. Transportation comes with your position."

Henri beamed. "*Merci*, Bastien! I be mighty fond of Russell."

"Russell?"

"*Oui.* That dappled Morgan. But it belongs to Monsieur Michel Andrews, like most of them. So—"

"I said I'd negotiate, didn't I?" He shot another sideways glance at Henri, who hadn't stopped grinning. "Who the hell names a horse Russell?"

Henri shrugged. "He answers to it, so no sense confusing him with a new name. Sure is a fine-moving gelding." He frowned. "But where would I keep him?"

Bastien cocked a brow. "You and your *maman* are still living over at René's townhouse, *non*?"

"*Oui*. Maman made a mighty fine home out of those old servants' quarters on the ground floor."

"Any empty stalls in the stables out back?"

"Two," Henri said.

"Well, there you go. Mayhap we can find you a nice little buggy or wagon, as well."

Henri let out a shout and, grinning at Bastien, danced a little jig.

The heat and conversation were exhausting, and Bastien burned to be alone. "Go on with you to Fontenot's now, before it gets too late."

Henri gave him a sailor's salute and took off at a run.

Bastien watched him vanish around the corner, then continued on his way to the shipping office, lost in his own muddled thoughts.

What the devil was wrong with him of late? Why had he taken Lily up on her offer to paint his portrait? He knew why, damn it. He'd used their time together as an excuse to study her while she worked, memorizing every lovely feature, every movement of her graceful hands.

Using the excuse to lounge around and bask in her presence had been a mistake. Her every nuance, her every movement had filled him with enough salacious thoughts to set both mind and body on edge.

Which had become a problem.

Because he wanted her. The urge to possess her, to pleasure her in intimate ways he knew only too well, was worsening by the day.

What was it about Lily that mesmerized him? Not only did he find her charming, intelligent, and growing more beautiful by the day, but she intrigued him. Her secrets captivated him. And whatever those secrets were, she was adept at keeping them hidden.

Shamefully, his growing attraction toward her wasn't new. That strange, magnetic hold her presence had on him had been triggered the moment she'd been seated in front of him back in his Jamaica office—back when she was so weak, she could barely hold up her head. Back when the poison running through her veins had caused her pupils to be so enlarged, he couldn't make out the color of her eyes. Though he wouldn't admit to himself her inexplicable appeal when they'd first met, he could no longer deny the powerful draw now.

Sacre bleu! He had no business desiring a woman under his care.

Doing so wasn't right.

Tell that to his fickle heart.

There were any number of women he could call on in town to satisfy his carnal needs. He could name a few who'd eagerly open their doors and arms to him without a moment's hesitation. But the idea of seeking out any one of them held no appeal. His peculiar response gave him pause.

Why Lily of all people?

Why now?

Women had always intrigued him. Hell, he'd barely been Henri's age when the allure of the feminine mystique captured him. He'd found females intoxicating in numerous ways—from their lovely curves, to their silken skin, to their sweet, velvet voices. In the past, he couldn't get enough of them—especially in bed. By his nineteenth birthday, he'd garnered a wicked reputation as being the erotic plaything of many a young widow in New Orleans. But there was more to his escapades than simple seduction—he'd intuitively understood what it took to meet the individual needs of any woman he'd bedded, and he'd reveled in the knowledge.

Christ. The mere thought of his torrid past soured his stomach. If there were one thing he could erase from his former life, it would be those randy episodes. In reality, he held a deep respect for the opposite sex that bordered on reverence. Yet, despite his love for women in general, he'd never spent any length of time entertaining one in particular. Never took a mistress—always left a part of himself detached.

There wasn't a thing he could do about his shameful past but continue to move forward in life in as respectable a manner as possible. That, and keep his lucrative investments expanding until he was as wealthy as his despicable father.

He'd been a damn fool marching into Lily's bedchamber today after she'd told him to keep out. It had taken all he had in him to slip that blasted key into her hand and make a hasty exit when all he'd wanted was to remain. When he'd paused at the door and glanced over his shoulder at her like some besotted fool, she'd stood in front of the window with her fingers touching her parted lips. The look on her face spoke volumes. She wouldn't have refused his kisses had he closed the distance between them, he was certain of it.

From now on, he'd make keeping distance between them a priority. He'd spend more time at work, leave Lily in his mother's care.

She doesn't like or trust Maman. Merde!

At last, he reached the shipping office, relieved to see there were no vessels at the docks requiring his attention. He stepped inside, only to find

that blasted cat, black as midnight, sitting in the middle of his desk and
staring at him with those unblinking golden eyes, his white-tipped tail
slowly twitching back and forth. "Get that *minou* off my desk!"

Felice grinned. "Why, good afternoon, Bastien. Might I remind you
the cat's name is Midnight? And I'll keep reminding you of the fact until
you get so sick of hearing me yammer at you, you'll be glad to call him
by his rightful name."

"Humph." The cat continued to stare at Bastien without moving. At
Bastien's approach, it stood, arched its back, and slipped off the desk, only
to set about twining itself through Bastien's legs and purring.

Bastien tried to outmaneuver the little beast and nearly tripped over
him. "Goddammit, he's getting hair all over my trousers."

René glanced up from whatever stack of papers he was going through.
"Should've let him be, *mon frère.*"

Felice stood, and as she headed toward Bastien, passed by René and
planted a kiss on his cheek. René grabbed her by the waist and gave her a
squeeze, the look in his eye a promise of things to come.

A wave of something undefinable washed through Bastien. "*Sacre bleu.*
Go home if you two can't keep your hands off each other."

Felice's soft laughter rang throughout the office. Lifting the cat from
around Bastien's legs, she set it outside. "Do your duty, Midnight. Catch
some nice, fat mice. And deposit your trophies at Master Bastien's feet."

"Not my *minou*," Bastien said.

"You love him, and you know it. Admit it, you're just so finicky about
your person and surroundings that a little cat hair disrupts your day."

She gave Bastien a peck on the cheek and whispered, "Why are you
suddenly against a man and wife showing a little affection to one another?"

He glanced up, caught a penetrating look in her eye that nearly made
him squirm. "I'm not," he muttered.

But he knew part of what bothered him about their affectionate ways
was his brother having married in the first place. While Felice was a fine
woman, and it was obvious she and his brother were deeply in love, Bastien
and René had made a pact years ago that neither would marry. Neither
would bring a child into the world to carry the blood of a despicable French
aristocrat and a voodoo priestess. And now, in a few months, René would
become a father, the ultimate betrayal of the pact they'd made.

Until this moment, he'd been unable to define his ambiguous feelings
toward the couple. Bastien felt betrayed. Well, at least he'd keep his part
of the bargain—he'd never marry. Nor would he bring another bastard

into the world. Despite his past philandering, he'd been careful to keep that from occurring.

"You've changed since returning from Jamaica," Felice said. "What happened there? Does it have anything to do with Miss Lily?"

Yes, and then some!

"*Non.* I did not sleep well—that is all."

Her lips pursed. "Of course."

René held up a large envelope. "This came for you. It's from Josette."

Bastien's bad mood dissipated like mist off a morning pond. He jumped to his feet and reached for the envelope.

A mischievous grin reached René's eyes. He yanked the envelope away from Bastien and wiggled it. "Why you be getting mail from our sister when I do not?"

Bastien growled and reached for it. "Because she loves me and barely tolerates you."

René wiggled the packet again. "What be in here, *mon frère*?"

"I'm warning you, René. I am in no mood for your hijinks."

Felice snatched the envelope out of her husband's hand and handed it to Bastien. "You know your brother isn't about to leave you alone until you tell us what's in there."

Bastien grunted. "I noticed you said 'us' and not 'him,' but it's a secret. I keep three things to myself, Felice. My love life, my money, and my next move."

"Oh, ho! Now you do have our curiosity piqued." Felice reached out and tenderly swept a lock of hair off Bastien's brow. "Now that I am wed to René, you are my brother as well, and I can tell by the look in your eye there is something in that envelope that has you excited. Open it. We'll wait."

"I'll do it at home."

Movement at the open door caught Bastien's attention. Justin Andrews walked in with Michel, Felice's brother, on his heels. Midnight, the cat, strolled through the door behind them and marched straight over to Bastien. He gave up and plopped the animal on his desk. Better there than winding around his legs and leaving hair all over him. The cat looked at him, curled into a ball in one corner, and gave a little meow that tugged at Bastien's heartstrings.

"Papa," Felice said, and peeking around him, spied her brother, the mayor. "What brings you two here? And looking so somber."

René and Bastien stood to greet them.

"I've just left Le Blanc House and a meeting with my British friends," Justin said. "I've come to discuss a few things with all of you."

Felice frowned. "And Michel merely happened by, or did you collect him along the way?"

Michel parked a hip on a corner of René's desk. "Will everyone please sit."

While the others took their seats, Justin remained standing. "My friends are to remain at Le Blanc House under our protection."

Bastien's heart kicked up a notch. "Protection?"

Justin nodded. "Specifically, Lily. Under no circumstances are any strangers to be allowed in the premises." He lifted a hand, silencing the open mouths ready to speak. "Nor are you to ask questions. Not yet, anyway. Everything will be made clear once we have the situation under control."

Felice threw her hands in the air. "Papa, you need to trust us. Tell us more."

"In good time, my dear. Suffice it to say that Michel and I will be working to find a solution to the rather dire predicament my friends find themselves in. I am asking you to be patient, to give them anything they might need. Lily is to remain confined to the house and gardens."

"Oh, that's fine," Felice snapped. "Just fine."

Justin turned pleading eyes to his daughter. "She could use a friend, Felice. Be one."

He turned to Bastien. "Words are not enough to express my gratitude for the way you took care of them, and for saving Lily's life. I wish there were something more I could offer you at the moment, other than to say thank you. Know that you have my greatest respect."

Bastien eyed the mail from Josette lying on the desk in front of him. Under the current circumstances, this might be the right time to find out if she'd agreed to his proposal. He tore open the envelope, quickly read over the contents, and swallowed a bark of laughter. "As a matter of fact, Monsieur Andrews, since we are all gathered here together, there might be something you can do for me, after all."

René leaned back in his chair and fixed a steady gaze on Bastien. "Go on."

Taking in a deep breath, he let it out as he spoke. "You are all aware that Le Blanc House originally belonged to my sister, Josette, after she inherited the mansion from her elderly first husband. Then there was the trouble with our pompous father harassing her and wanting to wrest it from her, intent on presenting it to his legitimate daughter as a wedding present."

Justin and Michel slowly nodded, while René's eyes narrowed.

Bastien directed his conversation to Justin. "Your nephew, Cameron, arranged matters so Josette could legally sell the home to your shipping company for one dollar, with the codicil that should she ever wish to buy it back, she could do so for the same one dollar."

René jumped to his feet. "Don't tell me she's decided to sell it to you for another dollar?"

Bastien grinned at his brother. "Our terms are private, but *oui*. She would like to sell the property to me for an undisclosed amount."

René cursed. "*Non*. You cannot be doing that."

Justin, Michel, and Felice looked at René and in unison, said, "Why not?"

René sputtered. "How much?"

Bastien laughed. "Did I ask you how much you paid for your luxurious townhouse?"

Felice looked from René to Bastien, then again to René. "For heaven's sake, husband. I've been hoping your brother would come to his senses and do more with himself than keep a rented suite at Le Blanc House. It hadn't crossed my mind Josette would want to sell the place, but the idea sits well with me."

"With me, as well," Michel said.

"I am particularly keen on the idea," Justin responded.

René paced a while longer, then paused, hands on hips. "What about our cousins Régine and Vivienne? What about the ship captains who lodge there when they are in port? What about the Talbots?"

Bastien swiped a hand across his weary brow and his Cajun accent thickened. "My owning the property will change nothing on the surface. It would be silly to have Régine cooking for only me and the staff, don'cha know?"

Justin walked over and shook hands with Bastien. "Then it's settled."

René reached for Josette's letter. "I would still like to know how much you are paying her for the finest mansion in all of New Orleans."

"You know full well I do not discuss two things with you, *mon frère*— my financial worth and my love life."

René leaned over and quietly said, "*Embrasse moi tchew*."

Bastien merely grinned and slipped Josette's letter into its envelope. "How about *you* kiss mine instead."

Felice looked at her father and shrugged. "Brothers. What can I say?"

Justin chuckled. "Of course, you were always such a sweet angel, never once taunting your brothers with snakes or frogs in their beds."

René looked at Felice, a grin working his mouth. "Do tell us more, Monsieur Andrews."

Justin waved them off. "I've an idea, Bastien. Would you consider having the papers drawn up in the morning, and then everyone can gather together in the evening for a nice family dinner to celebrate your new home?"

Michel stood. "I have a meeting to attend. Bastien, if you are up to my father's suggestion, I'll send word to Brenna."

"Bring the children," Bastien replied, his emotions threatening to overwhelm him. Purchasing Le Blanc House felt good. Felt solid. Soon, he would become the owner of the grandest estate in the Garden District—he, Bastien Thibodeaux, a bastard and French Cajun from the bayou who'd once been a dirt-poor, thieving cutpurse who'd seen the inside of every jail in the parish before his fifteenth birthday.

Michel started for the door, but Justin stopped him. Slowly, he looked into each of their eyes. "There's one more thing, gentlemen."

A chill snaked down Bastien's spine. He had a feeling he knew what was coming.

"I've another little journey I'd like the three of you to consider taking." They all nodded.

"When?" Bastien asked.

"Tomorrow night," Justin said. "Around midnight. After our family gathering."

So, celebrating Bastien's purchase of Le Blanc House wasn't the only reason Justin wanted a special dinner. He was asking the men to take part in yet another dangerous mission, one that could prove disastrous should their secret be exposed.

At least the journey would take him away from Lily for a while. With Rubio on hand to stand guard over Le Blanc House, Bastien could rest easy knowing she'd be kept safe.

Chapter Eleven

In that nocturnal realm between sleep and consciousness, deep terror rose up in Lily. Someone had opened the door to her bedchamber. She struggled to come fully awake, but was pinned to her bed as if by some invisible force.

Julian Stanhope crept into the room.

He stood in the shadows, watching her. She tried to reach beneath her pillow, to grab the knife hidden there, but she lay frozen in place. He moved to stand over her, his face twisted with hatred as his hands reached for her throat.

"Miss Lily! Wake up, Miss Lily!"

Lily's eyes fluttered open. It wasn't Julian leaning over her, but Allita shaking her awake and disentangling her from the bedclothes.

"Oh, God," Lily moaned.

The maid scurried around the room lighting candles and casting out shadows. "Another night terror, *si?*"

Lily rolled to a sitting position on the edge of the mattress, willing her labored breathing and racing pulse to settle. Would these nightmares never cease to haunt her? Would her upside-down life never be righted? When would she be able to properly mourn Papa's death? At the thought of never again seeing him, grief overwhelmed her fear.

"Go back to bed, Allita. Sorry to have bothered you."

"But—"

"Thank you for your concern, but I can take care of myself now." She gave her maid a weak smile and shooed her off with the wave of a hand. "Get some sleep or you'll be of no use to anyone on the morrow, especially to yourself."

"Should you need me—"

"I'll know where to find you. Please, I wish to be alone. I am fine, truly I am."

But she wasn't fine. Not at all. Lily waited until Allita disappeared into her own room, then paced the floor of her bedchamber, shaken to the core.

Bastien.

Every cell of her body cried out for him. For his protection. For the sheer comfort of his presence. She wanted—no, needed—him to help her settle the frantic blood pumping through her veins. She continued pacing, unable to gather courage enough to unlock the door and venture down the dark corridor.

What a frightened mouse she'd become.

And all because of you, Cousin Julian. Damn your wicked soul.

As dawn inched its way toward morning, she slipped into a robe, blew out the candles lighting the room, and tiptoed from her bedchamber. The soft glow of gas lamps at each end of the corridor lit a dim, shadow-filled path to Bastien's quarters. She reached his door and paused to contemplate the shiny brass lion's head affixed there. No sense waking the entire household. Lifting her trembling fingers, she scratched on the carved panel beneath the knocker—the usual custom in England.

"He's not in there," came his mother's curt voice.

Lily squealed and jumped around so fast her head banged against the door's hard brass knocker. Rubbing at the pain, she struggled to find words as Odalie's cold, piercing gaze took in Lily's dishabille.

"A ship came in," Odalie said through thinned lips. "He left for the docks hours ago. We do not expect his return until the eight o'clock dinner hour. What you be requiring of my son while others be sleeping, Madame Talbot?"

Heart still hammering, Lily met Odalie's gaze. She'd be damned if she'd allow this woman to intimidate her. Gathering her dignity around her like a protective cloak, Lily lifted her chin and swept past the woman.

"Nothing that cannot wait."

Returning to her bedchamber, she flung the curtains wide to the day's dawning, then collapsed on the bed. Her mind in a muddle, she stared blankly at the ceiling and waited for…nothing.

She spent most of the slow-moving day in private, working on the drawing of Bastien, unable to shake off the fear of the horrid nightmare. The knowledge that Bastien was not on the premises left her with a peculiar hollowness. Had she grown too close to him? His absence should not cause such a sorrowful state. How unlike her to become attached to anyone, let alone this sinfully handsome man who was merely passing through her life.

Oh, for pity's sake, his charm and disarming good looks had nothing to do with her present state of unrest. Not only had Bastien saved her life, but she'd been reliant on his healing treatments since boarding his ship in Jamaica. Her utter dependence on him for so long was what had her wanting to turn to him in a time of crisis. Nothing more.

In late afternoon, Madame Charmontès arrived with a new garment—a soft cotton the color of ripe raspberries—and held it up for Lily's inspection. She fell in love with it.

"It is zee new aniline dyes which create the vibrant color," Madame said. "The moment I spied this wonderful piece of fabric amongst my recent shipment, I knew it was meant for you, and voilà! I was right, *non?*"

"Madame Charmontès, you are a veritable genius."

"*Oui*, you speak zee truth." The tiny dressmaker, a French émigré claiming to be the finest modiste in all the world, kissed her own fingertips with a smacking noise and waved them in the air. "I was so eager to create zee perfect gown, I had my girls working late at night, cutting and stitching this *tissu fabuleux.*"

"Indeed, the cotton is fabulous, madame." Lily twirled in front of the full-length cheval mirror. "I shall wear your wonderful creation this evening."

Madame gave a brief bow of her head. "*Merci.*"

How would Bastien like it? Would he think the color fitting for her fair skin and hair? Lily dismissed the thought. What the blazes had gotten into her? She dressed according to her own preferences, not what another might think.

Especially *him*, for heaven's sake.

Nonetheless, when the clock struck the eight o'clock hour, and she made her way downstairs to the parlor, where both the Andrews and Thibodeaux clans were crowded, the first person she looked for was Bastien. He stood with his back to her, to the right of a blue velvet sofa, chatting with his brother and Justin Andrews.

Felice rushed through the noisy throng to Lily. "My dear, you look a vision. Madame Charmontès has outdone herself yet again. And your hair. How clever for Allita to twine tiny blue forget-me-nots through those gorgeous fair locks of yours. Who knew she had such talent?"

Felice slipped her hand through the bend in Lily's arm and gave a tug. "Come along. We shall first put a glass of champagne in your hand before we make our way around the room."

"I hadn't expected to see Michel and Brenna's children here," Lily said, greatly relieved to note Odalie's absence.

Michel's wife turned to Lily with a sparkle in her eye and spoke in a thick Irish brogue. "They are verra pleased to be here. My older boys are helpin' Régine and Vivienne lay out the feast in the dining room. My younger ones are…well…they've been taught manners, but in their eagerness to be a chattin' with ye, little feet might be stepping on a toe or two."

Colleen, a six-year-old with red hair and freckles to match her mother's, slipped her hand into Lily's and gave it a tug, her little pink tongue darting in and out through missing front teeth as she spoke. "Would ye like to thee my new kitten?"

Her mother touched the girl on her shoulder. "We're sure to be called to dinner soon. If'n she's a mind to, Miss Lily can meet yer new friend later."

"I should very much like to meet your new pet, Colleen. What have you named it?"

"Miss Lily. I named her after you."

"Oh, my!" Lily's hand flew to her chest. "I doubt I've ever had such a precious honor bestowed upon me. Now I *must* meet your little pet after dinner."

Her godfather approached and handed her a glass of champagne. "My dear, you look lovely—a stunning goddess once again."

"Indeed," Michel said as he joined them.

"I'm flattered. Thank you." Lily lifted the flute of champagne to her lips and glanced over Michel's shoulder to where René and Bastien appeared to be deep in conversation with the elder Mr. Andrews. René looked her way, said something to Bastien, and strode over to where she stood with the others.

Bastien glanced up. Their gazes locked for a brief moment, shooting a sizzling current through her. But he merely gave her a nod and returned to conversing with Mr. Andrews.

Lily's heart stuttered. Was it her imagination or had Bastien just given her the cut direct?

Donal, Brenna's eldest son, appeared at the threshold to the parlor and rang a bell to announce dinner.

"Shall we?" Michel held out his arm to Lily and proceeded to lead her into the elegant dining room with its grand décor, overhead twin chandeliers ablaze, and platters of aromatic food filling the table.

He held out a chair for her. "Since we've no assigned seats, would you mind if I sat beside you?"

"I'd be delighted."

At the other end of the long table, Bastien seated himself beside Brenna, not once glancing Lily's way. Puzzlement swirled in her brain, and the bright flame of anticipation lighting her heightened spirits flickered and died.

Henri approached to Lily's left. "I shall sit here, *s'il vous plaît?*"

Swallowing her disappointment, she smiled and patted the seat beside her. "I can think of no one I would rather have to keep me company."

* * * *

As the evening wore on, Lily was certain of her suspicion—Bastien was avoiding her. But why? Here it was, nearly ten of the evening, and not once during the entire meal had he glanced her way. What had she done to alienate him? What had changed since yesterday?

Confusion mixed with frustration. Her stomach revolted. Setting her knife and fork onto her plate, she folded her hands in her lap, careful to avoid the kitten asleep beneath her serviette. Earlier, Colleen, the little scamp, had crawled under the table and deposited the little beast in Lily's lap.

Perhaps Bastien was merely preoccupied with work. After all, he'd left before dawn and had barely returned in time for dinner. Or perhaps her imagination was playing tricks on her after the nightmare that still clung to her like a wet night rail.

The evening was growing late, and the children were restless despite the excitement of a family gathering the likes of which Lily had never before witnessed. Except for Odalie, the entire extended family was present. Even Allita and Rubio had been invited. Lily glanced at Rubio, seated next to a blushing Régine. Was love in the air for those two?

Lily had played host to many a formal dinner on her father's behalf, and painfully endured plenty of others elsewhere, but never had she been privy to anything such as this raucous spectacle. She rather liked it.

Wasn't Uncle shocked to see the entire Andrews and Thibodeaux family present. From Cousin Régine the cook, to Henri the apprentice and his mother, Cousin Monique, to Michel's children. Lily could tell by the set of Uncle's jaw, and the straight, thin line of his lips, that he was vexed. In England, children were swept away to the nursery; never were they allowed to dine with adults.

She'd nearly laughed aloud when mounds of steaming red crawdads appeared on the table and Donal, the eldest Andrews boy, proceeded to show Uncle how to snap off the head, suck out the insides, and then wrestle the meat from the tail. No doubt, Uncle would complain to her later.

Colleen wedged her way between Brenna and Bastien, said something to her mother, then turned to Bastien and leaned into him. He smiled, planted a kiss atop her head, then taking her small hands in his, twirled her in a circle. Colleen's giggles rang through the air.

Lily's heart pinched.

Years ago, when she'd been Colleen's very age, Papa had danced her around the kitchen in India while Mama and the servants looked on. Participating in such folly was beyond Mama's proper upbringing. Nonetheless, she'd stood to one side of the room, tapping a foot in time to Papa's raucous tunes.

Remembering that happy part of her life, Lily felt melancholy roll through her like a dismal mist. Suddenly, she wanted nothing more than to escape to her quarters.

As if Brenna heard Lily's thoughts, she glanced her way and tilted her head. Heat scorched Lily's cheeks at being caught staring at Bastien. Gently, she reached down and lifted the sleeping kitten into her arms and rubbed her cheek against its soft golden fur. When she looked up, she found Bastien watching her.

He turned away.

Her insides threatened to collapse. *He is ignoring me!*

Michel sent Brenna a speaking glance, then turned to Lily. "Time to get my small army home and into their beds. I'll have Colleen collect her pet."

"Truth be told, I've grown quite fond of my little namesake. She's purring quite nicely at the moment."

Michel grinned. "So I can hear."

Felice rose from her chair and stepped behind her father. She wrapped her arms around him, and resting her cheek against his, gave him a hug. Her father covered her hands with his own liver-spotted fingers. Lily used to offer her father affection in the same manner, especially after the evening meal, before she wheeled him off to bed in his special-made chair.

The tender sight landed as a cruel blow on an already battered heart. She closed her eyes against the pain engulfing her. Against a sudden sting of tears. She could take no more of this heartache. She shot to her feet, placed the kitten in Michel's arms, and rushed from the room, shoving her fist against her mouth to silence a sob that had been a long time coming.

Blindly, she flew to the first door she came to. The library. She rushed inside and closed the door behind her. Swallowing her sob, she moved to the large windows facing the garden and stared into the darkness.

"Oh, Papa, I miss you so. What am I going to do? Where shall I go once this nightmare ends? Or will I end up hanging for what Julian did to you?"

At the sound of the door opening and closing, her breath caught in her lungs. No need to turn around, she knew who it was even before his dark reflection appeared in the windows before her. Her heart thudding against her ribs, she tried to look past his looming image, out to some distant point in the night.

"Please, Bastien. Go away."

He paused directly behind her. The clean, masculine scent that was his alone surrounded her. "Lily? What be the matter, *chère?*"

The low timbre of his voice gave her belly a twist. His husky words told her of his concern—yet he'd avoided her all evening. She should be livid that he chose now to come to her. Instead, the sound of her name on his lips soaked right through her skin and washed away her anger. He was here, standing directly behind her in all his glorious beauty. Fool that she was, nothing else mattered.

She could hear her own harsh breathing, was acutely aware of a curious warmth spreading through her belly and leaving her weak in the knees. She brushed at a corner of her eye with the back of her hand. A snowy white handkerchief appeared over her shoulder. The heat of his large hand sent a current through her.

"Tell me, *chère*, what caused you to dash from the room?"

He stood so close, his sweet breath fanned over her cheek. A buzz slid across her skin. "I had another nightmare last night. I fear it's left me fatigued and out of sorts the day long. I'll be fine come the morrow."

"I think there is more to this. Tell me. Let me help."

When her mind struggled too long to find the right words to keep from divulging her secrets, he gripped her shoulders and gently forced her to turn and face him. "What could be causing this sadness in your eyes?"

At his tender touch, a needy desire, hot and dangerous, erupted inside her. She should remove herself from his presence. But leaving now was the last thing she wanted to do.

He gave her a gentle shake and took a step closer. "It pains me to see you so upset. What happened back there? Tell me."

She stared up into those fierce blue eyes while the heat of his body and the low rumble of his voice shut out the rest of the world. She was tired. So very tired of all she'd been through these many months. Suddenly, a deep need for his comfort overwhelmed all constraint. She collapsed into him.

He caught her.

"I...I cannot say," she said, choking out her words. "Please do not ask any more of me. Not yet, at least. Right now, what I need is for you to hold me. I confess, I am in dire need of comfort."

Stepping fully into him, she slid her arms about his waist, and set her cheek against his hard chest.

His entire body stiffened.

Then, with a low groan, he wrapped his arms around her and pulled her even closer, so close, the entire length of her body fitted snug against his. Holding her, he began a slow and gentle swaying, soothing her with the movement and his voice as he murmured in his Cajun tongue, words she did not understand, but could feel.

At once, he became a safe haven in the dark storm she'd weathered for so very long. She relaxed into him and floated in an ocean of tender warmth.

So good.

It felt so good to be held by him. To feel safe. To be cared for. He continued to murmur and rock her. With each unintelligible word, his mouth grazed the curve of her neck, the lobe of her ear, filling her with a want and need she'd never before known.

She held on tighter and a soft moan left her lips.

His heart kicked up a new rhythm, beating hard and strong against her cheek. Raising her head, she looked up into those liquid blue eyes and saw banked embers. She slid her hand upward and traced the curve of his lips, willing him to surrender to her sudden and desperate need to have his mouth on hers.

He sucked in a sharp breath. She felt restraint coil within him. He shifted, as if to distance himself.

"Don't leave me," she whispered and dropped her hand to his chest, splaying her fingers over his thrumming heart. "I want you to kiss me, Bastien. You cannot deny 'tis what we both want."

"I…" He shut his eyes tight for a moment. And then he opened them, those blue eyes now filled with his own pain. "Tell me the truth, Lily. Is Talbot your husband?"

I should walk away. But she could not to save her soul. She paused for a long while, lost in his essence, lost in her desire to have yet more of him. Finally, she gave her head a slight shake and whispered, "No."

His hard gaze licked across her skin like a hot flame. An incoherent sound left his throat; then he formed words, deep and husky. "I need the truth. Have you ever been anyone's wife?"

Lord in Heaven, she was losing her grip on her secrets, ready to toss them to the wind for the mere touch of his lips upon hers. She dropped her gaze from his and tried to find the will to walk away.

When she failed to respond, he gave her shoulders a squeeze. "Look at me, Lily."

Slowly, she raised her gaze to his, pausing first at his lush mouth, at lips separated to accommodate quickened breathing. Then her gaze reached his eyes, and she saw those banked embers ready to ignite.

"Have you ever been *anyone's* wife?"

The low rumble of his words pulsed in her breasts, then rode low in her belly. Good Lord, but this man did scandalous things to her insides, things she could not put a name to. Longing and desire, and a deep need for him rolled through her like a sudden storm. She shook her head. "No."

In the brief silence that followed, nothing existed but a world about to implode. His chest shuddered, and he released a soft groan as he lowered his mouth.

His lips brushed lightly over hers, and a hot shiver ran through her. "More," she whispered when he paused. "I want more."

He pulled his head back for a moment, his blue eyes smoldering a dark, liquid cobalt. "Oh, Lily, what you do to me."

He took command of her mouth, tasting her with sweet, hungry strokes of his tongue. She returned his kisses, greedily matching his movements. He took her breath into his own lungs and crushed her against him, so close there was no mistaking the result of his heated passion pushing hard against her belly.

Suddenly, he let out another groan and stepped away, his breath heaving. His lips glossed from their encounter, his eyes a dark blue storm of want, he raked his hand through his hair. "God forgive me, I cannot…we cannot… not now anyway."

"Bastien?" came a male voice from across the room.

He turned at the sound of René's voice coming from the library's entry and backed farther away from Lily.

"It's time," René said. He glanced from Lily to Bastien and back again, his brow furrowed.

Bastien nodded and strode from the room, his long legs eating up the distance between his brother and him.

Dazed, Lily stood in place for a long moment, staring at the empty hallway beyond the library.

Her godfather appeared at the open door and stepped into the room. "What in blazes is going on? What is wrong with you? What's happened?"

Aside from Odalie, here was the last person she wished to see. She rushed past him. "Merely another nightmare that has ruined this entire day. I'm off to bed."

Dashing from the room, she ran up the stairs to her bedchamber, and locked herself in. No doubt her godfather would be on her heels, demanding entry.

In moments, the door latch wiggled, followed by his loud demand. "Lily, open up."

"Blast it all." She marched to the door, flung it open and crossing her arms over her chest, spoke low. "I know you mean well, but there are times you smother me, and this is one of them. I wish to be alone. I shall see you in the morning. Good night and sleep well, because I certainly have need of a decent night's rest."

She made to close the door, but he stuck out his foot, ignoring her dismissal. "Mr. Andrews asked me to accompany him upriver for a couple of days. He wishes to show me around his plantation. I hesitated, thinking you needed me, but now I am reconsidering."

He swiped a hand across his brow and pinched the bridge of his nose. "Fool that I can be, I am doing my best to keep you safe, Lily. I only mean to protect you, not smother you."

Her heart tumbled about in her chest, and the heat of her anger dissipated. "I know you mean well," she said softly.

She kissed him on the cheek. "We've both been under a great deal of pressure. Your visiting your friend in his home might be just the thing for both of us. Now good night, dear one. I shall see you when you return. Rest assured, I am in good hands here. I am safe."

He lifted her hand and kissed its back. "I trust that you are, my dear."

She started to close the door, then stuck her head out and called to him. "Please ask Allita to tend to me immediately."

He nodded, gave her a jaunty wave, and headed for the stairs.

She closed the door and moved to the chaise lounge at the end of her bed. She picked up a book she'd found in the library, hoping to take her mind off the evening's events while she waited for Allita. Little good that did. Her body was still tingling from her encounter with Bastien, her lips still swollen.

Lord, but he was a powerful man. In even more ways than she'd imagined. What would it be like to lie with him, to stretch out naked alongside him? In his bed. She sucked in a breath. "Read, Lily. Read or go insane."

Allita appeared in the doorway leading to her room. "You sent for me, *si?*"

Lily nodded. "Help me with my hair and out of this gown, if you will."

She made her way to the dressing table, seated herself on the upholstered green velvet bench, and peered into the looking glass. Those once fresh forget-me-knots now drooped about her head and her eyes appeared puffy.

Allita removed the flowers, and as if sensing Lily's need for silence, uttered not a word while she slowly brushed Lily's hair.

Lulled by Allita's gentle ministrations, Lily closed her eyes and focused on each stroke of the brush, letting time pass without thought.

Muted voices caught her attention. Had several persons passed by her bedchamber at this hour? Curious, she rushed to her door and flung it open.

René, Michel, and Felice glanced her way just as Bastien opened the door to his quarters and, in the midst of donning a black jacket, stepped into the corridor. He wore dark breeches, black boots, a dark shirt and a wide-brimmed hat pulled low over his head. To Lily's shock, a gun belt rode low on his hips, a heavy firearm snug in its holster. René and Michel were dressed in a similar fashion. Each carried a large carpetbag. Why, they looked the embodiment of the gunslingers she'd seen featured in *The Times*.

He caught sight of her and paused in mid-step, flashed her a dark look, then joined the others. Bastien spoke low to Felice in his native tongue, words Lily could not quite catch.

Felice gave him a slight nod, watched as the three men disappeared down the stairs, then marched over to Lily. "Let's go inside."

Lily stood her ground, refusing to budge. "What's going on here? What's happening? Where are they off to?"

Felice backed Lily into the room, closed and locked the door, then dropped the key into her pocket. "We need to talk."

Chapter Twelve

Lily took note of Felice's scandalous apparel, from her tall leather boots and tan breeches that clung to her hips like a second skin, to her midnight-blue cotton shirt. She'd never seen a woman clad in such attire. "Why are those men dressed like thieves in the night? And look at your manly dress. What in blazes is going on?"

Felice glanced at the maid. "You may be excused, Allita. I'll help Mrs. Talbot out of her gown."

Allita looked to Lily for direction. She nodded. As soon as the maid disappeared, Lily crossed her arms with a huff and scowled at Felice. "Either tell me what's going on or leave this room at once."

"I ride astride, which accounts for my manner of dress," Felice said. "I also like taking midnight jaunts along the levees. Hence, my change of clothing."

"What of the men? What are they up to?"

"A ship's come in needing their attention."

"Balderdash." Frustrated, Lily tapped a foot. "I do not appreciate you treating me like a fool. Are they intending to rob a train?"

A sardonic smile tipped one corner of Felice's mouth. She moved to the window, pulled aside the curtain, and stared at the street below.

A new level of irritation set Lily to pacing. "Answer me, Felice. The tension in the air surrounding those three was so thick, a corpse could've felt it."

Felice said nothing for a long moment. Then she moved to a hard chair and sat. Balancing her elbows on her knees, she rested her chin in her hands, and studied Lily through pensive eyes. "You and Mr. Talbot have secrets. Secrets only my father and brother are privy to. Which gnaws at my craw something fierce."

"What in the world does anything concerning Mr. Talbot and me have to do with your family members leaving here at midnight dressed like marauding bandits?"

Felice leaned back in her chair and studied Lily for yet another long moment. "What if I were to tell you that you aren't the only one concealing something? What if I were to tell you that not only does my family have secrets, but they are very dark and dangerous ones?"

A chill ran down Lily's spine. "Would this mysterious something include Bastien and your husband?"

Felice gave a slow nod, her eyes never leaving Lily's. "What if I were to suggest we share confidences? I'd like to be your friend. Sharing a family secret is my way of saying you can trust me."

Lily blinked back a sudden sting of tears. "And if I cannot be trusted in return and were to reveal your secret?"

"Our entire family would be destroyed."

Lily flinched. "Everyone? Including Bastien and René?"

Again, Felice nodded.

As she paced, Lily rubbed at the chill bumps erupting on her arms. "Your family secret couldn't possibly be more destructive than mine should it leak out."

Felice's eyes narrowed. "On the contrary. The Andrews family is an old and highly respected entity here in Louisiana. Not to mention the stellar reputation of the Andrews Shipping Company."

"Are you so eager to learn my secret that you are willing to put your entire family at risk?"

Felice sat back, stretched out her legs and offered Lily a thoughtful look. "Perhaps I have other reasons for wanting to dig into your past."

It was Lily's turn to make her way to the window and peer into the darkness. Her reflection stared back at her. Months-long fatigue showed in her eyes. Honestly, she didn't know how much longer she could go on hiding her troubles. "I…I am not so sure if—"

"But you dearly want to, don't you?"

Curiosity and the sudden desire to divulge her secret ate at her insides. She'd spent her life caring for her father, had acted as his personal secretary in all his affairs, had been careful to present a pleasant but businesslike veneer to cover her lackluster personal life. She'd never actually had a close female friend—other than employees she'd personally hired and supervised.

A low cry escaped her throat. God in Heaven. Hers had been a life lived in luxury, yet what a pitiful and vacuous existence it had been.

"Do you ride, Lily?"

Lily jerked at the sudden interruption of her thoughts and turned to find Felice watching her with an intense gaze. "Indeed, I do. Pray tell, what do my equestrian abilities have to do with our mutually divulging secrets?"

Felice moved to the wardrobe and flung it open. "Being a proper Brit and all, you ride sidesaddle, I presume. A pity. Riding astride is much more stable."

Lily frowned. "Just what are you up to?"

Felice fished out a plain brown skirt and blouse and tossed them on the bed. "These should do."

The garments had been the first thing Madame Charmontès had brought to Lily. Even after a bit of white trim had been added, she still detested the drab apparel.

More than curious now, she was suddenly eager to escape the confines of the house. "You are quite aware that I've been restricted to the gardens. By your father's direct order."

Felice gave her a sly look. "Who's to see us? Most everyone is gone from the premises, including your Mr. Talbot and Odalie. Allita and Vivienne are snoring away, and Rubio is likely in the kitchen giving Régine...ahem...a helping hand. I can tell you find the idea of a bit of freedom rather attractive."

She was right. Lily was desperate to escape her prison. If only for a little while. "Just where might you be taking me?"

"Why, to reveal our family secret. And so you can share yours." Felice extended her hand. "What say you—shake on it?"

The hair rose on the back of Lily's neck. Nonetheless, she shook Felice's hand. "Help me out of this gown."

Once dressed in the drab clothing and wearing only a chemise and one petticoat for ease of movement, she followed Felice to the stables, where they collected their horses and the one sidesaddle available.

Leaving the mansion behind, they rode in silence along the grassy area dividing the boardwalk from the street, muffling what would otherwise have been a loud clip-clop of hooves amid deserted streets. Disobeying orders and leaving Le Blanc House should have left Lily feeling guilty and nervous. Instead, a sense of defiant exhilaration infused her.

It didn't take long for them to venture beyond the houses and lamplit streets. The thin crescent moon did little to light the starry sky, but Lily's gentle mare trotted confidently along behind Felice's gelding. It seemed a long while, but at last, they rounded a turn and left civilization behind.

Shrouded in darkness and with strange night sounds surrounding her, Lily began to lose her nerve. "Dash it all, where *are* you taking me?"

"We're nearly there," Felice called over her shoulder. "From here on out, no matter what happens, do not make a sound. René and Michel would have my neck if they found out I brought you here. Close your eyes for a moment. When you open them, they'll have adjusted to the darkness."

Lily did as she was told. To her surprise, the method worked. "I've never spent time outdoors in the dead of night."

"Hush." Felice said softly as she urged her horse onto a narrow dirt path and through a bottomland thicket smelling of loam and cypress. Lily's mare steadfastly followed. Soon, they emerged onto a grassy field fronting a bayou. Here and there, fireflies flitted about the meadow's tall grass.

"Amazing," Lily whispered.

"Shh," Felice responded. "We shouldn't have long to wait."

On the far reaches of the grassy field, beyond the waterway, the sliver of moon hovered above the treetops. A narrow ribbon of moonglow rippled across the slow-moving dark waters and touched the bank beyond. Stars peppered the sky.

Lily wanted to shout, *Why are we here?*

At a nudge from Felice, she nodded in reply. Felice pointed off to her right, to a wooded area on the other side of the bayou.

Lily thought she saw movement. She squinted into the night. Three silhouettes appeared, moving silently along the water's edge, then merged with the woods. Lily shot Felice a questioning look and whispered the names of Bastien, René, and Michel.

Felice nodded. "They had to first meet with one of the station masters for further directions. Since I've sneaked in here before, I figured we would beat them here. Now, hush." She placed a finger to her lips.

Soon the men reappeared, but this time they dragged something low into the water. A faint splash, and they climbed in. Two other figures appeared from the woods, pushed a larger boat into the water, and scrambled aboard. In moments, the five men floated silently out of sight.

Felice urged her horse forward. Lily followed. Halting at the water's edge, Felice motioned for Lily to bring her mare alongside. "You can speak now, but not much above a whisper. Sound travels a long way in the dead of night."

"What's happening? What are they up to?"

"They're on a mission. On my father's behalf." After a long silence, Felice turned to Lily. "We help slaves escape from their owners along secret routes."

"Oh, Lord in Heaven!" Lily's hand splayed across her chest. "You're abolitionists. And in the deep South no less."

Felice nodded. "My father helps operate something called the Underground Railroad."

Despite the warm night, a chill ran through Lily's bones. Her horse reacted to the change in her and danced sideways. She eased the mare back in place. "Your entire family is involved in this clandestine undertaking, aren't they?"

Felice's brows knitted together. "How are you, a Britisher, aware of the Underground Railroad?"

"I handled my father's business affairs," Lily said. "He donated money to a group in Montreal that aids in the resettlement of freed slaves. I know there are no actual physical trains, only secret routes. That, and my awareness of abolitionists up north, is the extent of my knowledge. Please, tell me more."

"My father is the station master for this particular route. You just witnessed five conductors off to remove some abused field hands from a particularly nasty plantation owner."

"But you...your family...you were born and raised on what I assume is still a working plantation, complete with slaves."

A low sound left Felice's throat. "Carlton Oaks happens to be a secret center for moving slaves along several routes north, and into Canada. Papa is a genius at this business of liberating the oppressed. We have workers who are legally free, but they choose to remain at Carlton Oaks in order to serve the cause. While visitors might remember a few faces in the big house, they pay no heed to those picking cotton, have no business venturing into the fields. The field hands are temporary, waiting to ride what they call the Gospel train north. When their time comes, they leave Carlton Oaks, and others rotate in. No one outside of our family is wise to the operation. Growing up at Carlton Oaks, I had no knowledge of what went on. Papa's machine was so well-oiled, he operated right under my naïve little nose."

"You had no idea?"

"None. My mother died when I was four. With grief overwhelming Papa, he spent his time freeing slaves, while I was left to my own devices. I was the only girl-child, with a nanny barely fifteen years old. I ran wild, mimicking my brothers' equally wild behavior."

"My mama died when I was seven," Lily blurted. "An accident. It left Papa paralyzed."

"Really? And you ended up taking care of your father's business. Are you good at math?"

"I suppose I'm rather efficient with numbers."

Felice smiled at her. "We have a lot in common, you and I."

"What of Bastien and René? Have they been involved in your father's endeavor all these years?"

Felice shook her head. "They were with another Underground Railroad prior to coming to work for the shipping company. Somehow, they figured out what Papa and Michel were about and eagerly joined up with them."

"I wonder what tempted them to take on something so dangerous when their reputations in the community were already tattered. You'd think they'd shy away from such perilous activities."

"They are Cajuns, Lily. They do not tolerate slavery in any form. They may live dirt-poor in the bayous, but they live free—fiercely free."

"So their heritage influenced them?"

"Their strong convictions can be traced back four generations to when the British military forced their ancestors out of Acadia. Families were torn apart. Homes and rich farmlands were confiscated. They were dragged from their homeland and onto ships with nothing but the clothes on their backs. Many of them were dumped in the bayous and left to fend for themselves."

Lily's stomach soured. "No wonder Bastien seems to set so little value on us British. Does René feel the same?"

"Even though the brothers are exceedingly close, Bastien's mother and grandmother had more influence on him during his early years," Felice said. "Odalie's grandfather was five years old when his family was torn from a good life in Acadia. His mother died on the ship and was tossed overboard without ceremony while he looked on. He grew into a bitter man alongside an equally bitter father, passing on his contempt of the British to his offspring. Odalie and her mother took up the banner. Because Bastien inherited their gift of healing, he spent more time with them than René. Hence the great negative influence. Bastien feels that had the British never come along, he would've lived a decent life growing up. He would not have been born a bastard, would not have been taught to steal for survival, and his mother would not have become a voodoo priestess. Most of all, he'd not have suffered rejection by an entire town."

"Oh, dear." They sat in silence for a long while as Lily digested what she'd heard.

Felice's soft laughter—anything but jovial—broke the silence. "Here we have Michel, mayor of New Orleans, and Papa, a highly respected plantation owner and head of a prosperous maritime operation. René and Bastien have finally earned their place in society. Can you imagine what would happen were anyone to learn of our clandestine activities? We'd likely be dead within days—long before we could be brought to trial."

"Have you ever gone with them on one of these journeys?"

Felice heaved a great sigh. "Once. The experience was so terrifying I didn't sleep soundly for months."

A selfish concern about Bastien being gone a long while crowded out the astonishment flowing through Lily. "Will the men take these people to Canada?"

"No. For security purposes, no one goes the entire way, nor do they divulge names or where they are from. They'll split up at some point. Come the morrow, an exhausted Michel will return home to tend to his family and mayoral duties as if nothing has occurred. René will go a little farther, taking a different route from Bastien. With the responsibilities of a family now, my husband will go no farther than just above Baton Rouge."

"What of Bastien?"

"He'll take on the most dangerous task. Might not return for two or three weeks—if at all."

"Don't say that!" Lily's mare quivered and danced sideways again. She reined the animal in and lowered her voice. "Why Bastien?"

Felice patted her belly. "René has a family to think of now, as well."

Surprise shot through Lily. She glanced at Felice's barely rounded belly. "I had no idea you were expecting."

Felice grinned. "Not only am I tall, with plenty of room inside, but I swear this babe is standing upright, holding on to my spine while dancing a jig on my bladder and beating her head against my stomach in time with her feet. René says if it's a girl, she's going to be just like me, with an independent streak and a passion for living."

"Congratulations." Lily grew quiet as a strange melancholy swept through her. What would become of her when all was said and done? She'd long ago accepted her lot as a spinster, had devoted her life to caring for her father ever since she was a child. She doubted anything much good would come of her life from here on out. After all, what did she have to look forward to but a lonely life in dreary Cowdrey Hall?

A frozen hell on earth. That's what the Haworth Moor in Yorkshire was.

A sigh escaped her lips. Better Cowdrey Hall than living in Mayfair, where she'd been held prisoner and Papa had been murdered.

In any case, it was her future, providing she didn't end up hanging for the crime her cousin had committed.

Chapter Thirteen

"Share your thoughts, Lily?"

Felice's words startled Lily out of her stupor. Heavens. She needed to change the subject, and fast. "Why did Odalie disappear before dinner?"

"She never joins the family. She was only in residence to care for you, but knowing he'd be away, Bastien gave Vivienne instructions and left the healing herbs in her care, so Odalie went home."

"I don't mean to be rude, seeing as how Odalie is your mother-in-law, but I find her to be a rather strange person."

"She is an odd one indeed," Felice said. "Like René and Bastien, I give the woman a wide berth, but I respect the fact that she is their mother. Also, as the reigning voodoo priestess, she is a very powerful person in these parts, with a strong following. Tread lightly."

"Why did Bastien bring her to me?"

"Despite the tension between Odalie and her sons, they honor her simply because she is their mother. But were she ever to challenge me, I would not back down."

"You have fire in your veins, Felice. So full of daring. I admire your spunk."

"What of you, Lily? Before you were poisoned, were you not daring? Did you not take chances in life? Did you not have a passion for living?"

A familiar guilt took hold of Lily. She stared out over the water. "I was once filled with a great passion for living. I was daring and foolish. Too foolish. My thirst for adventure caused my mother's death."

"What?" Felice frowned. "You said you were seven years old when she died. How could you have caused her death?"

"My father's adventurous spirit fed my own overzealous nature. He took the three of us on a buggy ride one day, recklessly dashing hither and yon about the countryside. I'd laugh and call out, 'Faster, Papa! Faster!' All the while Mama would cry, 'Slow down!'

"Papa did my bidding, not hers. We hit a rut in the road, one wheel flew off, as did the three of us. I was knocked unconscious but otherwise unharmed. When I awoke and staggered to my feet, I found my mother lying in the middle of the road, her neck broken. I heard my father's moans. Found him in a ditch with both his legs twisted at odd angles."

"Oh, my God, Lily. What did you do?"

"I ran down the road until I came to a house and called for help. Mama was dead, and Papa was paralyzed from the waist down."

"Oh, Lily. What happened was not your fault. It was an accident."

"Tell that to my guilt-ridden heart. Papa catered to me. Spoiled me. He'd do anything for me, and so he failed to heed my mother's cries to slow down. Had I not kept urging him onward, the accident would not have taken place."

"And you've carried this burden of guilt with you all these years. Is this why you devoted your life to taking care of your father?"

"It was the least I could do," Lily said and grew silent.

"One last question, Lily."

"What?"

"Is Mr. Talbot truly your husband?"

God no!

From somewhere deep in her heart, a silent cry tore loose and threatened to break the surface. She swallowed hard, sending the pain back down. But one thing she was certain of—she was a woman of her word. She'd promised to share confidences, hadn't she? After all, Felice had entrusted Lily with her secret. And a mighty one at that.

Taking in a deep breath for courage, she spoke. "He's my godfather. He's watched over me as best he could since my parents' accident. We didn't know for several weeks if my father would survive. I used to pray at his bedside. Promise God that if He'd let Papa live, I would care for him for the rest of his life. And so I did. Willingly."

"Then why did you flee England? Who poisoned you?"

It would be a relief to at last say something. "My greedy cousin couldn't wait for my father to die so he could inherit. When he found out Papa had legally bequeathed everything to me, Julian thought to take matters into his own hands. He poisoned both my father and me, which would have left him the sole survivor. Little by little, I sickened until I was too weak to leave my bed. Papa wasn't dying fast enough so Julian suffocated him with a pillow. Molly, our maid, saw the murder take place."

Lily looked at Felice. "Molly ran to my godfather in the dead of night, then promptly disappeared. We don't know if she is in hiding, or if my cousin did her in as well. Uncle...I call him Uncle...rushed to me, only to find Julian trying to smother me as well. He knocked Julian over the head and stole me away. When Julian regained consciousness, he went directly to two of his shady cronies: one a magistrate, the other a barrister. He told them he'd witnessed me killing my own father, and that I had run from the scene. With Julian roaming free and desperate to do me in, with a public warrant for my arrest posted in *The Times*, and with my health steadily worsening, Uncle panicked and brought me here, to his old friend—your father. Until we can locate Molly, he is keeping me safe from Julian."

"Oh, I'm so sorry. If only I could take away all you've been through, I would."

Close to tears, Lily murmured, "I should like to go home now...I mean back to Le Blanc House. Whatever you prefer to call my current residence."

"Well, since the new owner of Le Blanc House happens to be Bastien, I doubt he will turn you out anytime soon." Felice reached over and patted Lily on the hand. "Consider this a hug."

While they sat side by side on their horses, saying nothing, Lily's emotions went through a myriad of changes until she realized there was a long-hidden dream still beating in her heart. She'd lived a vacuous life all these years, bereft of the joy that had once flowed through her, as vital as the very air she breathed. Felice was right. It was time to let go of the past, time to find something of substance to make living worthwhile.

She felt her spine straighten, felt renewed vibrancy flow through her veins. "Where might I come by some of those breeches you are wearing?"

Felice gasped. And then she laughed. "Splendid, Miss Lily! Madame Charmontès takes great delight in making them for me."

"I should like a pair of boots as well. And a tailored blouse. And I want to learn to ride astride. Not only am I going on a few midnight rides with you, but I'd like to do something brave and different. I'll need help with that bit."

Felice continued laughing. "We shall breakfast out tomorrow. And I know just the place...an ice cream parlor."

"Ice cream for breakfast?"

"Indeed. They know me there. I have several pairs of breeches. I'll have Madame Charmontès alter one pair tomorrow and order more for you. I'll check the bootmaker's supplies on the morrow."

"Can't wait," Lily said and turned her horse around.

They returned to Le Blanc House in silence but before they led Lily's horse back into its stall, Felice hugged Lily. "You've a friend for life." She remounted, then paused, looking down at Lily. "I can sense a change in Bastien. He's bought this house, and according to Henri, is in the market for a fancy carriage and his own horse instead of riding whatever happens to be in the stable."

Lily's heart took a leap into her throat. "Why bring him up now?"

Felice's horse danced in place, eager to head for home. "At last, he's become the successful man he'd always dreamed of becoming, which gives him reason to take great care on this journey to free slaves. But I sense there is still an empty space inside him that none of what he's achieved has managed to fill."

Felice turned her horse toward the street and called over her shoulder. "He's lonely, Lily. And so are you. What do you intend to do about it? It's nice to see you've a new fire in your eyes, my dear. Sleep well."

Speechless, Lily watched Felice disappear. Fishing the key to the back door from the pocket in her skirt, she made her way inside, locked the door, and climbed the stairs to her room. Changing into a night rail, she crawled into bed and stared at the ceiling, her brain scrambled by Felice's parting words.

He's lonely. So are you. He's searching. It's nice to see you've a new fire in your eyes tonight, my dear. Sleep well.

Lily tossed back the covers and rolled out of bed. "Sleep well is not happening. At least not here."

She left her bedchamber, hurried down the corridor, and slipped into Bastien's room. Lighting the gas wall sconces, she locked the door behind her and leaned her back against the hard paneling.

And gave a soft gasp.

Why, his entire apartment was spectacular. It was a well-appointed suite with wide French doors opening onto a deep balcony overlooking the gardens. Her head buzzing and her heart in her throat, she moved through the sitting room lined with neatly filled bookcases into his bedroom, lighting the wall sconces as she went until the rooms were filled with a soft glow.

"My word," she whispered to herself. "Would you look at this."

A large, elaborately carved walnut bed was set against the back wall facing the balcony doors. A blue-on-blue French print covered the wide mattress. Matching dark walnut armoires flanked the walls adjacent to the bed. Here were more bookcases, the shelves containing fewer books, but holding what Lily recognized to be a priceless collection. A painting hung

on the wall behind a comfortable-looking chair. She moved to the table
beside the chair, picked up a book sitting at a neat angle and examined it.
Gulliver's Travels.
Warmth traveled through her chest. He'd read to her aboard ship. In
that deep, laconic, and melodious Cajun accent that calmed her. Even in
her weakened state, she'd been attracted to him.
She shouldn't be in here invading his space, touching his personal
things. Really, she shouldn't. But a hunger to find a part of him to cling
to kept her from leaving. Placing the book back where she'd found it, she
spied a door on either side of the bed. One had to be his dressing room,
but what was the other? Taking a guess that the door on the left, farthest
from the entry, would be where he dressed, she made her way to the door
on the right, opened it and stepped inside.
"Oh, my!"
Something more she hadn't expected. She stepped into a large bathing
chamber. Veined Italian marble lined the walls and paved the floor. A
large tub stood in the center of the room, a burgundy Persian rug before
it. Had he ever brought ladies here, she wondered? Most likely not, what
with the house a beehive of activity.
Leaving the bathing chamber, she made her way to his dressing room
and stepped inside. Closing her eyes, she breathed in his essence lingering
in the air, so real it was as if he might step forward at any moment.
And embrace her.
She'd never wanted a man before, but now that she did, the ache inside
her was sheer torment. She moved to yet another armoire, opened it and
found a number of neatly stacked shirts, folded just so. Everything about
his dress was carefully attended to. She'd noted that aboard ship—nothing
ever out of place. Did his penchant for neatness have something to do with
his sorry upbringing? Was his keen attention to his deportment a way of
making up for a life he'd despised as a child?
She picked up one of his shirts, wrapped her arms around it, and held it
to her chest as if it were Bastien she embraced. Then she buried her face
in the clean scent, one that was his alone.
Intending to place the shirt back where she'd found it, she was overcome
by a raw edge of want. With her breath clogging her lungs at what she was
about to do, she gave the folded shirt a shake, then shed her night rail and
donned Bastien's clean, soft, cotton shirt. The garment fell below her knees,
and the sleeves hung past her fingertips. She laughed softly. Hugging the
shirt to her body, she relived the dazzling moment when his lush mouth
had met hers, how the murmur of her name soaked right through her skin.

She turned a circle in front of the cheval mirror, the dizzying thrum of her blood beating a furious tattoo in her temple.

"I've gone mad," she whispered into the air. "But if this is madness, so be it. I want you, Bastien, and I think you want me back, so forgive the intrusion." Leaving the dressing room, she made her way over to his bed, where she pulled back the bedcovers and climbed in, bold as you please.

Chapter Fourteen

A sudden buzzing erupted in the low-lying brush. Bastien froze, one booted foot hovering in midair. Rattlers! And from the angry sound, a damn big nest of them. A bead of sweat rolled down his back. Inching to his right, he took care not to further disturb the slithering bastards and lifted the girl off the forest floor. He set her onto a low-lying branch, hoping she mistook the buzzing for cicadas. Either that or she was too busy nursing her babe to notice.

She regarded him through sad brown eyes. Fatigue etched deep furrows in her young face. "I cain't go no further, sir. Leave me here."

Like hell he'd be leaving her to the slave catchers. Bastien spoke in as calm a manner as he could muster. "*Non.* That will not do."

Her shoulders slumped. "But my feet, sir. I cain't walk no more."

"*Oui.* I know." Bastien removed a shirt from his carpetbag and slipped his Spanish *navaja* from its leather casing fitted inside his boot.

She glanced at the treacherous-looking knife and her big round eyes grew even bigger.

"I won't hurt you. You'll be safe with me." He had to hurry. Standing at the edge of the forest under a full moon meant taking a mighty risk, but he needed the light to tend to her.

"I'll be applying a salve to the bottoms of your feet. It'll sting at first, but soon, they'll feel cool." He tore the shirt into strips and used one length to clean each foot as best he could.

"What's your name?" he asked as he applied the salve.

She hissed and stiffened at the sting, then relaxed. "Bean."

He glanced up from his task and into her anxious eyes. "You be meaning the kind of bean a person eats?"

She nodded. "The big brown ones. Mama said that's about the size of me when I was birthed, so she called me her little bean."

His heart gave a squeeze. He wouldn't be asking her last name. It would be the same as that no-good plantation owner, as all his slaves were named. "What about your *maman*? Did she get left behind?"

Something passed through her eyes, then disappeared. She gave her head a little shake. "She got sold a while back."

Christ. He fell silent and went about the task of wrapping each foot in more cotton strips while the babe at her breast mewed and suckled. The mother couldn't be more than fifteen. All alone with a child. And scared to death.

She watched his every move. "What's your name, sir?"

"We don't use our given names," he said. "Keeps everyone safe that way. Call me Mister." Slipping the bandana from around his neck, he turned his attention to the babe. "If you'll hold her toward me, I'll diaper her."

Bean stilled. The look on her face telling him she was deciding whether or not to trust him. After a long moment, she held up the child as if offering him a gift.

Bastien drew in a slow breath to try to calm his roiling emotions. "What's your baby's name?"

"Child."

He lifted a brow. "Just Child, that's all?"

She shrugged. "Saw no sense namin' her when he was gonna sell her once she went off the tit."

Merde! He didn't have to ask who the child's father was, the dirty bastard. Bastien's heart lurched. Even a simpleton could tell she loved her little girl just by the sheer protective force emanating from her. "She's yours, Bean. No one will be taking her from you."

The moonlight reflected on tears in her eyes. She turned her head from his gaze and wiped at her eyes with her wrist. She hadn't broken all the way, but she was getting damn close.

He took out another shirt, his last one, wrapped the child in it, then setting the babe back in her mother's arms, used his knife to punch holes in the carpetbag.

Bean's stark gaze flitted from the bag to Bastien's face and back again. "What'cha doin'?"

"Making a cradle." He lifted the bag and turned it about for her inspection. "See where I made holes around the sides?"

Bean nodded.

"She'll breathe easy enough. If she cries, the heavy fabric will muffle her sounds until we can shush her. If I'm right, the bag will move in harmony with the rhythm of my footsteps. Soon, your little darlin' with the full tummy will be lulled into a sound sleep. You comfortable with that?"

She hesitated a moment, then nodded.

Bastien lifted the babe from her mother's arms and eased the child into the carpetbag. Turning, he presented his back to Bean. "Now pretend I'm a horse. Put your arms around my shoulders, wrap your legs around my waist, and hold on. We'll reach the safe house in no time."

"You expectin' to carry me the whole way on your back? That man what took the others said we had more than ten miles to go."

"*Oui.* You can't weigh much more than a mosquito. Come now—we need to disappear into the woods so we won't be seen."

Bean didn't hesitate. Wrapping her arms and legs around Bastien, she held on, clinging to him like a second skin. "You carryin' my child in harmony with your footsteps means somethin' good. Right, Mister?"

"*Oui.*"

She grew quiet, but Bastien sensed her restlessness.

"What exactly does *harmony* mean, Mister?"

"Peace and togetherness, I suppose." He moved deeper into the forest, where the overhead trees formed a canopy, blocking the moonlight. "We'll need to be silent from here on out."

"Yes, sir. I'll be quiet as a mouse peein' on cotton."

He chuckled. "Seeing as how you've nothing to do but hold on, why don't you rest your cheek on my shoulder and spend your time thinking about what to name your pretty little girl."

He thought he heard a sob.

Soon, they were shrouded in complete darkness as he followed the trail left by the other conductor—skunk piss dabbed on broken branches. Good thing there was no rain to wash away the stink or they'd be in big trouble, seeing as how he'd never taken this route before.

He hadn't expected to travel this far north. But when he'd handed over the rescued slaves to the conductor next in line, they'd heard the soft whimper of a baby. Stepping around a tall clump of bushes, they'd nearly stumbled over poor, bedraggled Bean. She hadn't been one of the number the third conductor had plucked off a cotton field. She'd been sitting off to one side, nursing her babe when the men hurried past. Shoeless, she'd waited until they were out of sight, then followed them.

Once the conductor had discovered she'd tagged along, he'd allowed her to remain, but when she gave up and sat down, he hadn't dared hold up the rest of the group. He told her to remain hidden and wait for the other conductor to come along. He'd promised to let the safe house know to expect her and the babe.

For a long while, Bastien trudged along in silence, the rhythm of his gait rocking the makeshift cradle. He heard Bean sigh.

With her hands clasped just below his Adam's apple, she propped her chin on his shoulder and murmured in his ear. "Mister?"

"What is it?" he murmured.

"We sure had us a big ole nest of rattlesnakes back there, didn't we?"

He would've laughed had he not been so weary. He barely managed a grunt in reply. Exhaustion gnawed at his bones. He concentrated on holding the fatigue in his mind, didn't dare let it seep into his leg muscles or they'd be done for. He couldn't remember catching more than an hour's sleep in one stretch since leaving New Orleans.

Merde.

He'd left the city when the moon was little more than a sliver in the sky. Now it had gone from full to beginning to wane, which meant he'd been away just over two weeks. Once he delivered mother and child to the safe house, he'd make his way to Memphis, catch the train that ran straight through to New Orleans. With all the stops, he might be home in a week.

Home.

To think he'd purchased Le Blanc House one afternoon only to depart by midnight. An image of Lily danced through his mind. Did she spend time in the garden? Had her health improved? Had her nightmares ceased? Would she even be there once he returned? The idea that she might have left for good produced a sudden void in him that ran too deep for words. Shoving the startling feeling aside, he focused on putting one foot in front of the other while keeping track of the smelly, torn branches.

By the time they emerged from the forest, dawn was breaking like a murky gray shawl covering the earth. He paused to take note of the slow-moving stream in front of him, one he'd been told to expect. To his left and up a gentle slope stood a white-washed clapboard farmhouse, a red barn, and several outbuildings. Sheep and cattle grazed over green rolling acreage while chickens roamed free around the barn and house. He caught the honking sound of geese.

This had to be the place. But what if he'd somehow gone wrong? Spotting movement on the back porch, he waited, ready to duck back into the woods. A tow-headed lad waved and pointed to Bastien's right. He spotted a small footbridge and made his way over it.

"Hallooo," the boy called as he ran to greet them. "My name's Will. William Jensen. We've been expecting you."

Bastien managed a crooked grin. The lad was about twelve or so. William might be the boy's Christian name, but Bastien would bet his life his last name wasn't Jensen. While all the conductors were called Mister, most of the Underground safe-house managers hid behind false names. Doing so kept their real titles safe within the community. "My name's Mister. On my back is Bean."

Will nodded. "Come along. Ma started cooking breakfast soon's we caught sight of you."

"Are the others still here?"

"Uh-uh. We moved them out quick. Before daylight. Pa took the last group to a safe house in Germantown. The first group went on to Jacob Burkle's place in Memphis. The conductors scattered to who knows where."

"How far away are those two towns from here?"

"Germantown is about six miles as the crow flies. Memphis is mayhap sixteen miles beyond there. Can I carry your bag?"

"I'd be pleased if you would. Take care, though. There's a babe inside."

Will's eyes flashed with excitement. Gingerly, he relieved Bastien of the bag, using both hands to grip the handle, and led them to the house.

They stepped through the back door and directly into a large kitchen filled with the heady aroma of bacon and eggs sizzling in a large cast-iron pan atop a wood stove. Sliced potatoes were frying next to them. Steam puffed a welcoming aroma from the spout of a blue enamel coffeepot near the back of the stove.

"My stomach just growled," Bean whispered.

"*Oui*. I heard it."

A sturdy, big-boned woman with graying hair and plump, rosy cheeks popped a loaf of bread from the oven onto a sideboard. Gathering up the bottom of a cotton apron buttoned to the top of her dress, she used a corner to wipe her hands. She turned to them with kind eyes. "Welcome to my home."

"There's a babe in here, Ma," Will announced as he gently set the carpetbag onto a long wooden table covered in a green-checked oilcloth. "And this here is Mister and Bean, the ones we've been expectin'."

She rushed to where Will stood.

"I'm Mrs. Jensen," she called over her shoulder while lifting the baby from the bag. "Feel free to hang your gear on that hook right behind you, Mister. Then you two sit yourselves down. I'll see to giving Bean and her dear little one a bath after you eat. Food first. Baths later. Will, put the plates on the table."

Mrs. Jensen glanced at Bean's wrapped feet and sent a speaking glance toward Bastien. He set Bean in a wooden chair at the table, then arched his rigid back while stifling a groan. Removing his hat and gun belt, he hung them on the one empty hook and took a seat across from Bean.

Bean opened her arms to the babe, her eyes alight with expectation.

"She's soaked through," Mrs. Jensen said.

"I don't care," Bean said, wriggling her fingers at the woman.

Bastien scrubbed a hand across his heavy beard. He hadn't shaved since he'd left New Orleans. What a god-awful sight he must look. "I noticed a pump out back which would suit me fine for cleaning up."

"Well water's mighty cold, Mister." Mrs. Jensen returned to the stove and went about filling a large oval platter with the savory foodstuff.

"Cold or hot makes no difference to me as long as I can get rid of some of this grit and manage a clean shave."

"You'll need to be swift about it then. No lingering outside during daylight hours with Pa and the farmhand not yet back. Will, go tell Oma breakfast is ready."

She set the steaming platter in the middle of the table. Next came the loaf of warm bread, the coffeepot, a pitcher of milk, two kinds of jam, butter, and a bowl of sugar.

This time, it was Bastien's stomach rumbling. He glanced up as Will led a little white-haired lady into the room. He seated her at the far end of the table.

Will said something to her in a language Bastien did not understand. She nodded.

"This is Oma," Will said, taking great care to ease her into her seat. "It means grandmother in German. She doesn't speak any English."

The old lady glanced at Bastien, gave him a nod, then settled her wizened gaze on Bean and the baby. She said something to Mrs. Jensen, who smiled. "She's my mother but we all call her Oma, which you have her permission to do, as well. Bean, you have been notified that after your baths, you are to feed the babe and then rest your weary body while Oma takes over."

Bean frowned. "Just what does takin' over mean?"

"It means Oma has spent many an hour right there in that rocking chair you see in the corner. Rocking her children and grandchildren is her specialty. It's a duty she's mighty proud of. I'm going to tell her that you said you are pleased to have her help you."

Bean looked from Oma to Mrs. Jensen to Bastien. And then a smile settled in her eyes. "I'd be most pleased."

Mrs. Jensen said something to Oma, who grinned and said, "*Ja. Sehr gut.*"

"Very good, she said." Mrs. Jensen glanced at her son. "Once you finish eating, fetch a towel and a bar of soap for Mister. Then get that strop and razor we keep for this sort of thing. May as well bring him some of your brother's clothes so I can wash what he's wearing."

She glanced at Bastien, and a touch of humor filled her eyes. "I imagine we can all tolerate the smell of you long enough to break our fast. Then I'll help bathe Bean and her baby, and we'll roust them up something to wear."

Bean spooned food onto her plate while holding on to her babe who, still soaked through, sucked on her little fist and gurgled contentedly.

"What's your little girl's name?" Mrs. Jensen asked.

"Harmony," Bean announced without hesitation.

Bastien paused with his forkful of food in midair.

Bean looked him straight in the eye. "Seems fittin' to me."

Girl, you be one strong survivor, don'cha know. "Nice name," he said and continued to fill his belly.

After breakfast, Bastien unwrapped the cloth strips and cleaned Bean's feet, then informed Mrs. Jensen that he'd tend to the girl's injuries once she'd bathed, but she could not be moved until she healed. Mrs. Jensen clucked her tongue but agreed to mother and child spending extra time in her home.

That settled, Bastien stepped onto the porch, where Will had set out the clothing, a bar of lye soap, and a thin towel. A bucket of water stood atop an old wooden chair next to a small, round mirror nailed to the clapboards. On the shelf lay the razor and strop. On closer inspection, Bastien realized that the Jensens had outfitted their home in several subtle ways in order to accommodate their "overnight guests."

He retrieved his own comb and toothbrush from a tin he'd tucked into one corner of the carpetbag along with another tin of healing herbs. Then he set about scraping the heavy beard off his face. With the door to the kitchen propped open, Mrs. Jensen could be heard humming as she bathed the baby in a galvanized washtub set atop the kitchen table.

Grateful for the privacy, Bastien finished shaving, shed his filthy clothing, then made his way around the house to the pump. He filled the tin bucket sitting next to it and dumped the freezing water over his head, sucking in a breath at the icy cold. Repeating the action, he soaped himself from head to toe, then rinsed himself clean.

Invigorated by the icy bath, he headed back to the porch and to the clothing Will had set out. A noisy goose met up with him, honking and waddling along behind.

Will sat on the wooden planks of the porch, his feet dangling off the edge, vigorously polishing Bastien's boots. He ignored Bastien's nakedness as if he'd witnessed the scenario many times over. "I'll have your boots ready for you in a bit, if you don't mind going barefoot for a while."

"*Non.* I like the feel of the ground on the bottom of my feet." He stepped behind Will and into a rough cotton homespun shirt and baggy pants. At least they fit. "Your brother must be a large man. Where is he?"

"My three sisters and two brothers are married and live hereabouts. Them and all their children." Will kept on polishing, putting a sheen to the boots that would make any man proud. "I'm the youngest. Since I'm the only one left, it's my turn to watch over Ma and Oma when Pa is off doing your kind of business. You should see the size of our gatherings here come Christmas and Easter."

Bastien sat down beside Will and listened to his chatter. Here indeed was a home filled with harmony. It felt pretty damn good to just sit and idly listen to a young lad eager to communicate.

As if Will read Bastien's mind, his cheeks flushed. "Pardon me for carrying on so. Ma says I'd talk to a fence post if one was nearby."

Bastien laughed. "I enjoy your company, Will, but I must speak with your *maman* for a moment."

He stepped into the kitchen and paused at the warm sight of Oma in the rocking chair with little Harmony asleep in her arms. To his surprise, what he'd thought was a shelf filled with supplies affixed to the wall was moveable. It had been pulled aside to reveal a small alcove fitted with a narrow bed and small cradle, where Bean, wearing a fresh day gown, lay sound asleep.

"It's the old larder," Mrs. Jensen said. "If anyone should happen along unannounced, we slide that shelf back over the opening with no one the wiser. Will's Pa fixed little breaks in the slats so the person inside can see what's going on. Bean and Harmony will be safe there. Will collected that old cradle from the attic. All my children used it. We keep it for our grandchildren now."

Oma studied Bastien with those intense, wizened eyes. Then she said something to her daughter. Mrs. Jensen smiled and kept her head down, peeling potatoes.

Oma spoke again, this time at length.

"She'll be talking about me, *non*?"

Mrs. Jensen's smile returned. "She thinks you are the most handsome man she's ever seen. The ladies must swoon over those blue eyes. How about a cup of coffee?"

Bastien felt the heat run up his neck and into his face. *"Oui. Merci."* He sat at the table, his cheeks still flushed, while Oma slowly rocked, watching him. He searched his mind for something to change the subject. "Will your husband and farmhands be back anytime soon?"

"Couple of days for Pa. Our two farmhands could show up at any time since they only took the one group to Germantown. You got a family, Mister?"

Bastien took a sip of coffee. *"Oui.* A brother and his wife. Also, a sister living in England. And Maman."

Mrs. Jensen paused. "No wife or children?"

A sharp image of Lily interrupted his thoughts. He shrugged. *"Non.* I've never been marriage-minded."

She said something in German to the grandmother, who clucked her tongue and responded in the same language.

"Oma thinks that's a shame. The way you've cared for Bean and Harmony, she says you're a family man through and through."

Weariness washed through him. Even with the kick of coffee running through his veins, Bastien rubbed a hand across his eyes. Eyes that suddenly seemed filled with sand.

Mrs. Jensen glanced over at him. "There's an extra bed in the bunkhouse. Why don't you rest before supper? Will can fetch you when it's ready."

Bastien glanced at the one empty corner of the kitchen. "I'll rest there. I need to keep an eye on Bean and her healing."

"We'll send for you if she needs anything."

"Non. She's my responsibility. I must see to her."

"But you said it could be five days or more. Surely, you don't intend to sleep there the entire time?"

"Oui. In case I am needed. She must keep off her feet, and I reckon she is stubborn enough to ignore my orders to stay put."

Will stepped inside carrying Bastien's shiny boots. His grandmother spoke to him. Will glanced at Bastien with a surprised look. He turned to his mother, who nodded. "Do as Oma says, please."

Will disappeared, quickly returning with a mound of bedding in his arms. He spread it out in the corner.

"They're feather ticks," Mrs. Jensen said. "Filled with goose down from that gaggle of geese running around. Ticks are meant to go onto mattresses, not the floor, but since you've insisted on bedding down here, they'll have to do."

Bastien settled in, barely able to keep his eyes open. It was there he intended to spend his nights until Bean's feet were healed enough for her to walk.

Over the next few days Bean blossomed under the Jensen family's care while little Harmony laughed and gurgled at everyone. Even Bastien found himself carrying her about or bouncing her on his knee. He felt oddly at home here, rested in the comfort of a family clearly devoted to each other, and to a cause they fiercely believed in.

But he was more than ready to return home. Mixed in with memories of home were unbidden recollections of Lily. It got so he could no longer separate the two. Hell, she probably wasn't even in residence any longer. God knew what had transpired in his absence. All the same, reflecting on their time together seemed to occupy a great part of his thoughts. Or was it his heart? He'd drift off to sleep at night with memories of her floating through his mind like a vision.

Mr. Jensen came and went. Will read to Bean in his free time, while Oma rocked the baby or spent her time unraveling old sweaters and using the yarn to knit new items for Harmony.

Bastien insisted on chopping wood for the kitchen stove and for every fireplace in the house, which gave him something to do when not tending to his patient. In the end, and much to Mr. Jensen's pleasure, Bastien had cut enough wood to see them through winter. Such a different life from that he knew in New Orleans, but he'd been right when he'd told Bean they'd find peace and harmony in this safe house. He hadn't expected it to apply to him as well.

At last, the time came for Mr. Jensen and the farmhand to transport Bean and Harmony to Memphis. From there, the next conductor would take her to Ohio, a free state. Once they reached Lake Erie, she'd be put on a boat to Canada.

At midnight, Bastien stood at the back end of the wagon and helped settle Bean and Harmony into the shallow compartment hidden beneath the belly of the wagon. They both had decent clothing. Bean wore Will's Sunday-go-to-meeting shoes, which fit just fine.

Bastien's heart felt as if it might burst. He took a deep breath to ease the discomfort. "Do you know what a promise means, Bean?"

"Yes, sir."

"I want you to give me your word that when you get to Canada, you'll learn to read. And you'll learn your numbers. Then promise me you'll read to Harmony every night. And as soon as she's old enough, you will teach her to read. Can you give me that promise?"

"Yes, sir."

He ignored the sound of tears clogging her throat and slipped a folded piece of paper into her hand. "Tuck that someplace safe."

"You mean in my bosom?"

"Wherever you think is safe. Once you reach Canada, show this to whoever takes you in. They'll see to it the person whose name is written on this note will get it. Instructions for him are inside. Be careful until you get there, Bean. Stay safe."

Christ. Why did he feel ready to weep? He nodded to Mr. Jensen, indicating it was time to move on. "You take care, Bean, you hear?"

As Mr. Jensen made to close the narrow opening, Bastien turned to leave. He couldn't bear to watch. The damn enclosure reminded him of a coffin.

"Mister?"

He turned. "What?"

She reached out, wiggling her fingers at him. "My heart sure does thank you."

He could only manage a nod. He squeezed her hand, then walked away, down to the edge of the stream, where he sat on a rock through half the night, his thoughts tumbling about in his head as if searching for something tangible. For what, he did not know. He'd been gone from home for nearly a month. Felt more like a year.

At dawn, he changed into his own clothing, pulled on his boots, strapped the gun belt on his hips, and thanked Mrs. Jensen for her hospitality. He shook hands with Will and kissed Oma on each cheek. Donning his hat, he made his way to the barn, where he saddled the gelding he'd been lent, and rode for Germantown.

Reaching the small township, he left the horse at a public stable where the Jensen farmhand would retrieve it, then rented another horse and rode the rest of the way into Memphis. He went straight to a haberdasher and purchased the finest the man had to offer—a soft white cotton shirt, gold brocaded vest, snowy cravat, and a plain black jacket. Locating the best hotel in town, he secured a large suite complete with its own bathing chamber.

That evening, he soaked in a grand porcelain tub, letting his mind drift wherever it might. Something had changed in him. He wasn't quite sure what, but he guessed once he reached home, he'd have all the time in the world to figure things out.

Come morning, Bastien boarded the train for New Orleans, and to a life that seemed a century ago. He settled into a private luxury car, and as the train rolled out of Memphis, he spent the journey staring out the window at the ever-changing landscape while he pondered his life thus far. In the end, one persistent thought drummed in his brain with the rhythmic clickety-clack of the train's steel wheels—Lily was no man's wife. Never had been.

Chapter Fifteen

"Finished." Lily placed her brush in the jar of linseed oil next to the portrait and took a step back. The image she'd painted of Bastien stared out at her through compelling blue eyes filled with the elusive emotion she'd been so keen on capturing. Exquisite heat coursed through her, tightened her breasts, and settled low in her belly.

She pulled a boudoir chair in front of the easel and sat. Wetting one corner of a cloth with the linseed oil, she went about the mindless task of cleaning her stained fingers whilst studying her completed piece, tilting her head this way and that, scrutinizing it from every angle.

"Definitely my best work," she murmured. An imposing figure even on canvas, Bastien stood on the deck of the ship that had transported them to New Orleans. To her great satisfaction, she'd managed to capture his potent vitality, a rare and barely disguised force she'd not seen in other men—except perhaps his brother. While René was an impressive man in his own right, he did nothing to elicit the delicious, erotic tension Bastien always stirred in her.

His booted feet planted wide apart on the wooden deck gave him a commanding air, triggering memories that spoke volumes to her heart. His large hands were fisted on either side of his narrow hips, while his open, unbuttoned jacket exposed a snowy white shirt and gold brocade waistcoat against a flat stomach. Fawn-colored breeches sheathed long, muscular legs. Behind him, full sails billowed against a cloud-studded sky, and a light breeze teased strands of raven hair across his forehead. The sun's rays filtering through a light haze created a nimbus around him. But, oh, those spectacular cobalt eyes rimmed in dark lashes—they appeared to bore straight into her, transmitting a mysterious raw emotion he'd not been quick enough to mask.

A wave of longing washed through her. She pressed a hand to her heart as if doing so might suppress its heightened beat. It had turned out that the charcoal drawing she'd previously sketched of him had been little more than practice for this almost life-sized portrait. What a wonderful surprise when Felice marched into Le Blanc House dragging this large canvas behind her, something she'd finagled from a reclusive artist she knew.

Lily let go a sigh. Had painting Bastien's portrait been prompted by some deep, soulful yearning for him? Something akin to melancholy gripped her. She wouldn't be in New Orleans for long. And upon her departure, the most enigmatic man she'd ever known would become little more than a memory. Well, wherever she was meant to end up, this likeness of him would go with her.

She would hang it in her bedchamber.

For her eyes only.

A small ache pinched her heart. Bastien had been gone nearly a month. Felice told Lily not to be concerned, that he'd disappeared in the past for longer periods. Nonetheless, Lily worried.

Even though she'd never once inquired as to his whereabouts, and even though she was supposedly married, everyone—Régine, Vivienne, Felice, René, even Michel's wife, Brenna—made a concerted effort to reassure her of Bastien's safe return. Good heavens. Were her growing feelings for him so transparent?

Not only had the lot of them become friendlier toward her, but they were clearly trying to make her feel at home, treating her like family. Even René was showing up unannounced on occasion, staying for dinner, and pointedly engaged her in light conversation. He'd also accompanied Felice and Lily on several midnight rides along the levee. Those late-night treks were a godsend. As were the early mornings when Rubio and Allita accompanied her the two blocks over to visit Brenna and her lively brood of seven, along with their menagerie. But best of all, Lily had been asked on more than one occasion to assist Felice in the shipping office during Bastien's absence. The tasks assigned to her were akin to those she'd often handled for her father's business ventures. She looked forward to the time she might again be asked to help out.

All told, Lily had grown rather content living at Le Blanc House. Were it not for the beastly hot weather, the idea of settling into her own home here would be appealing. If her legal troubles were ever resolved, that was.

Blast it all, she had no idea what her future might hold. One thing was certain—returning to London was out of the question. She recalled the lavish Mayfair townhome she'd once loved, forever banned to her by Cousin Julian's murderous actions. She pushed aside the anguish threatening to overwhelm her yet again and turned her thoughts to the Stanhope family's country seat—dreary Cowdrey Hall, set in bone-chilling Northern England. Despite her warm surroundings, a shiver ran through her. Was it simply thinking about the place that set her skin to prickling, or was it the horrifying ordeal she'd suffered?

Her stomach grumbled. Goodness. In her eagerness to complete the portrait, she'd ignored Allita's calls to dinner. Time to make her way to the kitchen and beg a morsel or two from Régine. Then, as Lily had been doing every night since Bastien's departure, she would secretly retreat to the comfort and safety of his luxurious suite. Unlike her assigned bedchamber, where night terrors still beset her, she'd curl up in his lush bed, enveloped in his very essence, and sleep soundly through the night. Drat it all, what would she do once he returned, when her brazen use of his private quarters must come to an end?

Pushing aside her unsettling thoughts, she rose. Turning the easel backward, she tucked the oil painting into one corner of the room, away from prying eyes. Then she moved to the windows, focused on drawing the curtains closed against the now darkened sky.

A gas streetlamp below cast a thin stream of light over her godfather and the elder Mr. Andrews exiting Le Blanc House. She paused to watch them clamber aboard an elegant open carriage drawn by two matching grays. So, Uncle was leaving for a few days without a proper goodbye, was he? Probably for the best. Things hadn't been the same between them since their heated exchange the night he'd gone upriver with the elder Mr. Andrews. Of late, Uncle was barely around, attending to a newfound business venture with Mr. Andrews while awaiting dispatches from the London detectives regarding their search for Molly. With Rubio protecting her, Uncle seemed comfortable putting some much-needed distance between him and Lily, which left him unaware of her activities this past month, and she was enjoying her newfound freedom. Except for the miserable night terrors she suffered in her bedchamber, Lily felt safe residing in this busy household.

When the elegant carriage pulled away from the house and disappeared into the darkness, she gripped the edge of the curtains and began to draw the panels closed. A movement across the street caught her attention. She paused. As she gazed into the darkness, her heart ticked up a beat. Nothing but blackness. She tugged on the curtain.

And froze in place.

A small red glow appeared, then grew a bit larger, as if someone were drawing on a cigarillo.

She squinted.

The shadowed outline of a hatted man faced Le Blanc House.

He was watching her!

With blood hammering in her ears, Lily managed to yank the curtains shut before her knees gave way.

That cannot be Julian!

"Oh, my God, no," she whispered as she slid to the floor. Stunned, she sat with her legs folded beneath her, unable to move. Unable to breathe.

This cannot be happening!

Scrambling to her feet, she turned off the gas lamps, then rushed from the darkened room to the stairs.

"Lily?" Rubio paused halfway up the steps, his brow furrowed. Then he took two at a time, racing toward her. "What's wrong?"

"Oh, Rubio." She forced air in and out of her lungs. "A man…he is out there…across the street…watching. Come."

She grabbed his arm and yanked him in the direction of her bedchamber.

He dug in his heels, stopping her. "If someone is out there watching you, his attention will be fixed on your window, not Allita's. Let's go to her room."

"Quite right." She clutched his arm and stumbled along behind him as they slipped into Allita's unlit chamber. Rubio made his way to the window, where the curtains had yet to be drawn for the night. He stood to the side, gazing down at the street. Lily hung back, her heart racing out of control, her blood still pounding in her ears.

Just when she was beginning to think she'd imagined things, Rubio stepped away from the side of the window and turned to her.

"Go to the kitchen with the others," he said. "Say nothing to alarm them. I'll leave through the servants' back entry and slip across the street."

"What of the front door? Mr. Andrews and—"

"I let the men out and locked the door behind them. Now go, Lily. And say nothing. Régine has made peach pies. Sit down and eat some as though hunger is what has your hands trembling. Can you do this for me?"

Still breathless, she nodded, and watched as he raced down the stairs and out of sight. Feeling even more terrified at being left alone on the upper floor, she gripped the handrail with shaky fingers and made for the kitchen. She paused to compose herself before stepping into the room. Then, as calmly as she could manage, she waltzed through to where Régine, Vivienne, and Allita were gathered, along with Henri, who was busy stuffing peach pie into his mouth.

"Whatever smells so divine?" She nearly choked out her words.

"Peach pie," Henri mumbled through his full mouth. "Ish real good."

Allita grinned. "Régine is making them to take to her papa tomorrow. Vivienne will accompany her to the countryside. With your permission, Miss Lily, I should like to tag along. I've never been anywhere outside of here, as you well know."

Vivienne glanced at Lily's hands. "You tremble, Miss Lily. Why is that?"

"I'm afraid I've waited too long to take my supper," she lied.

Régine silently ladled something aromatic into a bowl, then set it on the kitchen table along with a thick slab of bread. "Eat this first. It's shrimp gumbo."

Vivienne glanced at Régine. "Bastien's favorite, *oui?*"

"Bastien's favorite," Lily agreed. "I'll have a spot of tea with my pie if you don't mind." Delicious as the gumbo tasted, her stomach nearly rioted as it went down.

What is Rubio doing? What is happening out there in the dark?

She struggled to make light conversation. "You'll be visiting your father, Régine?"

Régine nodded. "We'll leave at the break of dawn and stay the night. You'll be fine with…" She paused to glance at Vivienne, who nodded and took up the conversation.

"You'll be fine with Rubio to watch over you," Vivienne said. "Perhaps you would consider allowing Miss Allita to join us? Henri has agreed to drive us, so it's safe, *non?*"

"Of course. Since I've dispensed with corsets and anything else that adds to this suffocating heat, I can well take care of dressing myself."

"What about your hair?" Allita asked.

Where oh where is Rubio? What the devil is taking him so long?

Lily forced down another mouthful of gumbo. "I'll merely draw a brush through it. After all, it will only be Rubio and myself here since Mr. Andrews and my…Mr. Talbot will be upriver again for a few days."

Vivienne scowled at her. "Is something wrong, Miss Lily?"

Rubio slipped into the kitchen and gave a surreptitious shake of his head to Lily, then made his way over to Régine. "Did you bake extra peach pies to leave behind?"

Régine laughed. "*Oui,* but you must take care that you and Miss Lily get your share. I fear that Henri will eat it all tonight."

While Rubio helped himself to a cup of tea and slid into the chair across from Lily, the others fell into an easy conversation. He leaned over and murmured, "It was nothing but a servant in the house across the street out for a smoke."

Lily set down her spoon and drew in a surreptitious breath. Would she always be so jittery at the slightest disruption in her surroundings? Would she forever harbor fears that Julian might show up at any moment? How could he know she was in this part of the world? Unless he'd hired someone to locate her, still intent on finishing what he'd begun. After all, with her permanently out of the way, he stood to inherit the entire Stanhope fortune and landholdings.

Fiddlesticks. Enough of thinking the worst.

She set down her spoon and rose. "If you don't mind, I shall take my piece of pie and tea to my room, and bid you a good night."

Allita stood to follow her.

"Stay and visit," Lily said. "I'm perfectly capable of getting myself ready for bed. Truly I am. Rubio, would you mind helping me with this tray?"

He jumped up, swallowed the last of his tea, and grabbing the silver salver from Vivienne, escorted Lily from the room.

Out of earshot, she said, "Who was it? What happened?"

He gave a shake of his head as they climbed the stairs. "Just as I said, a servant out for a smoke."

"What did he say?"

"Nothing. When I approached, he took his last drag, waved, and headed back to the house."

"How do you know he was a servant?" she demanded.

"Lily, calm down. He went around to the servants' entrance and waved at me once again before disappearing inside."

"But he was watching me. I could see his silhouette facing my way."

"Your curtains were open. Your lamp was on. Of course, he'd glance up when you stood at the window with the light shining behind you. Anyone would look your way, be it man or woman."

"You're right. My imagination still gets away from me." Hearing footsteps behind them, Lily glanced over her shoulder. She spied Allita climbing the stairs. "I'm fine. Go back and join the others."

"I shall take down your hair and get you ready for bed, Miss Lily. Then I shall feel free to rejoin the others, but not before."

"Stubborn woman," Lily muttered.

"*Sí*," Rubio responded. "Always has been. Always will be."

Entering the bedchamber, Rubio set down the tray, lit a gas lamp, and turned to leave, bidding Lily a good evening. As he exited the room, he shot Allita a speaking glance, his brow furrowed.

"What was that about?" Lily inquired.

"What was what about?" Allita responded.

"That glowering look."

"What look?"

Lily waved her hand in the air and took a seat at her boudoir table. "Never mind. When you get like this, I'd have to pull teeth to get anything out of you."

Lily closed her eyes and pressed her fingers to her temples. "I'm suddenly extremely fatigued, so please, do get on with my hair."

Allita removed the pins from Lily's hair, taking great care to brush her thick golden locks in long, soothing strokes, then laid out one of her more intricately made cotton night rails, along with a matching robe.

Lily glanced through the mirror at the clothing on the bed and managed a bit of a smile. "Trying to make up for your stubbornness? Or is it your way of thanking me for allowing you to visit the countryside?"

The color in Allita's cheeks heightened. "You're so beautiful tonight, Miss Lily. You should wear something a little special."

"Off with you," Lily scoffed. "Enjoy your time away. I shall see you in two days' time."

Allita broke into a wide grin and helped Lily into the night rail and matching robe before she fairly danced from the room.

She knows very well that I sneak into Bastien's bedchamber every night. Does she not think I am aware it is she who leaves a lamp lit for me? That she's the one who sees to it his shirts are laundered and put neatly away after I sleep in them? Lily doubted she'd ever find a wiser, more respectful lady's maid, despite her single-minded stubbornness. She'd miss Allita when she left here.

Dowsing the single lamp Rubio had lit, she slipped from her room, locking the door behind her. A furtive glance up and down the corridor told her she was alone. Barefoot, she hurried to the end of the corridor and let herself into Bastien's apartment.

A quick turn of the key and the rest of the world disappeared behind the carved panel. Gone were thoughts of the manservant who'd lingered in the dark across the street, whose presence had struck abject fear into her heart. Moving past the sitting room and into the bedchamber, she drew down the coverlet, then slipped into Bastien's dressing room, where she withdrew one of his perfectly folded shirts from the wardrobe. She laid it on the bed, ready to slip into after a tepid bath to cool her skin. But before she climbed in between the sheets of his large bed, she'd relax on the balcony, take in the heady scent of night jasmine, spend some time gazing at the moon.

"On with it, then." She marched to the bathing chamber and flung open the door.

And gasped.

Bastien stood with his back to her.

Naked.

Wet.

Glorious.

She sucked in a breath.

Good Lord!

He glanced over his shoulder and froze, a large Turkish towel held in midair. Dropping the thick cloth to his pelvis, he clutched the top half over his groin, and turned. "Lily."

The smooth, laconic drawl of her name in that deep voice soaked through her skin. Her belly gave a sharp twist. She stared at him, unable to move.

"You…you've returned."

He stared back. "*Oui.* I have returned."

Leave! Move! Get out of here, you ninny. But she could not force herself to take a single step. Her own harsh breathing rasped in her throat.

"You look well," he said. "Are…are you indeed well, Lily?"

Her head swam as she searched her brain for a response. "I…I am. Except for some residual nightmares, that is. And…and occasional tingling in my extremities."

He stared at her in silence for what seemed a long while. "I see…good to hear."

And then, the elusive look she'd strived so hard to capture in her painting flashed through his eyes. His body visibly relaxed, and he broke their locked gazes. The thick lashes framing those amazing, clear blue eyes lowered. Slowly, deliberately, he looked her over. She wasn't sure what he was thinking, but his heavy-lidded regard licked across her skin like a living flame.

Her breath stuttered, then clogged her lungs. A quivering warmth spread out from her belly and pulsed inside her skin. *Get out. Do not linger.* "Well…ahem…well then…welcome home. I shall leave you."

Before he could respond, she rushed to the door, unlocked it and raced down the corridor. Her fingers trembled as she struggled to fit her key into the lock. "Hells bells," she muttered. Shutting the door behind her, she leaned her back against it and pressed a hand to her chest. She closed her eyes against the heat of embarrassment flooding her cheeks, but all she could see behind her eyelids was that glorious naked man, a towel clutched over his most private parts, his golden, muscled body rivaling anything she'd seen in her art books.

"Gads…that's how I should've painted him." The stunning vision of him standing before her would be forever etched in her mind. "Michelangelo, had Bastien lived during your time, you would have snatched him up as your favorite subject."

A giddy laugh left her throat. "Oh, my word. What a gorgeous, gorgeous man." She walked over to the boudoir table and sat. Looking in the mirror, she noted her flushed cheeks, of the heated discomposure in her eyes. Had he seen it? This blatant passion that erupted at the mere sight of him?

Through the mirror, she caught the reflection of the silver tray sitting on a side table. A cup of tea. The uneaten pie. Why, the others must have known he'd come home. His favorite shrimp gumbo? His favorite dessert? How the devil long had he been here? Well, that's what she got for locking herself in her bedchamber to paint all day long.

Nervous laughter erupted again. While she'd been busy creating his likeness and pining away at his absence, he had returned. In the flesh. And what incredible flesh it was. Certainly, he'd been here long enough for Régine to have fixed his favorite food.

They knew.

Everyone but her knew.

And except for Rubio, who would likely remain downstairs in the servants' quarters, the lot of them would escape the premises at the crack of dawn.

The puzzle pieces fit. Something clicked in her brain. The food, the knowing glances Régine and Vivienne exchanged. The surly look Rubio had given Allita before exiting Lily's bedchamber—a warning not to spill the beans that Bastien was home? What were they up to? Had Bastien told them to say nothing? Were they leaving for the countryside so Bastien would be alone with her? On second thought, she'd bet Rubio would not be here come morning, either.

She paced the room.

Bastien knew where she was. He could've sent for her earlier. Did he not want to see her? That made no sense. Not after the sudden look that

crossed his face, that elusive one she knew by heart after spending hours...
no, several days...getting it down on canvas just so.

She was not naïve. He wanted her.

And she wanted him.

The idea at once both terrified and enthralled her.

No matter how many wealthy and not-so-wealthy men had tried to
curry her favor, she'd not cared for a one of them. Things changed when
Bastien came along. She'd been tired, so very tired of merely existing.
Now, she hungered to break free of the tedium that had ruled her life since
the terrible accident that had killed her mother and paralyzed her father.

Kaleidoscopic images of Bastien raced through her mind. Whatever
the intangible thread connecting the two of them was, she wanted to know
more of it—of him. The thought of lying in bed alongside him sent blood
pulsing through her veins. She yearned to experience something wild and
free with him. No, that wasn't quite right. What she wanted to do was set
herself free—free to be with him in whatever manner she might choose.
As they both might choose. He could teach her things. She wanted the
same fire to run through her veins that ran through Bastien's.

What would he do if she marched into his room right now and shamelessly
let her desires be known? The very idea set the fine hairs on her arms
atingle. Would he reject her? Or would he willingly share his bed with
her? In truth, sharing his bed, sharing the most intimate of intimacies with
him was what she desperately wanted. Only with Bastien had she felt this
overwhelming urge to touch and be touched.

Did she have it in her to boldly confront him with what she wanted and
needed? Could she act on her inner urgings with no expectations of him
whatsoever—now or in the future? What if he turned her away? Knowing
him, were he to reject her, he'd do so in a gentlemanly way. He'd see to it
she kept her dignity intact.

Following the dictates of her heart, she exited her bedchamber and
marched down the hall, her blood beating a furious tempo. Ignoring the
golden lion knocker attached to the door, she closed her fingers around
the brass handle, then paused to take in a long, fortifying breath. God help
her if she came to regret what she was about to do.

Willing her trembling fingers to still, she flung open the door.

Chapter Sixteen

Entering Bastien's suite, Lily moved beyond the sitting room and into his bedchamber. There Bastien stood, in the shadows of a single, flickering gas lamp. Bare chested, barefooted, he wore nothing but a pair of dark trousers slung low on his hips.

Their gazes locked.

The air around them grew heavy as the sheer power of his energy reached out and touched her.

As the seconds ticked by, she fought an impulse to rush to him. He studied her in that heavy-lidded way of his, saying nothing. What did she expect of him? That he would invite her in when she was already there? Her gaze slid the length of his glorious, well-made body—past his broad chest with its light dusting of hair, past the ribbons of muscle strapped beneath his naked belly—to the thin, dark line that disappeared beneath his trousers. Despite his calm exterior, there was no mistaking the wild and lethal grace coiled within him. Desire, hot and fierce, whipped through her.

He tilted his head as if reading her thoughts. "You turned down my bed, *chère*. Were you intending to sleep in here tonight?"

The low, smooth timbre of his voice gave her belly a sharp twist. "I had planned to." She gave a slight nod toward his bathing chamber. "After my evening bath, that is."

In two long strides, he closed the distance between them, his eyes flashing like cut sapphires. She caught his clean, fresh-washed scent, felt the electrifying force emanating from him.

"Have you done this before?" he asked. "Slept in my bed? Bathed in my tub?"

As she gazed into his eyes, it was as though she peered into his very soul. Thoughts scattered like so many dry leaves in an autumn wind. Her lungs surged in an uncontrollable rhythm, yet a steady calm thrummed through her veins.

At her silence, he hiked a brow. "Well, what say you?"

She lifted her chin. "I still have nightmares when I sleep in my own bedchamber, which is why I prefer your quarters. With the door locked."

There went that brow of his again. "You slept here the entire time I was away?"

She nodded. "Since the night you left."

He set his hands on his hips and studied her, his expression unreadable. "Tell me more."

"What is it you wish to know?"

"As your *traiteur*, you should tell me everything."

"There's something about the position of my chamber, facing the street, that causes me to feel vulnerable. But locked away in here at night, I sleep soundly. I also like your spacious balcony overlooking the garden since my bedchamber has none. I find the scents from below and the night air calming. Also, the tepid bath I take in your magnificent bathing chamber each evening cools my skin before climbing into your bed."

That elusive look she'd only today captured on canvas flashed through his eyes, then disappeared. "What do you intend to do now that I am here?"

Was there a challenge in his question? She'd known full well he might refuse her. She'd boldly taken the risk anyway—consequences be damned. "Must I spell it out for you, Bastien? I returned knowing you were here, did I not?"

His lips parted slightly, and his nostrils flared, as if catching her scent. "Tell me, *chère*—have you lain with a man before?"

She caught sight of his pulse pounding at the base of his throat. *If he intends to dismiss me, he's not taking it lightly.* "Whether I have or have not does not signify."

A muscle in his jaw rippled with tension. He shoved his hands in his pockets, as if to refrain from touching her, and swallowed. Hard. "You do not want to do this, *chère*."

"Oh, but you see, Bastien, I do."

His gaze left hers and struck the wall somewhere behind her. When he looked at her again, she swore she saw sadness in his eyes. "I am the last man you should take to your bed."

Admit it, you want this as much as I do. "Might I remind you it is your bed I am inviting myself into? With you in residence."

His breath was coming harder now, and the need to touch him rose on a higher tide of heat. Incapable of holding herself back, she reached out and laid a hand on his chest.

He hissed in a breath.

His skin felt as if a wildfire burned beneath the surface; his heart was beating like a drum. "I've missed you terribly, Bastien."

Clasping her hand in his, he slowly withdrew it from his hot flesh. "This would be a grave error, *chère*. We would both have regrets." The husky sound of his voice held layers—a smoky throatiness, a scrape of rawness that sent a quiver through her bones.

Pray, do not turn me away. "I know what I am about. I'll not allow myself to harbor a single regret, nor would I consider any action we undertake to be an error in judgment on my part," she said.

"Do not ask me to step into the most intimate part of your world, *chère*. I have a very dark past. I won't have its murky edges bleeding over onto you."

She scoffed. "Everyone has a past. While yours may have been muddied by the thieving life you left behind, mine happens to have been boring— exceedingly so. Something I fully intend to rectify."

He gave a small shake of his head. "Not with me. Never with me." The blue in his eyes deepened. "You deserve so much more than anything I could ever give you."

"I ask naught of you other than this one night."

When he said nothing, only studied her with an unreadable expression, she continued. "I am a woman who knows her own mind, not some young girl testing the waters. I have given a good deal of thought to my life of late. After my mother died and my father was left paralyzed, I lived a joyless, sheltered existence. A carefully tailored existence of my own making, I might add. At age seven, I ceased to be a child and became an adult in a young girl's body. I learned to look after Papa, insisted upon doing so. By age fourteen, I had a keen understanding of what it took to balance books, sharp instincts for what gave the greatest return on our investments, and whom to trust. At first, I handled his business dealings behind the scenes with no one the wiser. At twenty-one, we no longer hid my role as his partner. I also became his social hostess."

"Such a heavy burden you took on, *non?*"

She nodded. "I blamed myself for the accident that took my mother and crippled my father, so all those years, I was trying to make amends. Now I am making changes. I choose to view my ending up here as Providence. Once I am cleared of all charges back in England, I shall quit New Orleans. I do not know where I will eventually end up. Henceforth, I shall do as

I please and hold no one accountable for my actions but myself. What I want from you is this one night only."

Something akin to pain shot through Bastien's stormy eyes, surprising her. He stepped back, distancing himself. "*Non, chère.* Do not ask this of me. I will not risk hurting you."

She had no intention of begging. However, there was nothing wrong with speaking the truth. "I distinctly remember your touch while you were healing me. I want that touch again, but I want it differently—not as a healer to his patient, but as a man to a woman. I know you want me as I want you, so why can we not fill each other's needs for this one night?"

He turned away, his breath sounding heavy in his chest. Then he turned back to her and she was certain she saw a flash of pain again. "Take my bed tonight, Lily. I shall sleep in your bedchamber. On the morrow, I will have your things moved to the garden side of the house where you will feel safer."

Like the flutter of a candle's flame against a dark wall, a display of emotions flickered over Bastien's face. *He wants me as much as I want him, yet he holds back, putting himself in obvious distress. Dear Lord, what have I done, thinking only of myself?*

A soft sigh of disappointment escaped her lips. "I thank you for allowing me to sleep in your quarters for this night," she said. "I shall first take a tepid bath to cool my skin."

"You see, *chère*," he responded as she turned from him. "Even my refusal has wounded you. Believe me when I say this—were we to engage in any acts of intimacy, it would hurt you more than I could bear."

Lily paused to look over her shoulder at him, her heart falling into itself. "Your rejection did not injure me, sir. I think it is you, not I, who has been most hurt by my selfish actions. For that, I do apologize."

She turned and headed to the bathing chamber, tugging open her robe as she went, aware he watched her. As she stepped inside the room and let the diaphanous fabric fall to her feet, she thought she heard him sigh. And then the door to the corridor opened and closed behind him, his absence leaving a terrible void in the room.

She lit a single candle, then ran her bath, scattered a few drops of rose oil into the water, and put a thick towel on the ornate stool sitting beside the tub. Discarding her night rail, she slipped into the water.

She'd known full well the risk she'd taken when she'd entered his suite. Had been prepared for his rejection, certain if he did refuse her, he would do so in gentlemanly fashion. Never, in her wildest dreams, had she imagined her action might create pain for him. It was plain she'd upset him. Heaven help her, she had to somehow right this terrible wrong she'd done him.

In an attempt to relax, she closed her eyes and took a series of slow, deep breaths, hoping to dismiss her whirling thoughts, hoping to ease the emotional pain her unruly desires had inflicted upon them both. Clearing her mind did nothing to ease her burden. Bastien's presence in the house—*his home, not hers*—invaded the very depths of her being. Groaning aloud, she slid into the water up to her chin—still able to breathe, but feeling as if she were drowning inside.

Unaware of the passage of time, she was startled by the soft *snick* of the outer door opening and closing. She stilled. Had Bastien returned? The air left her lungs in a jagged exhale. Good heavens, she hadn't bothered shutting the inner door to the bathing chamber.

Rising from the tub, she wrapped the luxurious Turkish cloth around her body and stepped into the bedchamber. Bastien stood before her, one shoulder leaning against the wall, his arms crossed over his bare chest. His gaze moved over the length of her, then settled on her face. He seemed different from when he'd left her. While that unmistakable power still coiled in him, there was also a new kind of gentleness.

Heaven help her, were she made of wax, she would have melted at the sight of him. "I thought you had left," came her throaty whisper.

He shrugged. "I tried."

"I am so sorry," she blurted. "It was selfish of me to barge in here and expect you to fall at my feet with the same kind of need running through your veins as in mine. Please, forgive me."

Pushing away from the wall, he moved to stand in front of her. "Hush," he murmured. Curling a finger under her chin, he tilted her head and softly, ever so softly, touched his lips to hers. "*J'ai un besoin*—I have a need, as well."

Wrapping his arms around her, he tenderly pulled her into him, enveloped her in his warmth.

He stood there for a long while, saying nothing, not moving, simply holding her. Lord, but it felt good in his arms. Felt right to be held by him. *He* felt right.

He touched his forehead to hers. "Are you certain this is what you want, *chère*? To spend the night in each other's arms?"

A vivid image of the two of them naked swept through her mind. Arms and legs entangled. Her senses reeled. Good Lord, she could hardly breathe, let alone manage a coherent sentence. Easing her head back, she peered deep into his eyes. "Never in my life have I been more certain of anything."

Those sapphire eyes of his darkened, reminding her of a storm-swept sea. His sultry mouth tipped at one corner. "Then from this moment on, for this night only, I am yours and you are mine."

Lifting her in his arms, he carried her to the bed, where he tenderly laid her down, then stretched out alongside her.

She was going to let his slow seduction of her unfold his way entirely—in every sense of the word. A little thrill shivered over her skin. Why not seduce him right back?

Because she didn't know how.

Or did she? "I am in a towel while you are still wearing your trousers. Pardon my ignorance, but what comes next?"

As he tucked a strand of her hair behind her ear, his mouth twitched. "Let your instincts guide you."

"I am told it is painful the first time, and rather unremarkable thereafter."

"Not if done right."

His words sent a shiver of anticipation through her. "Show me."

"You require the right kiss, *chère*. The right touch. And you also need to touch me. You need to become familiar with my body, my scent, my taste. The secret to proper lovemaking is that you do the receiving of me. The time will be right for you to accept me only when you are completely ready."

At his words, her spine tingled and her breath escaped her lungs. "Lord, what you do to me, Bastien."

All the while he spoke, his fingers moved up and down her arm, serving to both soothe and excite her. "Tonight, I will do my best to honor every beautiful thing that you are. For now, *chère*, close your eyes and touch me. Take your time. Explore my body as you please."

His words stole her breath. "I am to touch you first?"

With a bare whisper of a touch, he traced the outer edges of her mouth with his thumb. *"Oui."*

A soft moan left her lips. She reached out and mirrored his actions. "Your trousers. You leave them on?"

A wisp of a smile touched his mouth. "You will be the one to remove them—when you are ready to do so."

Gently, he used his fingertips to ease her lids shut. "Touch me with your eyes closed."

Her fingers found the smooth, freshly shaved line of his jaw, then drifted down along his neck to a pulse beating hard. The embers burning in her belly burst into flame.

In the silence between them, slowly, gently, he stroked his fingers down her arm again, sending a thousand angels into flight. One hand slid behind her head, and then his mouth was on the curve of her neck, just below her ear. A fairy's kiss.

Did she moan or was that him?

"You drive me wild," he whispered in her ear, his words sending tremors quaking through her. "You unhinge me, Lily. You send me off someplace where I cannot manage to think straight."

You can't think straight? God, I am brainless.

She touched his belly, ran her fingers down his side, over his ribs, across the bands of muscle along his belly, pausing at the top of his trousers. Wanting more of him, she slipped her fingers under the waistband.

"Easy," he murmured, as he ran the tip of his tongue along the inside edge of her ear. "Take your time."

She gasped and shut out everything but the sensation of his mouth traveling to her throat. Opening her eyes, she reveled in the sheer sight of him.

He set his hands to her face, tilted it, and studied her while she swam in the depths of his sultry gaze. His mouth brushed against hers, a whisper of a kiss that left her boneless. She leaned into him for support. His arms swept around her, and she was enveloped—by his taste, his scent, the warmth of his skin.

But she wanted more of him. So much more. "Your kisses are so very, very wicked."

"As are yours, my love."

My love?

Those two words, like an unexpected silken caress, shifted the rhythm of her heart. Then he lifted his mouth from hers and a ghost of a smile, one that suggested all kinds of sinfulness, touched his lips. Once again, her fingers swept across his hard, flat stomach. Her breath hitched at the heat emanating from his smooth skin. Gripping his hip to steady herself, she sought his mouth and mumbled into it as she tasted his sweetness.

Her fingers found the top button to his trousers, worked it open. "Will you kiss me again?"

"*Non.* You keep kissing me, *chère.* Follow your instincts."

Instead of his mouth, she pressed her lips to his shoulder, scraped it with her teeth.

"That's it," he groaned. "You are very good at following your instincts."

"I feel as if I am about to implode...or explode," she murmured. "I...I cannot seem to tell which."

As her head lowered to his chest and to the hardened tips of his nipples, her hands found their way along his body to his hips once again. She found solid muscle, lean and all sinew. "God, what am I doing?"

"All the right things," came his deep groan.

She worked at the remaining buttons on his trousers, and as she made to slide them off, he moved to assist her. Then he tossed aside the towel she was wrapped in and pulled her naked body to the full length of his.

Skin to skin, she gasped. She wrapped her arms around his broad back and held him tight against her.

"Keep touching me," he murmured. "And I will do the same for you."

That wondrous feeling of touching him, of kissing him and nipping his skin had her on fire. When his hands found the most intimate parts of her body, she cried out from want of him. His hands and mouth found every sensitive spot she possessed, and when he turned her over and ran his fingers over the backs of her knees, she moaned.

Suddenly, he was over her, around her, enveloping her, and kissing every inch of her, until she was half crazed with desire. She cried out for him, not knowing what she wanted, but everywhere he touched, he set her aflame.

"Please," she whimpered. "I want more."

"You see, *chère*?" he murmured in her ear. "You needed the right kiss. The right touch." Hovering above her, ever so gently, he turned her on her back and eased inside her, pausing, murmuring between hot kisses, filling her up.

Something powerful, something she'd never known existed, took on a force of its own inside her. Wave after wave of ecstasy rolled through her, and as her heart, mind, and body opened fully to him, he plunged into her, only to still while sensation after sensation gripped her.

"My turn," he whispered. His hips began an easy roll, rocking gently into her as he held her and let another climax capture her.

Her teeth found his shoulder again and her fingers dug into his back. Exquisite pain. Lusty pain. A pain that caused no hurt, but sent her over the edge at the same time he whispered her name.

When her blood settled, when the rhythm of her heart returned to normal, she nestled her head in the crook of his shoulder and sighed.

His breath fell on her hair. "Did I hurt you?"

"No," she responded and raised her head to trace kisses along his neck. Those intimate imaginings that had kept her awake nights did no justice to this wonderful man lying beside her. "I already want more."

A deep chuckle left his throat. "*Oui.* I understand the feeling. Let me take care of you."

Touching his lips to her forehead, he slid off the bed and disappeared into the bathing chamber. Returning with a damp cloth, he kneeled before her and gently washed her clean. As she lay stretched out on his bed, watching his tender ministering, a thought seized her—she trusted him. Always had. In every sense of the word.

She was his now.

At least for however long this night lasted.

Chapter Seventeen

Early morning sunlight and sweet, melodious birdsong roused Bastien from a deep slumber. His first subtle awareness was of a profound sense of contentment. He stretched out a leg—and bumped up against something soft and feminine.

Lily!

His mind shot to full attention.

So did his body.

Memories of their steamy night together engulfed him. Her warm backside shifted, rubbed up against his belly. Blood rushed to his groin. A powerful urge to turn her over and sink deep inside her threatened to overtake the certainty that she'd be too tender after their long hours of lovemaking. Forcing aside raw desire, he enveloped her in his arms and simply held her, wishing he could transmit all the affection he was feeling through his skin into hers.

Christ, this feels good.

She feels good.

Too good.

He buried his face in her lush, blond curls, then touched his lips to the soft spot just below her ear.

A soft sigh escaped her lips. "Mmm," she murmured. "Don't stop."

But he had to stop before he lost control. "Hush," he whispered. "Go back to sleep."

Pressing a kiss to her cheek, he slid from the bed. He collected fresh clothing from his dressing room, then made his way to the bathing chamber, where he shaved and washed his body beneath the rain shower he'd recently installed.

Barefoot—always his preference—and wearing only a pair of linen trousers and a shirt rolled at the sleeves, he made his way downstairs to the kitchen. He'd fix breakfast for the two of them. Surprise her.

He fired up the wood stove and put on a pot of coffee. Stepping into the garden, he snipped a few herbs, plucked a couple of ripe peaches off a tree, and collected eggs from beneath a still-roosting chicken. Back inside, he gathered bread and ham from the larder and set about making the first meal of the day. It wasn't long before mundane food preparations had his mind wandering—straight to Lily.

Last night, he'd walked away from her at first, refused to involve her in an illicit affair. But there was one catch—he'd never desired a woman in the overwhelming way he desired Lily. Hell, he'd been oddly drawn to her from the moment their paths crossed.

Damn it, she'd been ill and under his care, a responsibility not lightly taken. However, the more time he spent with her, and the more her health improved, the more she captivated him. To make matters worse, he'd missed the hell out of her while he'd been gone. And when she'd waltzed into his room last night, boldly declaring her purpose, it had taken every measure of discipline he possessed to walk away. He'd had every intention of spending the night in a different bedchamber. Alone.

God help him, he'd failed.

Had his return to her been a mistake? Their sensuous night together sure as hell didn't feel wrong. In fact, nothing in his life had ever felt more right. Something remarkable seemed to be at work here. Something deeper than two lusty people fornicating, and he didn't quite know what to make of it.

A noise in the corridor leading to the kitchen snapped him back into the moment. "Lily?"

Rubio stepped through the doorway. "At the moment, she is taking a shower, señor."

Bastien frowned. "How the hell would you know what she's up to?"

"I was airing out the bedchambers in Vivienne's absence when Miss Lily caught up with me. She wanted to know how to use your fancy contraption."

Bastien grabbed two mugs from the cupboard and set them near the stove. "I thought you meant to take your leave with the others."

"I changed my mind."

Something in Rubio's tone gave Bastien pause. "Why? You appeared eager enough last night, when I said I could watch over Lily."

"After you retired to your quarters, Miss Lily rushed from her chamber in a frenzy. Said she'd seen a man across the street watching her."

Icy fingers ran down Bastien's spine. "Did you investigate?"

"*Sí.*" Rubio waved a hand in the air. "It was nothing. Merely the neighbor's servant out for a smoke."

Bastien poured two cups of café noir and handing one to Rubio, nodded toward the cream and sugar. "Then what changed your mind about leaving with the others?"

Rubio helped himself to two lumps and a good splash of cream. "I do not rightly know, señor. The man seemed friendly enough before returning to the servants' entrance. Later, I got to thinking. Something didn't sit right with me, so I decided to remain behind and sleep down here in the servants' quarters. Watch over things."

Trusting Rubio's instincts, he decided the incident required further investigation. "Why don't you pay our neighbors a visit? Make a few inquiries of the staff."

"Me?" Rubio scoffed. "I am not acquainted with those people, señor. Who am I to be knocking on the door of a home in this part of the city?"

"The Bartletts know me," Bastien said. "Tell them you are my secretary, and I sent you to inquire."

"Your secretary?" Rubio sucked in a breath. "Such a position a man like me could only dream of." He took a swallow of coffee, tension bunching his shoulders.

It didn't take much for Bastien to deduce what was bothering the man. He poured more coffee into each of their cups, then set about making another pot. "You're keen on my cousin Régine, *non?*"

Rubio's cheeks flushed. "*Sí, señor.* I do not expect you to understand, but I feel it is our destiny to spend our lives together."

Perhaps I am beginning to understand. "You wish to take Régine back to Jamaica?"

"Oh, no, señor! I would very much like to remain here with her. However, I need steady employment if I am to make a family. Which is something I do not presently possess. I took great care with your most beautiful gardens while you were away. I would very much like to take on the duties of the workers you currently employ."

"You are asking to perform the duties of three men?"

"*Sí.* I have been careful to watch all they do." He placed a hand over his heart and shot Bastien a wide grin. "You do not need three men to do what Rubio can do alone."

Despite the levity in his last remark, Bastien caught the quiet desperation in Rubio's eyes. "The garden is full of plantings I've collected from my travels. Some are quite rare, and I am particular about their maintenance. Do you think you could learn their proper care?"

"*Sí.* I learn quickly. What I did not know, Régine showed me." A nervous smile touched Rubio's lips. "We very much enjoy the garden together."

Bastien chuckled. "You have lost your heart to her, *non?*"

Rubio's cheeks turned crimson. "I do believe her heart to be a mirror to mine."

Bastien studied the Spaniard for a long moment while he contemplated what marriage between the two might bring. They'd have children together. Perhaps many. Odd, but the idea of little ones running about seemed suddenly appealing. Hell, the entire third floor of his ridiculously vast home lay empty—it could easily be turned into proper quarters to accommodate a large family. Pleased with the idea, he said, "Does your aunt expect to return to Jamaica?"

"There is nothing back there for either of us, señor. My aunt would be content to continue looking after Miss Lily. Perhaps Miss Lily will remain, as well?"

Bastien's chest constricted. "*Non.* She does not wish to settle here permanently."

Rubio shifted his stance. "We have all hoped she would remain here… with you."

Christ! He turned his back to Rubio and busied himself setting out cooking utensils. "All of you? My cousins, as well?"

"*Sí, señor.* We were hoping…well…my apologies. It is none of our concern. Perhaps when Miss Lily takes her leave, my aunt could assume the duties of those who come to clean for you."

Bastien grunted. "Allita has no need to undertake such tedious work at her age. Vivienne can find plenty to keep her busy." He glanced over at Rubio. "The third floor is vacant. If the idea of turning it into a home suits you and Régine, then it is yours for the taking."

A stunned expression froze Rubio's features. He stepped to the window and stared out at the garden. "I…I do not know what to say, señor."

He caught Rubio's misty-eyed reflection in the glass and decided on a lighthearted response. "I have no intention of losing the best cook in all of Louisiana, don'cha know. Now, come along. Let's walk and talk about this idea of yours."

Rubio grinned and headed for the back door.

Together, they wandered about the grounds while Bastien explained the origins and care of the various plants they came across. Pleased with the garden's condition, he said, "You've done a fine job in my absence, Rubio. If you'd be willing to act as both my secretary and overseer, we can discuss your wages on the morrow."

Rubio halted. He stood before Bastien in a long moment of awkward silence. When he finally spoke, his voice cracked. "Régine returns on the morrow. I shall ask for her hand. If she agrees, then I must go to her father and ask his permission to wed his daughter."

An odd emotion filled Bastien, one he could not name. "You're a good and honorable man, Rubio. You will make a fine husband for my cousin."

"Thank you for believing in me, señor. I will not let you down."

Suddenly, it was Bastien's turn to be at a loss for words.

Régine.

Married.

He was glad she'd found a good man. God knew she deserved it. So why was he suddenly feeling hollow inside? Casting aside the foreign emotion, he continued their walk. Reaching the largest oak tree in the yard, he glanced up and halted. "What the devil is *that?*"

Rubio laughed. "A tree house of sorts. Miss Brenna brings her many children here to visit. Miss Lily had this idea...well...I can remove it if you are not pleased."

He gave the ladder attached to the tree's trunk a shake, testing it. "This was Lily's idea?"

"*Sí.* Miss Lily, she has changed a lot in your absence."

"How so?"

Rubio shrugged. "It is hard to say, exactly. She seems more lighthearted. She takes great delight in Brenna's children, and all the little critters they bring along. Also, she smiles and laughs more."

He handed his cup to Rubio. "Hold this, *s'il vous plaît.*" He climbed far enough up the ladder to inspect the wooden platform built into the wide crotch of the tree. "You built this?"

"*Sí, señor.*"

"Has Miss Lily ever ventured up here?"

"*Sí.* When the children come to play. At times she spreads out quilts for them to lie on and reads to them. Other times, Miss Felice and Miss Brenna join her up there for tea."

Bastien grinned. "I'll be damned."

"Shall I remove the platform, señor?"

"Oh, hell no." He made his way down the ladder, the seed of an idea germinating. Retrieving his cup from Rubio, he took a swallow of the now cold coffee. "Do you know where Vivienne keeps those quilts?"

"*Sí.*"

"Will you spread out a few up there for me, *s'il vous plaît?*"

"May I ask why, señor?"

Bastien couldn't help but smile. "I'll be taking breakfast with Miss Lily in the trees today."

Grinning, Rubio trotted off. He returned with the colorful quilts, laid them out, then departed to inquire about the neighbor's servants before heading to the shipping office to inform René of his brother's return.

Rubio hadn't been gone a half hour when Lily wandered into the kitchen, barefoot and wearing a thin frock with little beneath it—certainly no corset. Her hair hung like a golden halo about her shoulders. Something achingly sweet bloomed in Bastien's chest.

She was so damn beautiful.

Non. She was more than that.

She was dazzling.

"Bonjour, ma douce."

Instead of a sunny greeting in return, uncertainty clouded her lovely features. What the devil? Was she uncomfortable facing him after last night's torrid encounter? He wanted to say something to put her at ease, but couldn't come up with anything clever and was left feeling dumb as an ox.

Her gaze moved across his face, as if she were looking for the meaning behind his greeting. Her hand was splayed across her midsection. "Oh, Bastien, what have we done?"

Merde! This would not do. He moved to where she stood, and taking her by the waist, lifted her onto the kitchen table. *"Oui.* What have we done, *chère?"* He touched his lips to hers and tucked a strand of hair behind her ear. "And when do we get to do it again?"

"Oh!" she gasped.

He grinned and kissed one corner of her mouth, then the other. "I shall not allow you to regret our time together. You are forbidden to make bad memories of something beautiful." He kissed the tip of her nose. "With regret will come sadness, which serves neither of us. Is this what you want? *Non, chère.* I think you desire pleasant memories."

"Which is why you gave me such a shocking response?"

"But of course." Easing her legs apart, he stepped in between them, slid his arms around her, and traced his lips along the soft curve of her neck. "Were you not the one who made the announcement that there were to be no expectations or regrets come the morrow?"

When she failed to respond, he leaned his head back, slipped a curled finger under her chin, and tilting her face upward, studied her through heavy-lidded eyes. "Do you, *chère?"*

"Do I what?"

"Have regrets?"

Her shoulders slumped, and she rested her head against his shoulder. "I could never regret the magic that happened between us." Relief bloomed in his chest. "It was good what we had together, *oui?*" She sighed. "*Good* cannot begin to describe what spending the night with you was like. What we shared was far more than anything I could have anticipated."

At her response, heat coursed through his body, settled in his chest and pelvis. "Then what be the problem, *chère?*"

"I fear a wanton has been let loose in me, for all I can think of is getting back into your bed. With you in it. And quickly."

The tension left his bones, and an urgency to accommodate her desires pulsed through his veins.

Not now.

Not so soon.

Fighting the impulse to carry her right back upstairs and into bed, he ran the backs of his knuckles along the thin cotton of her bodice, passing over one pert breast. The tip hardened, and gooseflesh rose on her arms. "This might be my favorite gown," he teased. "Barely there, and with little beneath. It does wonders for my imagination."

Lily let go another sigh. Her sweet breath fell upon his mouth. "Since I've not tolerated this blasted heat well, and since I go nowhere, Mademoiselle Charmontès took it upon herself to create a few day gowns using her thinnest fabric. I can at least feel the breeze touch my skin, which helps me avoid the fainting couch."

Oh, the things he wanted to do to her. He stepped back. "But it also gives me bad thoughts, *chère.* Very bad thoughts, indeed."

She gazed at him through smoldering amber eyes and placed a hand flat against his chest. "I think I would like to experience those very bad thoughts."

Her simple touch heated his skin and all manner of places deep in his belly. He backed away before he lost all control. "Sit right where you are, *chère.*"

He moved to the stove and proceeded to fix their meal. "Do not speak. Let yourself take in the moment. Enjoy all that is in it."

She watched him dip thick slices of bread into a pan of beaten eggs. "What are you doing?"

He tossed the coated bread into a sizzling iron skillet. "I am making *pain perdu.* It's what we Cajuns do when the bread is not fresh."

He grinned at her and placed two pieces of ham in another pan. "Régine took all the fresh bread with her."

Lily sat quietly atop the table watching his every move, her hands folded in her lap, her bare feet swinging lazily back and forth.

A satisfying sense of well-being washed over him. It was a grand idea, this feeding her. "Coffee, tea, or lemonade?"

"Lemonade, please. I cannot fathom drinking anything hot."

"I can make the tea cold if it pleases you. There is still a bit of ice in the storage room out back."

She waved him off with her hand. "Have you forgotten I'm British? We drink our tea hot or not at all."

Damn, she was enticing. "Then lemonade it is."

He proceeded to fill two plates, then set them on a large oval platter along with their drinks, and a bowl of sliced peaches. "Come along, *chère.*"

"Hmm," she said, and with a playful sparkle to her eyes, slid from the table and followed him to the tree; he paused at the base. "We're to break our fast here, in the children's tree house?"

"You take tea up there with my brother's wife and Brenna, *non?*"

She laughed. "You and Rubio have been gossiping."

Balancing the tray in one hand, he started up the ladder. "I must go first so as to preserve your dignity."

"Brilliant move." She followed along behind him. "How clever of you to have thought of this. I've grown quite weary of always having to be correct, of adhering to society's boring dictates. I wanted to be impulsive and adventurous, so I began by having Rubio build this little tree house. I dare say it has turned out to be as much for my enjoyment as for Brenna's little ones."

They settled on opposite sides of the quilt. He showed her how to dip the slices of the *pain perdu* into a bowl of sweet syrup, then licked his fingers clean. "Now, what shall we talk about while we break our fast together?"

She leaned back against a thick branch of the tree. A lazy smile touched her lips as she mirrored his actions and slowly licked the syrup off the tips of her fingers. "You go first."

"*Non.* Let's start with why you have pretended to be the wife of a man old enough to be your grandfather…no, don't leave or you might fall down and break something…perhaps your pretty neck."

She returned to sitting with her back against the tree and studied him. "You think my neck pretty?"

"I think everything about you is pretty." He heard the raw, husky edge to his own voice. "*Non.* Not quite the right word. Dazzling is better. You dazzle me."

A small smile touched the corners of her mouth. "Are you flirting with me, Monsieur Thibodeaux?"

"Merely being honest. Flirting means there is a goal, an end to a game one plays. I am playing no games with you, my sweet."

A tilt of her head, a ghost of a smile, and she studied him for a long while. "Are you in the habit of playing games with the opposite sex?"

He stuffed a slice of fruit into his mouth and licked his fingers again. "Not anymore."

"But you used to. Is that what you are implying?"

"Not implying anything. I speak with honesty, and with no game in mind. I am simply having breakfast with a lady I find mighty pleasing to be around, *non*?"

"Oh." It was her turn to toy with her food. "You have a reputation for breaking hearts, so I have heard."

In her eyes he saw a light that spoke of a new passion for living. A rogue thought slid into his thoughts—what if she stayed? What if she never wanted to leave?

Setting aside his plate, he opened his arms to her. "Come, *ma petite*. You are much too far from me, and I have grown quite lonely."

She crawled into his arms, her light laughter filtering through the trees. "You are indeed flirting with me, Monsieur Thibodeaux."

He parted his legs wide enough to fit her in between them, then turned her around so her back rested against his chest. He slid his arms around her, just beneath the swell of her enticing breasts, and rested his chin atop her head. The light, clean fragrance surrounding her sent his mind back to his bed, back to the two of them wrapped in each other's arms. "We had a night of it, didn't we, *chère*? One I know I shall never forget, with another promised for tonight, yet I still do not know your rightful name. Tell me, Lily. Who are you? Why are you really here?"

When she didn't answer, he slowly ran his fingers through her tresses in long, soothing strokes. Then, with gentle fingers he massaged her temples, and waited.

A soft sigh escaped her lips. "For all you have done for me, and for all we have shared, you deserve to know the truth. I am Lady Liliana Stanhope. My father, James Stanhope, was murdered by my cousin, Julian, who then tried to rid the world of me by using the deadly poisons you discovered in me."

A hitch in her voice caused Bastien to pull her tighter against him. "You don't have to—"

She covered his hands with her own. "I would like to finish what I have to say. Julian's aim was to inherit the Stanhope fortune. I went on the run to escape him, but also to escape being hanged because of his accusations that it was I who murdered my beloved father—accusations I could not refute because the one witness who saw what really happened disappeared."

"I assume there was a substantial fortune if he was willing to commit murder for it, *non?*"

"Indeed. You might've been familiar with our family shipping concern since we contracted with your company for a steady supply of cotton. We also bought your rum, which my father favored."

Stunned, he searched his mind for any Stanhope company in their shipping records. "The name is familiar but I cannot place your company."

"Cowdrey Imports. Named for my father's title as Earl of Cowdrey."

His heart skipped a beat. He grew still. "*Oui.* I am very familiar with this name. But I do not recall working directly with him or seeing his name anywhere."

"Actually, it was I who ran the business on my father's behalf. We worked closely together, but I negotiated and signed all contracts and bills of lading. I tended to the accounting, as well as most anything that needed doing. My father considered me rather brilliant in my ability to increase profits, which pleased me no end."

Christ. It can't be. She can't be. "You…you mentioned you are Lady Liliana Stanhope. By any chance did you sign all documents, 'L. L. Stanhope'?"

Soft laughter escaped her lips. "You've an excellent head for detail, Monsieur Thibodeaux. Had anyone we did business with known that L. L. Stanhope was a female, they would not have taken me seriously. My father and I enjoyed our little secret."

God Almighty. He'd known the name, yet he'd never imagined L. L. Stanhope was a woman, let alone the woman in his arms. For a long moment, heavy silence permeated the garden. Had even the birds stopped singing?

All thoughts of her remaining in New Orleans dissipated like morning mist on a lake. He was a Cajun bastard raised in a bayou shanty. She was a woman of high nobility, the daughter of a wealthy earl. She lived in manor houses, rode in gilded carriages attended by footmen in proper livery. She ate with a silver spoon. There wasn't any goddamn way anything good could come of their being together. This was all a make-believe world he'd been playing around in. And it had just come crashing down around him.

He forced his voice to remain steady. "Who is the man you passed off as your husband?"

"My godfather. Charles Langdon, Earl Chamberlain. He helped my father to raise me after my parents' accident. Saw to my education when my father could not."

At a loss for words, Bastien sat with his arms still around Lily—Lady Liliana Stanhope—wondering how he might gracefully extricate himself and disappear while he put the pieces of his mind and heart back together.

"Bastien?" She slid from his hold and faced him. "You've turned cold. What is it?"

Thunder roared in his ears. What the hell was he to say to her when he couldn't manage to string two sentences together?

She leaned over and laid her hand against his cheek. "Say something."

He wanted to shrug off her tender touch. Instead, he forced himself to hold steady. "I need a bit of time to collect my thoughts."

She scooted away from him, gave him space. "You are beginning to frighten me."

Rubio rushed into the garden and to the base of the tree, breaking the stark tension of the moment. "Might I speak with you, señor? Your brother requests your presence for a necessary bit of business regarding the *Aria*. Also, there is something I need to discuss with you, which I do not wish to impose upon Miss Lily."

The servant across the street! "I'll be right down." Bastien turned to Lily. "I'll return in an hour or two. We shall talk then. Would you like to remain here for a while, or would you prefer that I help you down?"

She looked puzzled. And hurt. The sadness in her eyes shredded his insides, but he was desperate to learn what Rubio had to say.

And he needed to think.

Needed to collect himself.

"Please, go about your business," she said. "I am quite good at getting down on my own. For now, I'd like to remain and enjoy the garden from above."

"As you wish." He followed Rubio into the house. "What have you learned?"

Rubio shook his head. "The only male servant in the Bartletts' employ is the butler, and he is a rather robust fellow with a head of white hair. He showed me the entrance to the servants' quarters, which has a deep inset leading to the door. I am afraid my visit left him quite concerned, too, señor."

"*Merde.*" Bastien sucked in a deep breath. "I'll speak to him. When does Monsieur Talbot...Christ, what a mess...I just learned his real name is Lord Chamberlain...when does he plan to return? Do you know?"

"He and Mr. Andrews indicated they'd be gone upriver three to five days."

Bastien raked a hand through his hair. "What does my brother want?"

"The *Aria*, she is ready for your private purchase, but the sale requires both your brother's signature and yours. The deadline for transfer without incurring interest was yesterday. René managed to get an extension, but in twenty-four hours, the penalty interest will go into effect."

Bastien cursed and headed up the stairs for a change of clothing. "It may not be certain, but I suspect the man you saw last night was Julian Stanhope, Miss Lily's cousin. He is the one who poisoned her."

It was Rubio's turn to release a string of curses. "How did he find her here?"

"I do not rightly know. Do you know where my weapons are kept?"

"*Sí.* I also keep my special knife in my boot. Do not worry, señor. I will keep her safe."

Bastien raced up the stairs. "I'll return in two hours. Say nothing to Miss Lily. The man would be a fool to try anything in broad daylight. Nonetheless, close and lock the downstairs windows. Alert the stable boy. He is to allow no one through the side gate. Should he find a stranger lurking about, tell him to ring the bell in the stable tower three times to bring you running."

He paused on the stairs. "I want both of you armed. If Julian Stanhope enters my property, you have my permission to shoot the bastard."

Chapter Eighteen

Still bewildered by the sudden shift in Bastien's demeanor, Lily sat on the balcony of his suite overlooking the lush gardens. Her colorful silk fan did little to allay the sultry afternoon heat. Surely her status as the daughter of a wealthy earl would not intimidate a wildly successful and confidant man like Bastien. Or would it? Oh, bother…he'd said they'd chat once he returned. No sense belaboring whatever had caused their special morning to turn sour.

Heaving a sigh, she set the nearly useless fan atop the open book in her lap. Something akin to forlornness settled in her bones. One way or another, she'd soon be gone from here. Her leaving meant Bastien would no longer be part of her life. She closed her eyes against the melancholy her thoughts produced. Her action only served to bring the mental image of him into sharper focus. For a moment, her mind played tricks on her as the memory of his marvelous touch and wickedly enticing scent became so real, he might as well have been sitting alongside her. Despite the heat, her skin prickled.

The man certainly possessed talented hands. Back when she'd been so terribly ill, there were times her mind failed to so much as grasp his name, yet she never forgot his gentle but powerful healing touch. Nor was she likely to ever forget his magical caresses last night—an altogether different experience from when he was her healer. All the while he made love to her with a sweet tenderness that nearly brought her to tears, a fevered passion had coursed through him, igniting a consuming fire in her as well. But there had been more—his exquisite lovemaking fanned the flames of a burning hunger that left her desperate to connect with him on a deeper level. Saints help her, she wanted to dive in, wanted to recklessly explore life's glorious, fathomless depths with him. Which made his sudden coldness even harder to bear.

A noise behind her pulled her from her reverie. She glanced over her shoulder and watched Rubio circle the room, then march right back out. What the devil had gotten into him? This was his third trip in here. And why was he sporting that surly expression? She opened her mouth to call out to him, then changed her mind, deciding she didn't care to engage in a conversation requiring some long-winded explanation. Picking up the open book, she went back to reading the same paragraph of *Gulliver's Travels* yet again.

"Hell's bells." Giving up, she closed the pages. She took a sip of lemonade, wrinkled her nose, then set the glass back on the parquetry table beside the discarded book.

Ice.

The drink needs ice.

This was a craving fairly new to her palate; after all, she hailed from cool England where people relished hot beverages. Not knowing the first thing about the proper collection of ice from the storage hut, she dared not venture out there on her own and risk mucking things up. Where was Rubio when she needed him? Deciding to go find him, she snatched up her fan and glass of lemonade, and exited Bastien's quarters. All along both sides of the corridor, every chamber door and window stood open. Obviously Rubio's doing. Fancy that. He'd created a nice cross-breeze throughout the entire second floor.

As she passed her godfather's bedchamber, she caught sight of his desk strewn with papers. "Oh, for heaven's sake, I only just organized your mess."

Backtracking, she entered his room. The familiar fragrance of shaving soap and cherry-scented pipe tobacco hung in the air.

She made her way to the oversized oak desk and surveyed the disarray. How the man managed to know exactly where everything was would forever puzzle her. However, these documents were vital communications between Charles and the London detectives scouring England for the servant who'd witnessed her father's murder, and needed to be kept in order. The investigators also served as intermediaries between Lily and her company's solicitors who were monitoring the operations of Cowdrey Imports on her behalf. Regular reports were sent to her by way of the detectives, and she would respond in kind. Thus, her whereabouts were kept secret.

* * * *

Setting down the glass of lemonade, she went to work creating two stacks of documents according to dates. One pile contained copies of letters from Charles to the investigative agency. The other consisted of correspondence received from London.

Despite the free-flowing air through the open windows and door, her activity had brought a sheen to her skin. Deciding to relax a moment before heading downstairs, she vacated the hard chair for a more comfortable seat near the window, across from his bed. A flick of her wrist set her fan in motion. She leaned her head back against the plush, blue velvet settee.

Had it been only a day since Charles and Justin Andrews had gone upriver? A pang of guilt squeezed her heart. Had she been too harsh with her godfather? Probably so. Although she owed him no apologies for their falling out, she would probably be the one taking the first steps to settle their differences.

Her gaze swept across his ornate oak bed, topped with a muted red and gold paisley counterpane. The slight depression in the right side of the mattress, created by his hefty form, brought another smile to her lips. She dipped her head and squinted at the floor, spotting what appeared to be the corner of a small ornate box peeking out from beneath the patterned coverlet. She tilted her head back and forth for a better look. Definitely a box. And from what she could make out, a lovely deep purple cloisonné. Curious, she made her way across the room, bent down, and retrieved the ornate container.

A mere six inches long, and no more than four high, it was a lovely little piece. She recognized the pattern from some of the cloisonné items her parents had collected while in India, which Papa had brought back to England with him. A brass key hung in the lock. She could not recollect ever seeing this item among Charles's belongings. It had to have some special meaning to bother bringing it with him to America. Especially since they'd left in such a hurry.

She was no snoop by nature, but curiosity got the best of her. Shrugging off a thread of guilt, she perched on the edge of the bed and eased open the box. Inside, she found five parchment letters bound together with a pink silk ribbon. She lifted out the packet and a light, floral scent followed—a scent at once oddly familiar.

Definitely writings from a lady.

How curious. She'd never known her godfather to show any special interest in a woman other than as an occasional companion to those needing an escort to a social event. Had he a secret mistress she'd never known about?

Well, why ever not, since he was a confirmed bachelor who vowed never to wed. She slipped the ribbon from the packet and opened the first missive.

My dearest Charles,
Oh, my sweet, sweet love, how terribly I miss you and your loving arms.
Lily froze.

And then her fingers trembled.

This was her mother's handwriting!

She glanced at the grand flourish of the signature. She knew every stroke of Mama's pen from the letter she'd written Lily the day she was born, welcoming her into the world. The cherished epistle had become so fragile over time that Lily only read it on her birthday.

Bringing Charles's letter to her nose, she caught the faint scent of her mother's favorite floral perfume. She knew this fragrance well, having kept a prized bottle on her dresser for years, until a housemaid had dropped and broken it.

She read one letter after another, stunned by the contents. Mama and Charles had been engaged to be married once he returned to Delhi from a military assignment in Kashmir. Then why had she married Papa?

As she reached the fifth letter, she heard Rubio's booted feet pounding down the corridor...or was that Bastien returning? Quickly, she stuffed everything but the final letter back into the box, slid it under the bed, and thrust the fifth one under a pillow.

Rubio paused at the threshold, his face still a mask of concern. "Can I help you with anything, Miss Lily?"

"No, thank you. I was merely tidying up Mr. Talbot's messy desk when the heat got to me. I need to sit awhile."

Rubio scowled at her, then grunted. "Mr. Talbot?"

She scowled right back. "What in heaven's name has gotten into you? It's as though you are pacing the entire house like a sentry keeping watch. Is there something going on I should know about?"

His back straightened and his cheeks flushed. "As of this morning, I have been hired on as Bastien's overseer. I must...everyone is gone but the two of us. I have decided to practice my new assignment in their absence by looking after you and the premises. Please have patience with me while I do so."

"Yes. Right-oh. Brilliant decision." Not for one moment did she believe his excuse for roaming the corridors and acting so strangely. "You have a new position, you say? Well, congratulations."

Desperate to escape to her quarters, she conjured up her own fib. "I've a bit of a headache. If you'll excuse me, I'll be seeking out my own bedchamber."

"Of course." He turned on his heel and disappeared down the hall.

Heart racing, she snatched the letter from beneath the pillow, and hiding it in the folds of her gown, raced to her quarters and shut the door. Quickly, she moved to the window and unfolded the last letter.

My darling Charles,

It is with a heavy heart that I must inform you that our dear and loyal friend, James Stanhope, and I have wed. Oh, my darling, please hear me out. I am with child. It happened the night before you left for Kashmir. Since there was no way for you to return to Delhi in a timely manner, James stepped forward to avoid a nasty scandal, which neither you nor I would have been able to overcome, given our elevated social standing.

My love, you have known James all your life, so you know him to be a right and honorable man. My mother does not know the truth, but Papa does. He, too, feels our action was the only thing to do.

James intends to pen a letter to you in good time. I hope you will find at least a modicum of comfort in a promise he makes: You will be named the child's godfather; you will help to raise up our child. We will work together as a united family.

My dearest, I shall love you always,

Jocelyn, (now) Lady Stanhope

Lily could not breathe. She tried gulping in air, but it went no farther than her throat. Dizzy, she made a fist, pushed it into her stomach, and forced a gasp. Mama and Charles were expecting a child together and her father… God in Heaven…James Stanhope was not her father!

Despite the heat in the room, a chill swept through her as a thousand questions crowded her mind. "Is this why you were always around, Charles? To raise me alongside my father…or my make-believe father?"

More discordant thoughts tumbled into her mind in jagged pieces. Had Papa really loved her? Surely, he must have. He'd always demonstrated as much. She pressed her trembling fingers to her temples. Why hadn't she been told?

She tried to stand. Her legs wouldn't hold her. Dropping back onto the bed, she buried her face in her hands and wept until all that was left were dry, hacking sobs. She didn't know how much time had passed when Rubio pounded on the door and called out.

"Miss Lily, are you all right?" He kept pounding, now sounding frantic. "Miss Lily, answer me this second, or I am coming in."

"Enter," she called out and stuffed the letter under her own pillow. Rubio raced into the room, wide-eyed and looking worried. "Oh, Rubio. I'm afraid I fell sound asleep."

"Your eyes are swollen. Have you been crying?"

"No…well, maybe a little. Do not be alarmed, Rubio. I am being a silly goose, worrying about something that is merely a figment of my imagination."

Rubio's brows stitched together. "What…what do you mean, Miss Lily?"

"Nothing to concern yourself with. Something I said distracted Bastien before he left." She swiped a hand across her damp brow. "It's sweltering in here. When he returns, would you tell him I am out back on the swinging bench?"

Rubio paled. "That…that's quite far to the rear of the garden, Miss Lily. Perhaps you'd be more comfortable a bit closer?"

"Pish posh. I'll be just fine. What the devil's gotten into you?"

When he failed to respond, her frazzled temper threatened to get the best of her. "I'll tell you what *is* far back in the garden." She paused to take in a calming breath. "The shed where the ice blocks are kept. The ice box in the kitchen is empty. I think Vivienne forgot to fill it before they left. Would you be a dear and fetch me a bucketful? I'd like some more lemonade. This time with ice."

"That wouldn't be a good idea."

Any moment now, she'd come apart and end up in a heap on the floor. She stood and forced a smile. "Come, we shall go together, and you can meet me back at the bench with the ice."

She brushed past him and marched down the hall. He scrambled to join her. They made their way through the kitchen, pausing long enough for Lily to pour herself a fresh glass of lemonade and for Rubio to grab an empty bucket for the ice. Together, they walked through the garden to Lily's favorite bench. She sat down, snapped open her fan and, looking up at Rubio, forced another casual smile. "Thank you for putting up with my wicked mood today. I fear this miserable heat has me quite undone."

He studied her for a long moment through narrowed eyes, then raked a hand through his dark hair and glanced around. "I'll be right back. Please, Miss Lily, stay seated right where you are."

Too flustered to string together the words it would take to challenge his strange request, she nodded. "I shan't be going anywhere."

He nodded and strode off, his pounding footsteps fading away behind her. She released a sigh of relief. Setting the glass of lemonade and fan on the bench beside her, she closed her eyes and tried putting the fractured pieces of her thoughts back into some semblance of order. What would she do once Charles returned? How should she confront him? Should she hand him the box of letters to indicate she knew the contents, then simply walk away and wait for him to respond?

Suddenly sick to her stomach, and with a head that felt stuffed with cotton, she buried her face in her hands. At last, she caught the sound of Rubio's footsteps as he approached from along the path behind her. She would use some of the ice on her nape to cool and soothe her.

"Thank you," she said. "I fear I am not feeling well at all. I could use—"

"Hello, Liliana."

Julian!

Terror stole her breath.

There stood her cousin, eyes glistening like hot amber stones, a hank of blond hair pasted to his sweaty forehead.

She couldn't move.

Couldn't speak.

Couldn't get air into her lungs.

Finally, she opened her mouth to scream for Rubio but Julian clapped a hand over it and shoved her hard against the bench. "I wouldn't do that if I were you. While it won't rouse your sleeping guard, it might bring the neighbors running."

She bit down on his fingers, clawed at his face, and kicked at him with her bare feet.

He laughed, and sinking a knee into her stomach, used it to imprison her hands against her belly. Yanking her head back with a snap, he pulled a silk scarf from inside his pants pocket and tied it around her mouth.

"Rubio. Where is Rubio!" she mumbled through the cloth.

Julian took a swipe at the blood trickling down his cheek. "Your friend is having a bit of a sleep in the shed out back. I must say, I found the hut made rather comfortable quarters last night. I jolly well had the coolest room in town. Tell me, Cousin. Since you don't get out much, have you been to the bayou? Seen the alligators? Interesting beasts. I know of a special spot where we can watch them *snap, snap, snap.*" He made a comical display of slapping one palm against the other.

In one dreadful moment, she understood her cousin's intentions to be rid of her once and for all. He bound her ankles and hands, then tossed her over his shoulder and carried her to a wooden utility wagon inside the stable. The young stable hand lay sprawled on the hay. His eyes were closed, and blood smeared his nose and cheek.

Heaven help us.

A strangled noise left her throat.

"Not to fret, Liliana. The lad merely sleeps. Diethyl ether was such a lovely invention. I was first introduced to the stuff by a dentist in London. I immediately realized it would make a useful tool once I located you. I

hadn't realized exactly how useful it would be until I watched the comings
and goings of this little household. You are quite alone now, Cousin, so do
not resist me lest you find yourself with a fractured bone or two."

He started to lift her into the wagon bed. Even with her ankles bound
she managed to kick at him, barring his efforts.

He cursed and slammed her against the side of the cart.

Her legs buckled.

She slid to the ground, the rough wood driving needle-like slivers into
her back. She clenched her jaw and fought against crying out in pain.

When he spoke, his words were quieter, more venomous. *"Tsk. Tsk.* You
never were one for being told what to do, were you? And you always were
a deplorable little female."

He held her against the side of the wagon while he retrieved a small
amber bottle from his pocket. Removing the cork, he sprinkled some of
the contents over the gag covering her nose and mouth.

Their gazes locked.

She held her breath for as long as she was able while the cold bite of fear
gripped her nape and slid down her spine. His eyes, glittering with hatred
and…and what? Fascination? The man enjoyed torturing her!

Despite her held breath, the sweet-smelling fumes seeped into her nostrils.
A roaring began in each ear. Louder and louder the two noises circled
her head, until the sounds crashed together like a pair of giant cymbals,
battering her senses. No longer could she keep her eyes open, and his voice
now sounded far away.

But her mind still worked.

He'd nearly destroyed her once, and it had changed her. Forever. Something
savage ignited in her.

A ferocious sensation rose up from somewhere deep inside.

I must survive.

And then something else broke loose.

Rage.

A rage so powerful, it fed her soul. Somehow, she would find a way
to survive. Somehow it would be his life that ended, not hers. She forced
open her eyes, and even as her vision tunneled, and she could no longer
hold her breath, she glared at him, cursing him with her eyes, wishing him
into the fires of hell.

"Are you thinking I'm about to kill you?" Julian smiled and dimples
appeared in each cheek. "Well, I won't. But the alligators will. Eventually."

Chapter Nineteen

Bastien exited the Bank of New Orleans with the signed documents transferring ownership of the *Aria* to René and himself. Tucking the sheaf of papers into a leather saddlebag, he mounted his roan and headed for the shipping office. He'd like nothing better than to race to his destination, but he didn't dare risk overheating the horse in this hellishly hot weather. The leisurely *clip-clop* of hooves echoing in the near-empty streets did nothing to improve his mood.

Intelligent people retreat to their homes during the heat of the day. Which is where I ought to be, goddamn it.

A muscle worked in his tight jaw. By rights, he should be eager to feast his eyes on the ship, which had been refurbished during his month-long absence. He should be eager to learn whether his stubborn brother had adhered to their agreed-upon interior renovation plan. He should also be keen to celebrate yet another milestone. Christ, not only were he and René part owners of a shipping empire, something few men ever hoped to achieve, they now owned a luxury ship for their private use. Now, however, reveling in material gain came secondary to more pressing matters.

Go home.

He shrugged off a persistent gnawing in his gut that he should bypass the office and forced common sense to prevail. Rubio would protect both Lily and Le Blanc House and do so with an iron fist. As for guarding the stable, Armand, the lad he'd hired on six months ago, was as tenacious as a dog defending a bone.

By the time Bastien neared the docks, he'd convinced himself that his uneasiness arose from the shock of learning Lily's true identity. God Almighty, a woman of her ilk was so far out of reach for a no-account

Cajun like him, she might as well be queen of England. What had he been thinking, taking her to his bed, when nothing good could come of it? Giving in to his desires had been a mistake of the worst kind. It didn't matter that their night together had been like nothing he'd ever experienced. *Merde*, but the woman did things to his insides.

Reaching the rear of the shipping office, he dismounted, tied up his horse in the shade next to a water trough, and removed the saddle and blanket. He slipped the bank documents from the saddlebag and stepped around the corner.

And whistled out a breath.

The majestic *Aria* floated dockside, her sleek hull and masts painted a shiny black with gold trim. Twin golden rams carved from large hunks of wood hugged either side of the bow to form the figurehead.

Humph.

The golden rams had to be Felice's idea. She'd insisted on taking charge of that part of the ship's refurbishing. He'd figured she'd choose a female or angelic figure for good luck, but not his brother's plucky wife. She'd hired an artist to create two stubborn, heading-butting sheep—no doubt to represent him and his brother. The scamp. At least in Greek mythology the golden ram could fly, and the *Aria* could indeed reach exhilarating speeds. In any event, there'd be no mistaking this beauty whenever she sailed into a foreign port.

Directly behind the *Aria*, the cutter *Celine* floated high in the water. Which meant the ship had been emptied of cargo. Judging by the glistening exterior, she'd recently been scrubbed clean.

He stepped into the office and paused at the entrance. René stood with his back to Bastien, facing Felice at her desk, obscuring her from view. Beside him stood her brother Michel, mayor of New Orleans. Donal, Michel's eldest son, stood with them. All four were in deep conversation.

At the sight of them, an overwhelming sense of pride gripped him. This was *his family*. Soon, Rubio and Allita would add to the growing number as well. As would René and Felice's babe when it came along.

But not Lily.

Never Lily.

What the hell was wrong with him? He never meant to marry. And she had no intention of remaining in sweltering New Orleans. He shoved aside his unproductive thoughts and concentrated on the people standing before him. This was his clan, and he needed them. Needed their help.

"*Bonjour*," he said, and stepped into the room.

They all turned at once. After a brief pause, a cacophony of greetings filled the room as everyone spoke at once. Bastien managed a small grin and nod in reply, then strode to René's desk, where he slapped the papers down. Felice bolted from her desk and rushed into his arms, nearly toppling him over.

"I thought never to see you again!" She dropped a kiss on each cheek, then moved in closer to give him a hug...well, as much of a hug as her expanding belly allowed.

She gripped both his arms and gazed deep into his eyes. "It is so very good to see you, dear Bastien."

He smiled down at her. "And you as well."

She glanced at the documents he'd set on René's desk. "We must have a celebration this evening. In your home, since Lily does not get out much."

"We have a problem," he said.

Felice stepped back, her brow furrowing. "What's wrong?"

He shoved a hand through his hair and glowered at Michel. "Not only did your father know the true identity of the people staying with me, he also advised you of the particulars. Correct?"

Michel nodded. "As mayor, I need to be advised of anything having to do with investigations and legalities. I am also required to keep such matters confidential, particularly when a woman's safety is at risk."

René stepped forward. "What the devil are you getting at, Bastien? What problem do we have?"

Bastien walked to the cabinet holding the legal files. He removed one thick packet and spread out the documents across René's desk.

Everyone crowded around the table; their brows furrowed. Felice shrugged and glanced at Bastien. "They're the Cowdrey shipping agreements. What does this have to do with Lily and Talbot?"

Michel's cheeks turned a darker hue. He said, "Tell them what you know."

Bastien flipped through a couple pages and ran a finger down the document, pausing at the bottom lines. He swallowed a curse at the sight of his name written directly below Lily's.

"See this signature, L. L. Stanhope?"

They all nodded.

"It belongs to none other than Lady Liliana Stanhope, daughter to the Earl of Cowdrey. It seems Lady Liliana oversaw every aspect of the business on behalf of her father."

He took his time and settled a hard look on each person. "She is also a guest in my home. Along with her godfather, who is not Mr. Percival Talbot, but Charles Langdon, Earl Chamberlain."

"Good heavens," Felice murmured.

"How did this come about?" René asked, his Cajun accent deepening to reveal a slow rise of temper. "Why did these people choose to come to N'awlins in disguise?"

Bastien turned to Michel, who looked suddenly green. "You knew everything, didn't you?"

Michel raised a hand, palm out, and shook his head. "I had no idea that L. L. Stanhope was our Miss Lily."

Bastien slapped a hand atop the documents. "It sure as hell would've been helpful for me to know that Lily's cousin had murdered her father. That he's the one who poisoned her and likely did away with the housemaid, the one person who could point a finger at him."

He took in a deep breath to calm himself. "Now we come to the part where I said we have a problem. Rubio spotted a man lurking outside my home last evening, watching Lily. When Rubio went out to check, the man acknowledged him, then retreated across the street and disappeared into the neighbor's servants' entry. However, when I sent Rubio over to check with the neighbor, he was told no such person is employed in their household. The man had an English accent, by the way. Anyone care to wager that the lurker is Lily's cousin?"

Felice gasped. "Do something, Michel." She turned to her husband. "René?"

"I've got things under control," Bastien said. "For the moment, anyway. Rubio and the stable boy are armed and watching the property."

Michel pinched the bridge of his nose and paced the room. "I'll go straightaway to the constable. I'll see to it he has guards positioned around your home day and night."

He glanced at Bastien and paused. "For what it's worth, Father's orders were to keep things secret. I was aware Cowdrey Shipping belonged to my father's lifelong friend, James Stanhope. I also knew we were shielding his daughter from her cousin, but I will tell you again, I had no idea that L. L. Stanhope was, in fact, our Lily."

A sense of betrayal bit at Bastien's gut. "You also knew this Talbot was, in fact, Charles Langdon, Earl Chamberlain."

"Stanhope, Langdon, and my father were old friends. They'd formed a pact more than forty years ago that they'd be there for each other in a time of need. Which is why Langdon sailed for New Orleans. He sought my father's help. Both men pleaded with me to keep the circumstances secret so nothing would accidentally leak out while investigators in England searched for the housemaid who was witness to Julian Stanhope's crimes."

Pain filled Michel's eyes. "I am sorry, my friend. Not only did you and René perform a great service to my aging father when you came to work here, but once your brother married my sister, we became family. And family means loyalty. I should have insisted upon telling you, especially since Lily and Chamberlain moved into your home."

Michel turned to Felice. "When are Langdon and our father due to return?"

"Not for three or four days."

"Probably better that way," René said. "We should take care of things on our own and not let those meddling old fools try to take charge."

"May I be a part of this, Papa?" fourteen-year-old Donal asked, his cheeks as flaming red as his hair.

Michel nodded. "Run home and tell your mother we'll be having dinner at Bastien's—"

"Vivienne and Régine are gone until the morrow," Bastien said. "We have no one to do the cooking."

Michel turned back to Donal. "Stop by Antoine's Restaurant on your way home. Tell Antoine to either send a chef over to cook in Bastien's kitchen, or prepare enough food for a small army. We'll have guards to feed, as well."

"But don't tell Antoine about the guards," Felice put in. "The man is aware of the size of our family, and that the sea captains board at Le Blanc House, so he'll think nothing of the order."

"Christ," Bastien muttered. "I forgot about both the captains." He raked his hand through his hair again. "I intended to tell you before I traveled up north last month that since I'm now sole owner of Le Banc House, I'd rather it be kept for private use. Would it be a problem for the captains to board at the company townhouse?"

René and Michel nodded in agreement.

Michel turned to Donal. "After you've notified Antoine and your mother, I'd like you to ask around at the hotels to find out if an Englishman has been in residence. If they ask why you want to know, tell them it's your father, the mayor, doing the inquiring. Can you manage everything?"

"Yes, sir!" Donal's spine straightened, his chin lifted, and with a proud nod, he disappeared out the door, only to backtrack at the sound of hoofbeats. "It's Rubio. He's all bloody!"

* * * *

A damp, stale smell of old dirt filled Lily's nostrils. She tried to move and swallowed a moan. Everything hurt. She tried to raise her head. A furious throbbing raged inside her skull. She winced at the pain and let her cheek fall back onto the musty earth. As she lay there, her mind sharpened and memories of what Julian had done came into focus.

Where am I?

Ignoring the pounding in her head, she forced open her eyes. Thin, sunless light filtered through wooden slats. This was some kind of shack. She tried to rise again, but her pitiful attempt was pointless. Her muscles refused to work. A violent shudder ran through her and she plopped back onto the dirt floor with a painful thud.

She lay quiet and listened.

Was that a choir of frogs bringing in the night? Wherever she was, it had to be near water. Had Julian taken her to a bayou?

Alligators.

He'd spoken of alligators.

Oh, dear Lord!

Mosquitoes buzzed about her head and bit at her arms. She tried to swat at them, only to realize her hands and legs were bound. No wonder she couldn't move. A rustling sounded from somewhere outside. She stilled. Was that someone humming?

The rickety door creaked open, and Julian strode in. "Ah, you are awake."

He kneeled down and removed the gag from her mouth, then ran a hand lightly over her hair in something resembling familial affection. "How are you feeling, Cousin?"

She stared up at him and said nothing.

He winked at her, and with a saucy grin lifted her onto a wooden chair. "Oh, you have no fight left in you? So soon?"

Mark my words, you insane bastard. I have only begun to fight.

She swept her gaze over him, slowly and meaningfully. "If I am not meant to survive, then why in the world would I fight you?" she lied. And then a bubble of laughter rolled through her.

He scowled at her. "What the bloody hell do you find so amusing?"

"Oh, Julian, this is rich. So very rich. You were always such an impossible child. Too impatient to wait for anything, no matter how worthwhile it might be. Had you only been a little more patient, you wouldn't have had to murder my father, nor do me in to get your hands on the inheritance rightfully coming to you."

He grabbed the sides of the chair and shook it so hard her teeth rattled. "You choose this of all times to mock me? Well, I won't fall for your taunts. There is no way you can convince me to let you live."

A kind of hysteria rose up in her, to the point that she started laughing and couldn't stop. "I only today learned that Lord Chamberlain is not my godfather. I am, in fact, his daughter. Which means, I am no blood relation to your uncle, James Stanhope."

Defiance rose up in her and she leaned forward as if wanting to charge full force into him. "Not one drop of Stanhope blood flows through my veins. You, Julian Stanhope, are the sole heir to everything. *Tsk. Tsk. Tsk.* Papa's—or should I say, your uncle's—health was rapidly failing. He wanted no one to know."

She leaned back and tilted her head up at him, a small smile forming on her lips. "He changed his will to give everything to me, but you see, I have no claim to it."

"You knew all along you were not his daughter?"

"No. I just told you, I only recently found out. So whether you choose to let me go, or toss me to the alligators, in the end it makes no difference, because it's too late for you, Julian. Too many people know what you did. You will never inherit. You pitiful excuse of a human being. You killed the one man who was destined to leave you a fortune, one you had only to wait to land on your doorstep. And for that, you will hang by the neck until you are dead."

She didn't see it coming.

The back of his hand connected to the side of her face, tumbling her over. Her head hit the floor with a heavy thud.

He said nothing as he unbound her ankles and lifted her to her feet. Then he grinned again. An almost feverish light settled in his gaze. "Come along," he said. "I've something to show you."

He guided her out the door and onto a grassy slope. In the dimming light, fireflies danced in the air and the chorus of frogs grew louder, resonating up and down the banks of a slow-moving body of water.

"So, this must be a bayou," she said, boldly ignoring his bullying.

Julian chuckled. "Brilliant deduction, Cousin."

He paused and dramatically placed a hand over his heart. "Egad, but I have erred. You are no longer my relative. Nor are you Liliana Stanhope. How shall I address you, then?"

A dramatic sigh left his lips. "Simply Lily will have to do. Although I find the nickname distasteful. So very plebeian, don't you think? Or is it because I've always detested you?"

He shrugged and waved a hand through the air. "Oh, well. No need to concern ourselves with such trivialities since our time together is rather limited."

Slowly, she took in a deep breath to steady herself, refusing to give in to his taunting. She looked up and down the bayou, seeing nothing but trees and swampland. Not another building in sight. Before them, a narrow bridge connected to another shore. Beyond the bridge, a dirt path disappeared around a bend.

"How did you come to find this place?" she asked, trying to sound casual as she sized up anything and everything that might give her a way to escape.

"Rented it from some mudbug Cajun selling his wares in the marketplace in town. Told him I was writing a jolly good book and required some creative privacy." He laughed. "I gave him plenty of coin and told a good tale about needing my solitude, which included no interruptions from him. Here, look at this."

He turned to an old wooden bench and picked up something white.

A dead chicken.

He shook it in her face.

She turned her head to the side, away from the stench of blood. "If you intend to bully me with that thing, you will be sorely disappointed. I've seen plenty in our kitchens. Even plucked a few myself."

A frenetic look glistened in his eyes. "Oh, no, Lily. Here's what we do with the little bird."

Gripping her arm with his free hand, he led her to the middle of the bridge. "Look down there, Lily. Alligators. It's getting a bit dark, but if you peer into the water, you can see their shadows beneath the surface, and their snouts just above the water. Now watch."

He tossed the chicken into the still waters and a frenzy ensued as the beasts rolled about in a battle to claim the dead bird.

Her heart jumped into her throat and stole her breath.

Lord help me.

This is what he intended long before he stole me away.

Julian grinned. "Snap. Snap. Snap, Lily. Fascinating creatures, aren't they? Like something out of prehistoric times."

She clamped her teeth together, refused to give him the satisfaction of seeing the fear in her. She would not cry out—not even if he gave her a push over the edge.

He glanced around. "My, but it's grown near to dark on us, which would spoil all my entertainment." He grinned again, and gripping her by the shoulders, leaned her over the footbridge. "Snap. Snap. Snap, Lily."

Her breath froze at the sight of the dark shadows lurking below. Nonetheless, she managed to remain silent.

"Bloody hell," he said. "Your false bravado doesn't fool me one bit. Now, let us venture inside, where I shall bundle you up nice and tight so you cannot escape. Then I shall return to my boarding house for the night."

Shoving her back through the door, he bound and gagged her once more, tied her to a post, and with a jaunty good evening, left her alone. Something dark and queasy swept through her. Bile washed up into her throat as reality hit her—painful and real as a slap to the face—no one was coming for her.

How could they when they didn't know where she was?

Chapter Twenty

Bastien retrieved a pair of clean cotton gloves from his dressing room and went in search of something Lily had recently worn next to her skin. Passing by his bathing chamber, he caught sight of her peach-colored night rail draped across the boudoir chair.

"That'll do," he muttered and backtracked into the room. Following the constable's instructions, he donned the gloves before touching the garment—less confusing for the bloodhounds, the officer had said. He picked up the gown and memories assailed him—of their exquisite night together, of their tender morning spent in the treehouse. His chest tightened, constricting his lungs.

Stay safe, Lily. Do whatever you can to stay alive.

He left his suite, and made his way downstairs and into the gardens, all the while sending a silent call to the heavens for her safe return. When was the last time he'd prayed for anything? He couldn't recall, but he was damn well doing it now.

He reached the swinging bench where Rubio had last seen her and halted. On the ground nearby, an army of red ants overran a shattered drinking glass. Lily's colorful silk fan lay a few feet away, crushed beneath the imprint of a large boot. An open book, its pages mangled, hung askew off the bench. Terror settled like hot coals in the pit of his stomach.

"Christ." He set the carefully folded night rail on the bench beside the book and stepped back to survey the scene once again. A movement off to the right caught his eye. Rubio appeared from the direction of the stables. He halted beside Bastien.

"Don't touch anything," Bastien said. "The bloodhounds need to catch a good scent. Also, we do not know what the constable might notice which we do not see."

Rubio stood for a long moment, staring at the disarray. "Miss Lily did not go easily with him, señor." A small groan left his lips. "I should never have left her alone to fetch ice for her drink."

Bastien waved him off. "Do not blame yourself, *mon ami*. We both thought her safe here. Did you find any sign of what might have become of Armand?"

Rubio shook his head and winced. He touched the back of his skull and his fingertips came away smeared with blood. "The service cart is missing. So is the gray, but no sign of the boy, nor the pistol I gave him. I did take note of a smelly rag in the hay. I was careful not to touch it. Looked like what was tied around my mouth when I woke up. Smelled the same when I put my nose near it."

Bastien closed his eyes against a blast of pain. "What the hell did that son of a bitch do with Armand? The boy is barely thirteen. If that. To think I plucked the little thief off the streets to give him a better life, and then to have him end up a victim of Lily's goddamn cutthroat cousin."

"I can't figure how the man got in here, or when," Rubio said. "Armand saddled your horse before you left for town, right?"

Bastien nodded. "*Oui.*"

"Then Stanhope must have slipped into the garden through the stable soon after you left. Probably didn't take much to overwhelm little Armand. Especially if the man came up behind him as he did to me. Or could he have been lurking in the stable while you two were in there together?"

Bastien shook his head. "Had he been hiding in a stall, the horses would've grown nervous and alerted us." Tension and frustration built in him like a storm about to erupt. He blew out a hard, frustrated breath. "Come along. Let us see to putting a few stitches in that gash in your head while we wait for the constable with the dogs."

No sooner had they made their way through the back door and into the kitchen than Michel and René walked in, coming from the direction of the front of the house.

Bastien scowled. "How the hell did you get in here?"

René flashed a brass key. "I still have one of these."

"Since you no longer live here, *mon frère*, hand it over." On second thought, it was probably a good thing his brother had a key. "Or perhaps you should provide me with a key to your home should there be an emergency."

René shoved the object in question back in his pocket. "We're here to wait for the constable with the bloodhounds, and then we shall go with you, *oui?*" He wandered over to where Bastien tended to the back of Rubio's head and looked over his brother's shoulder. "Looks like he be needing about five stitches, *non?*"

That storm of frustration building in Bastien crackled to the surface like lightning and thunder combined. He shot a hard look at his brother, paused the needle and thread in midair, and let loose with a litany of Cajun curse words.

Michel snorted and headed for the larder. "While you two relieve yourselves of some of your pent-up tension, I shall see if there's any ham for sandwiches."

Bastien cursed again. "You think of food at a time like this?"

"It's getting late," Michel responded. "We should all eat something before we set out. No telling when we'll return."

"Régine always has ham," Rubio said.

"I know." Michel tossed a large slab of Cajun tasso, smoked and spiced ham, on the table, retrieved a large knife, and began slicing. "Someone mind grabbing the bread and condiments?"

"Since I am somewhat busy," Bastien replied, "and since Rubio is the one being tended to, that would leave my brother, who is standing around doing nothing, to do your bidding. Get to it, *mon frère.*"

"*Embrasse mon tchew,*" René replied and moved to where Michel worked on assembling the meal.

Bastien snorted. "Since this is my home you've invaded, how about you kiss mine."

"You two settle down before your bickering gets out of hand." Michel kept slicing the ham while directing his next words at Rubio. "Close as two peas in a pod, those two. Or a cat and dog wrestling in a sack. Depends on how far they take things."

"*Humph,*" René and Bastien responded in unison.

Bad-tempered as Bastien felt at the moment, he'd been mighty relieved to see René and Michel appear. Michel was right—bickering was a learned response between two brothers who'd fended for themselves during their growing years. Whatever one called their disputes, they released pent-up frustrations, even when their squabbles turned physical. "Did you two bring weapons?"

"Of course," René mumbled through a mouthful of food. "Your sandwich is on the table if I don't get to it first."

Bastien ignored his brother's taunt. "Finished. Eat something, Rubio."

"You, too," René said.

As much as Bastien's stomach rebelled against putting food in it, Michel was right—no one could predict how long they'd be out looking for Lily. His head buzzed. *Is she hungry? What has that bastard done with her? With Armand?*

A banging on the front door sounded and they all took off at a run. Bastien yanked open the door to find the constable holding a single bloodhound on a leash. Behind him stood five uniformed officers.

"What the hell, only one dog?" Bastien blurted.

"Indeed," the constable responded. "A pack of hounds are a noisy lot. They bark constantly when on a hunt, sending signals back and forth to each other. You'd hear them coming for miles. On the other hand, a single hound is silent, keeps his nose to the ground and soldiers on. This here is Old Red, the best of the lot."

He reached out and shook Bastien's hand. "I am Constable Dewey. We'll be traveling on foot. If you wish to ride, you'd best get your horses ready while my men and I inspect the scene where the lady was taken and collect an article of her clothing."

"We'll be walking with you." The thought of again viewing the scene in the garden had Bastien's stomach revolting. He looked to Rubio. "Let them in through the stable while I get our firearms."

* * * *

Lily gave up trying to free her wrists and ankles from the rough ropes. The useless effort only managed to scrape her skin raw, generating even more blood for the nasty buzzing insects to feed on. She slumped in the chair she'd been tied to, and for the first time since her ordeal began, the feeble hope that she'd somehow be rescued drained away.

A lone tear slid down her cheek. The sting and buzz of mosquitoes made her want to cry out in despair, but she doubted she had any voice left. She tried closing her mind to the irritating noise when a rustling sound coming from outside the cabin caught her attention.

She froze and held her breath, trying to hear despite the pounding of blood in her ears.

Another bit of rustling, and her throat went dry.

An animal? Had to be. Julian had left the area a while ago. She'd heard his feet pound across the footbridge and then fade away. Besides, he was too much of a coward to venture into the bushes. Especially when daylight no longer filtered through the spaces between the shack's wooden slats.

A loud roar shook the ground and walls around her. She jumped and the ropes dug in anew.

What in the world was that horrid sound? A bear?

"Oh, Lord, help me," she whimpered, her heart pounding a furious beat. Whatever was out there, it was big. And fierce. No wonder Julian hadn't bothered with the gag. She'd cried out until hoarse after he'd left, but there'd been no one to hear her calls for help. Now, with the bellowing outside, she wasn't about to draw attention to herself.

The cabin door flew open and a silhouette appeared against the evening sky. "Miss Lily?"

"Armand?" she managed to squeak out.

"*Oui.* I am here for you." In the dim light, she made out some kind of club in his hand. He hurried to her side, dropped the cudgel, and went to work untying the ropes.

"How…how did you find me?"

"Your cousin thought he knocked me out, but by the time he returned to the stable and tossed you into the wagon, I was awake and only pretending. When he drove away, I quick-like slid beneath the undercarriage and hung on. Then when he took you inside this here shack, I ran around to the side and found this club. I knowed I'd be findin' one around here somewhere."

"The club…how…what is that—"

"This place we be in is a crawdad and frog gigger's shack. They always keeps a club with 'em when they dig and gig. Use it to beat off snakes and gators. Or kill a few catfish they manage to catch with their hands."

"Oh, Armand, you are my savior. You must get us out of here immediately, before my cousin returns."

"*Non.* We cannot leave until mornin', Miss Lily."

Fear shot through her anew. "Julian plans to return at dawn. We must leave now."

Armand shook his head, his shoulder-length black hair whipping about his head. "I don' know my way back in the dark. Besides, there be snakes and bears and big ole cats we don' wanna be runnin' into."

"Then how did Julian find his way to town in the dark when he doesn't know the bayou as you do?"

"He unhitched that ole mare from the wagon, let her have her lead. She'll know her way back."

Another roar sounded, so loud the wooden shack trembled.

"My Lord in Heaven, what is that awful noise?"

"A bull gator. He won't be trying to come in here." Armand moved to the side of the small room and flung open a rickety shutter. "There's a full moon a comin' up. Your eyes will adjust so we'll be fine until the dawn breaks. Don' you worry none, Miss Lily. I be takin' good care of you. Remember, I know the bayou. And I know her secrets. We go at the first break of light."

She swatted at the buzzing around her head. "If my body isn't drained of blood by then."

He scrambled to his feet. "I can be handlin' that for you right quick." He picked up the club and sprinted out the door. In moments, he was back with the big stick tucked under his arm and his hands full of bayou mud. "It'll be a stinkin' mess, but it'll keep those nasty *moustiques* off you. Can I be havin' permission to touch you so I can get this mess smeared on you?"

"Oh, please do. I fear I'm about to expire from these flying vampires."

By the time the boy returned several times with enough mud to coat her lower extremities, arms and face, even the stinging and itching had become bearable. Actually, the gray, oozing mud caking her skin produced a soothing effect. "You're a clever lad," she said. "What would I do without you?"

"*Tu emportes ta chance là où tu la trouves,*" he responded, and plunked down on the floor in front of her, his skinny legs crossed, the club across his lap.

"Hmm, there's a phrase I understand, but gracious, how does it apply here?"

He shrugged. "It means you take your good fortune where you can find it, *oui*?"

Still puzzled, she nodded.

He tipped his head to the side and something resembling a smile flitted across his mouth. "Well, tonight you have good fortune because bayou mud, it be better than finding gold, *oui*?"

"Indeed." Eyes now adjusted to the dark, she studied the boy in front of her by the shaft of moonlight filtering through the open shutter. "How old are you, Armand?"

"Twelve or thirteen. Or thereabouts. Lost count after Maman died."

"Oh, dear. If you don't mind my asking, when did she pass?"

"When I was about six or seven. Mayhap five. Don' remember."

He'd been an orphan roaming the streets all this while? Her heart squeezed. Despite his bad grammar, his voice held that lovely Cajun French lilt she found oddly calming, something her nerves desperately needed.

"What happened to your mother?"

"Fever."

"And your father?"

"Never knew him. Not like Bastien and René. Even though that high-hat French papa of theirs won't lay claim to them, at least they don' have to wonder who they came from."

Once again, her heart went out to him. He was a small, wiry boy, perhaps too small for his age because he'd been living on the streets for so many years. Lord knew how he'd managed to survive. "Tell me how you came to act as Bastien's stable hand."

"He pulled me off the streets near six months ago, when he caught me liftin' a lady's fancy reticule. Lickety-slick he was, grabbin' my wrist and wrenchin' my arm behind my back afore I knowed he was even there. Said he knowed more tricks of the trade than I could ever think of doin'. Imagine that, he called my thievin' a trade."

"So instead of turning you over to the authorities, he hired you?"

"Yes, ma'mselle. Ain't no better a man what lives than Monsieur Thibodeaux. He told me I would not be survivin' the streets much longer. He said sooner or later someone would toss me to the gators…sorry, Miss Lily. Anyway, he took me in, taught me about takin' proper care of his horses. Said he wanted to set me on the straight and narrow. He said he'd been better off than me when he was my age because he had sisters, and a *maman*. But most of all, he had a brother who saw to it he went to school to learn readin' and writin'."

"Did you ever go to school?"

"*Non*. Bastien, he brings in a schoolmarm. He knows I don' fit in with them in the classroom. Before you come along, most nights we met in the library, where he'd read to me, and then have me read to him. That was real nice."

"I am truly sorry my presence in the household stole such pleasure from you."

He shook his head. "*Non*. We'll start up again once things get back to normal."

Get back to normal. Meaning when she was gone from Bastien's life—something she no longer wanted to happen. A shaft of pain shot like an arrow through her heart. Why was she concerning herself with such thoughts? She'd likely not see another evening or sunset if they didn't manage to escape before Julian returned.

"I should hush now and let you rest, Miss Lily. I've been blither-blatherin' too much."

She managed a shaky breath. "Oh, no, Armand. Please, do keep talking. Your words are exceedingly interesting. Not only do they keep me from losing my sanity, they help to pass the time."

And so it went for hours—he spoke of his life, of the bayou, and of the man who'd not only rescued him from a life of crime, but saved Lily's life in yet another way. When she'd asked the boy why Bastien made him sleep in the stable, the boy said doing so was his choice, that Bastien had given him the assignment of caring for the horses, and care for them he would, day and night.

Weary, nearly numb with fatigue and spent emotions, Lily dozed off here and there while Armand watched over her like a good soldier, never wavering in his words or care. When he suddenly went quiet, the silence startled her to attention.

He was on his feet, club in hand, peering between the slats.

Fear shot through her anew. "What is it?" she whispered.

"Someone comes. I see a torchlight."

"Oh, my God, Armand!"

He put a finger to his lips and spoke soft and low. "Won't be your cousin, Miss Lily. He couldn't find his way here 'til light. Mayhap the man who owns this place comes to hunt crawdads."

Armand gripped the club with both hands and, lifting it on his shoulder, shifted over to one side of the door. "Quiet now. There be more than one."

"Leave, Armand. Crawl through the window and hide where they can't see you."

"*Non.* I will not leave you. Now get yourself in the far corner, and don' say a word."

It was plain the boy, half her age, intended to protect her with his life. Lily bit her bottom lip to keep from crying out, and with legs shaking so badly she could barely stand, she kept her back against the wall and moved to the darkest corner of the room.

And then she heard them.

Barely a sound at first, but it was there, foreign to the bayou noises she'd grown accustomed to during the night.

She covered her mouth with both hands to keep from crying out. Held her breath. Listened so hard her ears rang.

A loud crash splintered the door and sent it flying open. Lily swallowed a scream and pressed her back hard against the wall as if trying to disappear into the wood.

A man stood in the doorway, his large form silhouetted against the backdrop of torches and lanterns.

Armand stepped forward and swung his club at the figure.

The man grabbed it with ease and sent the boy flying.

Armand landed on the dirt floor with a grunt, came up on one knee, then squinted at the figure. "Bastien?"

"Armand?" Bastien rushed into the room. "Christ, I could've killed you!" Someone else moved into the room, his lantern flooding the shack's dark corners with light.

"Thank Heaven you found us," Lily cried out. Relief swamped her. Exhaustion swept her legs out from under her. She closed her eyes and sank to the dirt floor.

Chapter Twenty-One

"Good God, Lily!" Bastien rushed to the corner of the room and knelt in front of her, his heart near to bursting.

She sat with her back against the wall, hugging her drawn-up legs. "I'm fine now that you're here," she muttered, the exhaustion in her voice belying her claim. "How did you find us?"

"Bloodhound." Bastien curled a finger beneath her chin and easing it upward, studied her face. A thin film of dried mud resembling gray lacework clung to her cheeks and forehead. He glanced over his shoulder at Armand. "This be your doing?"

"*Oui.*"

"*Bien.*" Bastien tilted Lily's head to the side. He caught sight of a dark bruise beneath the caked dirt. Fury lit a fire in him, hot and dangerous. "The bastard struck you, didn't he?"

She rested her chin atop her knees and considered him through weary eyes. "Does something so obvious require a response?"

A powerful urge to gather her up in his arms gripped him. Instead, he brushed a hank of matted hair off her face with a gentle sweep of his fingers. "Your pardon, *chère.*"

René strode into the room with Michel at his heels. "We couldn't locate Stanhope."

"He done unhitched the mare and rode to town," Armand responded. "That capon, that coward, he be comin' back on the morrow, don'cha know. Say he gonna feed Miss Lily to the gators."

Bastien sucked in a hard breath that stuck in his throat.

Armand scooted over to sit beside him. "Not to worry, *mischie.* He doan know I sneaked a ride under the wagon and hid out 'til he left. Soon's daylight come along, I was gonna see her back to Le Blanc House afore he showed up. Didn't matter none dat he stole the pistol Rubio gave me, 'cuz I found this here club. Ain't no way I was gonna let that *bon rien* hurt her."

"A good-for-nothing, indeed." Michel lifted his lantern high. Getting a good look at Lily, he cursed softly. "We need to get her out of here before that beast—"

"I shan't be going anywhere." Lily shook her head and dismissed Michel's words with a sweep of her hand. She leaned away from the wall, her back straight, her voice filled with renewed vigor. "I intend to see this horrible nightmare through to the very end. My cousin upended my life, killed my...my father, and nearly did me in—not once but twice. I shall be the one to greet Julian when he steps onto that bridge. I shall be the one to coax a confession out of the rat. I need those of you who remain to stay out of sight and act as witnesses—"

"*Non, chère.* Your plan is too dangerous."

She pressed her fingers to Bastien's mouth. "Hush. I am quite aware of my country's laws. I shan't return to England unless I can be cleared of all charges, which requires Julian's confession. Lacking his admission, it would take years to clear my name."

She'll be leaving. Her words sent a dull ache pulsing through Bastien. As if touching her might somehow ease her suffering as well as his own private pain, he took her hands in his and inspected her wrists. "Bring the light closer, Michel."

At the sight of dried blood mingling with the mud caking her wrists, Bastien bit his tongue against the raw language wanting to spew forth. He sat back on his heels and paused to bank the fresh onslaught of rage boiling his blood. "Are you in pain?"

"In truth, I no longer know. Thankfully, Armand knew to cover me in mud, or the mosquitoes would've carried me off. Now that the mire has begun to flake off, the bites are beginning to itch again."

"I have something at home to remove the sting once and for all." Again, he resisted the urge to gather her into his arms. Instead, he gave her hands a squeeze. "Are you certain you do not wish for Rubio to take you and Armand home while the rest of us lie in wait for your cousin? We know how to extract a confession from him."

She managed a beleaguered smile. "You should know me better by now than to suggest such folly."

Despite the dirt outlining her mouth, he wanted to bend his head and press his lips to hers. "You're a stubborn one, don'cha know."

She turned to Armand. "After all we've been through, what say you—
would you care to take your leave now?"

"*Non*, Miss Lily. Same as you, I wish to be here when the constable
takes that motherless goatherd to the gallows."

Constable Dewey stepped forward and held his lantern over Armand.
"Say, isn't this the little cutpurse I used to chase through the streets?"

A quick glance at the open window, and Armand's body shifted, poised
for a quick getaway.

"Leave him be," Bastien growled. "He's my ward."

Armand's eyes widened. "I am?"

"*Oui*." He regarded Dewey. "I take full responsibility for him."

The boy's mouth fell open. "You do?"

"*Oui*."

The constable's gaze darted back and forth between the two. "Is he
your legal ward? If not, there are—"

Bastien waved Dewey off with a flip of his wrist. "Once this is all
settled, I'll make his situation with me legal. And permanent. I'll say it
one more time—he is my concern, so leave him be."

Armand, catching Bastien's full meaning, let out a soft gasp. He glanced
from René to Michel, as if seeking their approval. Each, in turn, gave him
a short nod. He lowered his head and his quivering bottom lip disappeared
between his teeth.

Dewey cleared his throat. "Well, then. We need to return the bloodhound
to the kennel. Morrison, you remain here with me. The rest of you take
the dog and go on ahead."

René leaned his shoulder against the wall and looked from Michel to
Rubio, then shot Bastien a speaking glance.

Bastien gave a small nod. "Seems to me there be plenty of us here to
bring Stanhope in, Constable. No need for you to spend the next few hours
waiting around."

A sarcastic chuckle escaped Dewey's mouth. "Oh, I know you Thibodeaux
brothers only too well. Mr. Stanhope would never make it to the jail."

Michel blew out a frustrated exhale. "Now see here, Dewey. I'm the
goddamn mayor. And in case you've forgotten, my sister is the wife of one
of these Thibodeaux brothers you just demeaned. As respected partners
in the Andrews Shipping Company, they've proven themselves to be fine
upstanding citizens. I'll not have you besmirch them. Which, by the way,
is also a direct reflection on me."

A crimson flush crept up Dewey's neck, reaching his face. A muscle
twitched along his jaw. "My apologies, Mayor. Officer Morrison and I

shall endeavor to act as proper legal witnesses on the lady's behalf." He turned to the other officers. "You may take your leave."

When the room cleared of so many people, Bastien stood and surveyed the shanty. A narrow cot was shoved sideways against one wall with a chair and rickety wooden table nearby. Rough-hewn shelves held tins and utensils. A blue enamel coffeepot sat atop a small potbellied stove. Scant items of clothing hung on hooks. The door he'd kicked to pieces hung by a single hinge. It was a wonder he hadn't smashed more than the door. He'd have the sorry-looking thing replaced.

"This is someone's home," he said. "How did Stanhope come by it, I wonder?"

Lily sighed. "He rented it from the owner. Mentioned something about running into the man selling crawdads in the marketplace. He gave him a good amount of coin to keep him off the property for a month."

"Stanhope lived here?"

"Heavens, no. Such a meager dwelling would never serve my cousin. I expect he lives in the lap of luxury in some hotel. Or, knowing him, he finagled his way into someone's fine home as an exalted English guest. He has a most persuasive way whenever it suits him."

A chill raised the hairs on the back of Bastien's neck. If Stanhope had rented this hovel for so long a time, what kind of menace did he have planned for Lily? He studied the weariness written all over her countenance. She didn't deserve to be here. Didn't deserve any further suffering. "Would you care to have a lie-down on the cot?"

She wrinkled her nose at the faded quilt atop the bed. Leaning her back against the wooden wall, she sighed yet again. "I think not. And don't bother offering the chair. Julian had me tied to it until Armand set me free. I do have a concern though—since I intend to be waiting just outside the entry when Julian crosses the bridge, how will we know he's arrived until he is upon us?"

"You see, *chère*? Your plan, it be far too dangerous a way of dealing with him," Bastien said.

"Not if I don't allow him to get too close to me before he makes his confession. Afterward, the constable and his man can collect him."

"*Non.* It's reckless and I insist—"

"Bastien," René interrupted. "The lady knows her mind. And we know how to lie in wait in the shadows, *non*?"

Damn it, René was right. Nonetheless, Bastien scowled at his brother and cursed under his breath.

Armand scrambled to his feet. "I got me an idea. Anyone know how to make a bayou hooty-owl call?"

"*Oui.*" René shoved his hands in his pockets and turned his attention to the boy.

"When dawn breaks," Armand explained, "I'll head down the path a ways. Once I spy him a comin', I'll backtrack close enough so's you can hear my hooty-owl. Then you hooty-owl back to let me know you is awake and ready for him."

Bastien studied Armand, who appeared eager to please despite looking as exhausted as Lily. His heart pinched. What a hell of a life the boy must have lived in order to survive. "You took good care of Miss Lily. I'm proud of you."

Armand's cheeks flushed. "*Merci.*"

Rubio snatched the quilt off the cot, and stepping outside, gave it a good shake. A cloud of dust swirled in the air around him. He coughed. Soft chuckles swept through the room, easing tensions. He spread the coverlet back over the cot and, seating himself at one end, patted the bed. "There's room for two more to sit while we produce a plan."

Lily remained on the floor, her eyes shuttered as the others proceeded with a plan of action based on her terms. Once done, conversation trickled to a halt. Rubio, Michel, and Dewey sat sideways on the cot, arms crossed over their chests, eyes closed. Monroe slumped in the chair, his elbow propped on the table, and leaned his cheek in his hand while Armand curled up in one corner. René had stepped outside.

A balmy breeze swept through the gaping entry. The flames in the oil lamps flickered and swayed. Bastien turned off one lantern, set the other on the table, and lowered the wick, creating a faint glow in the room. Taking to the floor beside Lily, he whispered, "Would you care to rest your head on my shoulder?"

She offered him a tired smile. "If you don't mind, I'd rather use your lap as a pillow. I care not about how improper my request might be. I doubt I've the strength to remain upright much longer."

"Of course." He slipped an arm around her and eased her to him.

Uttering a soft "Thank you," she curled up with her head on his lap, her golden lashes fanning across her cheeks as her lids fluttered shut.

"Rest." He gently worked his fingers through her tangled hair and tenderly stroked her brow. "Soon, this will all be in the past."

"Keep doing that," Lily murmured. "It's soothing."

A curious, welcome warmth spread through him, something he'd not experienced before, yet somehow, the feeling seemed familiar. And natural.

He continued to brush his fingers across her brow and through her hair, using tender strokes.

Who would've thought the sickly woman who'd boarded his ship back in Jamaica would turn out to be a British heiress running from a murderous cousin? And who would've thought she'd end up on the dirt floor of a bayou shanty with her head in the lap of a man not worthy to so much as touch her, let alone bed her.

Memories of their glorious night together swam through his head, filling him with a strange fever that transcended lust. He was damn well going to hurt when she left. Drawing in a slow, deep breath, as deep as he could manage without disturbing her, he held it and used his inflated lungs to compress his heart, as if doing so might force out the sudden pain.

He spied René leaning against the wall next to the table, studying Bastien through hooded eyes. When had his brother slipped back into the room? Nothing in René's composed face reflected his thoughts, but after a lifetime together, Bastien could tell René was now aware of what Bastien didn't want anyone to know—that he was in danger of losing his heart to a woman he could never call his.

"Shut off the damn lantern all the way," he grumbled in Cajun. "No sense wasting oil when dawn will soon be upon us."

René's lips twitched. Slowly, he lifted his shoulder off the wall, leaned over the table and lowered the lamp's wick, shuttering the room in darkness.

Bastien leaned his head against the wall and closed his eyes while a world of confusion hammered his thoughts and knotted his brain.

He didn't know if he'd fallen asleep or had merely dozed when sweet birdsong roused him. He opened his eyes. The pale light of dawn greeted him. Easing Lily from his lap, he slipped outside. He stood at the water's edge and breathed in the fresh, morning air. A few feet away, an enormous bull alligator glided slowly past, his big head and snout floating just above the surface of the still water, his green eyes fixed on Bastien. The bayou was a beautiful world if a person knew its secrets, but deadly if one was a stranger to it. No matter that he wouldn't have chosen a life here; he'd been born to it and learned its ways. At least the shanty he'd been raised in had a wooden floor. And bedrooms. Maman kept the home spotless, and some of the furnishings were worth a good deal of coin—thanks to his good-fornaught wealthy French father, who thought nothing of keeping her as his mistress while refusing to take her out of the bayou and into a better life.

René stepped from the shanty and joined him beside the water.

"I want five minutes alone with Stanhope," Bastien said.

"*Non, mon frère.* Granting such a request would be far too dangerous. You have worked too hard, gained too much to give it all up for what five minutes alone with the devil would cost you." He nodded toward the bull gator floating in front of them. "It would be less perilous to tangle with that beast down there, don'cha know."

Bastien grunted. René was right—he'd likely lose his head and end up hanging for Stanhope's murder. "We did wrestle a few of those monsters when we were young and foolish, *non?*"

René chuckled. "*Oui.* Let's hope we are no longer so reckless in our actions."

Before Bastien had a chance to respond, Armand emerged from inside the shanty, his cudgel in hand. He disappeared around the corner. Reappearing, he hurried to where René and Bastien stood, buttoning his trousers along the way. "Coo-wee! Look at the size of dat gator. Some good eatin' in dat tail, *non?*"

Armand paled when he realized what he'd said. "Shouldn't have said dat. Jess the thought of Stanhope meanin' to serve Lily to the gators raises some *freesons* on my flesh."

His stomach growled.

"Christ," René said. "Give the lad some food. His gut sounds like the mating call of one of these gators."

A belly laugh erupted from Armand. He started for the bridge. "I can fill me a-plenty once we be done here. I best be gittin' along down the path. Doan be forgettin' dat no-good cousin of hers stole the pistol Rubio gave me. I saw him slide it in the back of his trousers. And don' be forgettin' to listen to my hooty-owl, René."

"I'm listening already," René responded. He shoved his hands in his pockets and slipped into the Cajun tongue as his gaze followed the boy running across the bridge. "Look at the size of him. Do you think he's really thirteen? More like ten, I'd say."

Bastien shrugged, but he'd been wondering the same thing. "I don't think he truly knows. Could be his growth's been stunted from not enough food over the years. That's what Régine and Vivienne think. Damn shame to live on the streets the way he did. No clue as to who his father might be or even his last name. Says his *maman* only called him Armand and he can't remember ever hearing anything else."

"You figuring on legally giving him ours? Making him a Thibodeaux?"

Bastien's chest squeezed so tight, he had to take a moment before responding. "Thinking on it. Providing he wants that."

René hiked a brow, then turned on his heel. "You might think about giving someone else your name as well."

Christ! René's words nearly knocked Bastien off his feet. His brother couldn't have been referring to anyone but Lily, and his words were damn cruel. Lady Liliana Stanhope would soon be free to return to England, and to a life so far removed from his, they might as well be living on separate planets. It didn't matter that René had picked up on how Bastien was feeling a few hours ago. They were only feelings. And feelings were elusive emotions that in time passed from his life. They always did. Once this day was over, he'd treat Lily's injuries, act as her *traiteur* once again, and distance himself emotionally.

He stood along the water's edge for a long while, listening to the familiar morning bayou sounds, watching the fish, the alligators, and letting his thoughts roam. From the edges of his mind, a vision of young Bean and her babe, Harmony, formed. When he'd last seen them, they'd been tucked away in the flat bottom of a wooden wagon. Had they managed to reach Canada? Had she delivered the note he'd given her for McGregor? Or had she lost it along the way? Surely the retired ship's bosun would've sent a telegraph by now had she arrived. At least she hadn't been caught and returned to the plantation or he'd have heard about it from the Underground.

The soft sound of an owl hooting caught his attention. René sprang from the shanty and hooted back. He turned to Bastien. "It's time. Come along inside."

Lily stepped outside. Their gazes caught and his heart jumped to his throat. He gripped her shoulders and pressed his forehead to hers. "You don't have to do this."

"But I do," she said. "If it makes you feel any better, I trust you and the others to keep me from harm. All I need is Julian's confession and he's yours."

Dewey and Morrison, rifles in hand, took their places on either side of the shanty, hidden from view. Bastien stepped inside and positioned himself next to the doorway, the spaces between the shanty's boards giving him and the others a good view.

Within moments, a tall, fashionably dressed man came into view.

"Stanhope," Rubio whispered. "I recognize him from that night on the street in front of Le Blanc House."

Bastien didn't know what he'd expected. Certainly not a dashing, fine figure of a man, handsome by any measure. And harmless looking. "Christ. Would you look at the dandy."

Stanhope was halfway across the bridge when he spied Lily and stumbled to a halt. "Sink me, you got yourself loose."

"I did." Her spine stiffened, and by the tilt of her head, Bastien knew she'd lifted her chin in defiance.

"Well, aren't you a bloody mess?" He let out a hoot of laughter. "You look like a ragamuffin straight out of Whitechapel."

"What did you expect, Julian? That I would look fresh as a lady in waiting for the queen?"

Bastien was surprised when Stanhope grinned and dimples formed on the man's clean-shaven cheeks. Stanhope had to be swimming in insanity, but with his blond locks and glowing smile, he could've passed for a saint.

"You cannot think to run off, Lily." Glancing around, her cousin made a dramatic sweep of his hand. "There's no place for you to go..." He tilted his head toward the water. "Except down there, where one, no two, or is it three of those prehistoric beasts linger in wait."

Bastien set his jaw to keep from cursing, his hands opening and closing into fists that wanted to pummel the son of a bitch. René set his hand on Bastien's shoulder and gave it a squeeze.

"You can let me go, Julian. You legally inherit everything."

Stanhope shifted his stance, and a cloud of irritation descended upon his countenance. "You intend to keep flapping your mouth to the bitter end, don't you? I would never do such a thing as set you free, dear cousin. You'd continue to wag your chin to whomever would listen about what we both know to be true, and that simply would never do."

"Tell me, Julian, what happened to Molly?"

"Who's Molly?"

"My lady's maid. She saw you kill my father. You found her and did her in, didn't you?"

He reached up and scratched his head. "*Tsk. Tsk. Tsk.* Let me see. Oh, yes, *that* worker bee. Such a stupid girl. Not only ignorant, but alas, the pudding head couldn't swim."

A strange smile touched his mouth, one that failed to reach his stone-cold eyes. "Do *you* know how to swim, Lily?" He shrugged. "Doesn't matter. Those beasts lurking below don't give a fig if you can swim or not."

A movement behind Stanhope caught Bastien's eye. He drew in a sharp breath. Armand, club in his hand, slowly crept onto the bridge.

"*Merde*," Bastien hissed through his teeth. "What the devil is the fool up to? He's going to get himself killed."

René touched a finger to his lips and shook his head for silence.

Lily shifted her stance and her voice grew stronger. "Do you enjoy toying with me, Cousin? Like a cat playing with a mouse before it pounces?"

He laughed, his face lighting up with what appeared to be sheer joy. "Quite right. Rather immensely. I suppose we had better get on with things before the blasted sun gets too hot. I don't much care for the heat here. Never liked it in India, either."

He started to step forward. She held up her hand. "The least you can do is tell me about my father—your uncle—and why you felt the need to suffocate him with a pillow when you could've merely poisoned him as you did me."

"Oh, I did have a good go at dosing him with the same stuff I gave you, but the bastard didn't react quickly enough to suit. In the end, I lost patience and simply did him in. I should've used his pillow in the first place and not wasted my time on the slow-acting poison."

"There's the confession she needs." Bastien signaled to his brother, Rubio, and Michel. Together, they stepped from the shanty behind Lily. Dewey and Morrison, rifles aimed at Stanhope, stepped from around each corner of the building.

Stanhope gasped. In a flash, he reached behind himself, snatching a pistol tucked in the top of his trousers.

Before the others could act, Armand swung his cudgel, hitting Stanhope's arm with a loud *thwack*.

The gun went flying.

Stanhope twisted around to look behind him.

He slipped.

Eyes wide, arms and legs flailing like windmills, he gave a loud screech and tumbled off the bridge.

Bastien pulled Lily into his arms and buried her face against his chest. "Don't look."

Stanhope hit the water. A great roiling and boiling of the waters rose up. One gator after another sank razor-sharp teeth into him, and the churning waters turned crimson. Blood-curdling screams turned into hideous begging. Then the bull gator swept in and went to war for dominance.

Dewey stepped to the edge of the bridge. He raised his rifle. One shot and Stanhope's horrifying cries went silent.

As the gators took Stanhope under and the waters stilled, Dewey turned to Bastien, his face pasty white, his hands shaking. "I had to put him out of his misery."

"You did him a favor." Bastien spied Armand standing stock-still behind Dewey, his eyes wide and swimming with tears. "Good God!"

Lily lifted her head. "Go to him, Bastien. He needs you."

René stepped forward. "Lily's right. I'll see she's safe."

Bastien started for Armand but he turned and ran. Bastien's booted feet pounded the earth, his long strides catching up with the boy just around the bend in the path.

"I kilt him." He swiped at a cascade of tears. "I didn't mean to. Never kilt no man."

"*Non*, Armand. This was not your fault. He tripped and fell. He came to murder Lily in one of the cruelest ways possible. Providence took over, and he ended up being the one to meet the fate he had planned for his cousin."

"I did wrong." Tears continued to streak down Armand's dirty face, leaving clean tracks and dripping off his chin. "Now I ain't got no right to be your ward."

Bastien threw his arms around the boy. "It was an accident. Stanhope shouldn't have been on the bridge with bad intentions. Now let's go get Miss Lily and take her home."

"Home?"

"*Oui*. Home. How would you like to be more than my ward?" Bastien swallowed hard. *Merde*. Why were his emotions getting away from him? "How..." He paused to clear his throat. "How would you like it if I were to adopt you? Give you my name?"

Armand stepped back, staring at Bastien for a long moment. "Does that mean you'd be my pa?"

Bastien bit back his own tears. "*Oui*. I would be."

Armand sniffed and took another swipe at his dirty cheeks. "How you gonna go about being my pa, and showin' me how to be your kid when you ain't never had none?"

"Hell if I know. Since I never had a father to show me how to be one, I can only promise that I will give it a damn good try. Do you think you can meet me halfway?"

Armand stared at Bastien for another long moment, as if he were peeling away layers and looking deep into Bastien's heart. And then he sniffed, wiped his cheeks with his dirty fist and grinned. "I'd be likin' dat a whole lot. Now let's go get Miss Lily and take her home with us. Where she belongs."

Where she belongs.

Bastien's chest shuddered on the intake of a harsh breath. Those words sure as hell felt right. If only they could be made true.

Chapter Twenty-Two

A cool breeze washed over Lily, waking her. The too-long nap had left her feeling lethargic and foggy headed. She lay atop the bedcovers, absentmindedly observing dust motes dancing about in a stream of late afternoon sun. When had the weather shifted? And why did she feel so downcast? Shouldn't she be filled with a glorious sense of victory since she no longer had her monstrous cousin to fear? And now she was free to return to her life in England.

I have no life in England.

Nothing to return to.

James Stanhope was not my father.

She squeezed her eyes shut against the sharp pain slicing through her. She had no legal right to anything belonging to him. Not so much as a tuppence. Not so much as the porcelain music box she'd left behind in London. He had no heirs, which meant his entire estate would revert to the Crown. What a pity. Should she pretend to be ignorant of her true heritage and unlawfully inherit?

She could not live with such deceit. Not at all.

She needed to confront Charles.

A wave of melancholy washed over her. When all was said and done, would she end up having to turn to him for shelter—a father who'd betrayed her with his silence all these years? By no means did she wish to succumb to such a fate. In fact, she doubted she'd forgive him any time soon for the terrible secret he'd kept, let alone reside in his household. Blast it all, she must also forgive both James and her long-dead mother for their deceit as well.

Her mood sank even lower as she sat up on the side of the bed with a soft grunt and inspected the gauze bandages wrapped neatly around her wrists.

And therein lies the greatest reason for my misery.

Bastien had tended to these injuries. But he'd done so in a cold and detached manner, damn the man. Gone was the warm, compassionate lover who'd protected her in the bayou. Once home, he'd turned her care over to Allita and Vivienne. At the time, she'd thought nothing of his action since she required a bath and needed to have her hair washed. But upon completion of her toilette, an aloof Bastien returned, once again acting the consummate professional *traiteur.* After he'd applied an unguent and wrapped her wrists, he'd advised Vivienne on Lily's further care and promptly departed. The intimacy they'd shared so recently was nowhere to be seen.

A wall now stood between them.

One Bastien alone had built.

His bewildering conduct left a tremendous void in her.

Her nerves in a jangle, she stood, brushed the wrinkles from her sprigged muslin day gown, and headed down to the kitchen.

Régine and Vivienne sat at the table along with Allita, Rubio, and Armand. A large pot of café au lait and a round platter of beignets rested in the center of the table. At the cozy sight of this eclectic group, Lily's heart pinched. Her mood plummeted even further. She'd soon be leaving them behind. But to go where?

"How you be feeling, Miss Lily?" Armand mumbled through a mouthful of Régine's tasty French fritters.

Lily tensed. And then she realized he referred to her injuries not her mood. She eased out a held breath. "Much better than the past twenty-four hours, thank you."

Armand grinned, sheer contentment radiating from him.

Her heart gave another squeeze. *He feels safe knowing he has a permanent home.* No longer did he refuse to remain inside. Gone were the days when he'd dash back to the stable with food in hand and consume it alone. Poor dear. What horrors he must've suffered trying to survive alone on the streets for so long.

She folded her hands in front of her and offered him a smile. "It's good to see you sitting at the table with everyone, Armand. But should you be drinking coffee at such a young age?"

"*Humph.* I be Cajun, Miss Lily. We start drinkin' this fine tastin' stuff in the cradle. That's how café au lait came to be, don'cha know."

Even stoic Vivienne laughed. "That's not quite the way of things, Armand. Won't you join us, Miss Lily?"

Lily shook her head. "Not just yet. Do you know where I might find Bastien?"

Rubio swallowed a gulp of coffee. "He went off to the shipping office to check on things. Then he and Henri were to meet up with a horse trader. After that, he'll see a gentleman who makes fine carriages. Won't be home until late, he said."

"I see." Disappointment flooded Lily. It took all she had not to turn on her heel and race to her bedchamber. Instead, she forced herself to join them, poured a cup of coffee and helped herself to a beignet.

Once their afternoon repast was over, Vivienne asked to see Lily's wrists. Chairs scraped along the floor as the others scrambled to take their leave. Unwrapping the gauze, Vivienne gave a nod. "*Bien.* I will discard these bandages. The salve Bastien applied worked to close the abraded skin. Now we shall allow the air to do the rest of the healing. On the morrow, I shall look in on you before the noon hour. Then Bastien will check your progress before you retire for the night."

A chill ran down Lily's spine. He didn't intend to meet with her until late tomorrow? *What is going on? Why is he avoiding me?* Frustration got the best of her. "No, he will not," she snapped.

Vivienne's spine stiffened. She sat back with a frown and clasped her hands in her lap. "Why not?"

Oh, dear. What have I gone and done, losing my temper? I must've lost my wits. "You…you are doing a fine job with my care. Bastien is a busy man who has done quite enough for me. Hereafter, if you feel uncomfortable tending to me, then please send for his mother."

Vivienne studied her for a long moment through narrowed eyes. Then she rose and, with her chin in the air and her back ramrod straight, proceeded to make her exit. "As you wish."

Left to her own devices, Lily stepped into the garden. Chills skittered down her spine. Julian had kidnapped her out here. She made a hasty retreat and decided to visit the library while she awaited Bastien's return—waited to get to the bottom of his curious behavior. However, no matter which book she chose, concentrating on so much as a single paragraph proved fruitless, so after returning one book after another to the shelf, she gave up. Nothing she attempted settled her nerves. Not even pacing the floor. The mellow sound of the library's pendulum clock marked the hour of ten, striking a dull chord in her chest.

Still no Bastien.

Dejected, she gave up and climbed the stairs to her bedchamber, where she slipped into a silk peignoir. The fabric, delicate as an aqua mist, grazed her skin. A buzz ran across her flesh and into her belly. The sensation was too reminiscent of Bastien's erotic touch. She missed him. Blast it all, there was no denying it—his avoiding her hurt something terrible.

Cursing under her breath, she removed the gown and donned a nondescript thin cotton night rail. This, too, brushed across her skin, leaving a tingling in its wake. Frustrated, she left the garment on and took to her bed.

In moments, her tossing about left the covers in disarray. In a miserable huff, she got to her feet, snatched a woolen shawl from her wardrobe, and marched down the corridor into Bastien's quarters. Turning a single gaslight on low, she retreated to the balcony and settled into one of the chaise lounges.

Try as she might to calm her restless thoughts, not even the starry sky or jasmine-scented air served to calm her. Just when she was ready to give up and seek her bed once again, the soft snick of the door opening and closing caught her ear.

He's returned.

She felt the air stir, felt Bastien's powerful presence before he silently stepped onto the balcony. She looked up at him. He stood before her clothed in his usual dark trousers and a white shirt open at the collar with sleeves rolled. At the sheer sight of him, a curious, liquid warmth spread from her belly and pulsed inside her skin. Fighting the urge to jump up and rush into his arms, she remained in place, refusing to speak first.

Their gazes locked.

He fisted his hands on his hips and said nothing, but a flurry of emotions ran through those fierce blue eyes of his, none of which she could name. Then his mouth twitched. "Vivienne says you've sacked me. Why is that?"

So, they were to get right to the meat of the conversation. *Well then, honesty it shall be.* "I do not wish to see the remote and professional *traiteur.* What I need is what we've shared in the past. Thus, if Vivienne refuses to treat me, I prefer your mother."

He grunted. "You don't even like Maman."

The low, smooth timbre of his voice gave her belly a twist. She shrugged. "I believe the feeling might be mutual."

He stood before her for a long while, saying nothing, but those expressive eyes told their own tale. Something shifted in him and his pupils flared, deepening in color.

She rose from the chaise and approached him. "What causes the storm in your eyes, Bastien?"

When his silence continued, she leaned in and placed a hand flat against his hard chest. He stood unmoving, more marble than man. Fear skittered through her but she forced down her rising distress.

"I could use one of your long hugs," she said. "The kind that makes me forget all the danger I have been through."

Something shifted in him anew. He lowered his lids, shuttering the emotion in his eyes. When he spoke, his voice held a huskier tone. "I give you that kind of hug, do I?"

She'd heard that rasp in his voice before. So, he was not unaffected by her presence after all. Her heartbeat kicked up against her ribs. "You do."

He sucked in a deep, shaky breath, then slashing her a dark look, turned on his heel and strode back into his bedchamber. "You should leave. You have packing to do."

What? A shockwave ran through her, making her head swim. Had he just dismissed her?

Dear God, she'd only just found him and already she was losing him. Could feel him slipping away from her. The angry thrum of her blood rose up to beat a furious tattoo in her temple. Suddenly her heart felt like a bleeding wound inside her chest.

Ask me to stay.

She heard her own harsh breathing. Could feel her heart racing in panic. No, she couldn't panic—she *wouldn't* panic. Her breath clogged her lungs. She swallowed hard. "I don't understand. Why are you asking me to leave?"

He kept his back to her, his fingers flexing, his fists clenching and unclenching. "Your dilemma is over, Lily. You are now free to return to England. A ship leaves port a week from tomorrow for London. I've booked passage on it for you and Chamberlain."

What's over? You and me? Or Julian? I have no home in England. I am not Lady Liliana Stanhope, damn it!

She dared not confess her new dilemma just yet. Not until she'd confronted Charles regarding her true parentage. And she dared not inform Bastien for fear he would interpret the news as a plea to take her in. Well, she was no bloody, homeless orphan on the begging end of life.

At his insolent words, she unraveled. Waves of anger washed over her, and her tongue refused to be silent. "For God's sake, Bastien. We've not been playing a game of naked chess where you decide to announce a stalemate, then hand over my clothes and send me off with a handshake and an *adieu*."

She wanted to cry out that she loved him, but her heart told her no.

Bastien was right. She was free to leave. And hadn't he once said he had no inclination to wed? If he were ever to decide he wanted a life with her, he had to come to that decision alone.

Move your feet. Walk away.

"I have one question. If I am not departing until next week, why pull away now? Why not thoroughly enjoy each other until I take my leave? Why not take joy in each other's company with no holds barred? No regrets."

His back was to her, but he visibly stiffened. "I've never believed in lengthy goodbyes, Lily. You should leave."

The low rumble of his command shut out the world around her. She stood stoic, unmoving while she raged inwardly, trying to gather strength enough to make her exit.

"You are free as a bird to explore the city at your leisure before returning to your home in England," came his voice from the shadows. "What we had together amounted to no more than a bit of pleasure-seeking between us. But now that you are about to take your leave, I see no sense in carrying on."

That did it. Rage took over. "That's just plain silly." Lily yanked the door open so hard it hit the wall with a bang. "I abhor infantile thinking. You, sir, can take your nonsensical, idiotic way of thinking and shove it right up your—"

He moved like lightning, slamming the door shut, and nearly knocking her backward. Swinging her around, he slapped the flat of his hands against the wall on either side of her, caging her in. His eyes, piercing sapphire flames, locked onto hers. "Right up my what?"

In that wild moment, and despite her raging temper, a bubble of laughter crawled up her throat. She couldn't help the grin that escaped. "Your bum."

The very air around them stilled. Seemed to hold its breath along with hers, waiting for his response. A shadow moved across his face. He stood over her, saying nothing for what felt like an eternity.

And then something profound shifted in him.

The tension in his entire body seemed to give way. The muscles in his face and along his jaw relaxed. His lips, thinned by emotion, softened and parted. Turned lush and ripe, ready to be tasted. The edges of his eyes softened and the blue deepened, his gaze turning hot, licking across her skin like a living flame.

God help me, perhaps I haven't lost him after all.

He seemed to struggle for words.

She waited, saying nothing.

And then, the cold wall he'd built between them gave way. Crumbled to dust. He pressed his forehead to hers. "Do you care for me, Lily?"

Care for you? Silly fool, I've fallen stupidly, madly in love with you.

But she couldn't say those words. The sudden change in him had just given her hope, but he had to know his own heart. Speak his own truth. With no urging on her part. She cared deeply for him—an elephant in the room couldn't be more obvious. But if he failed to declare his love for her first, she would walk away. And if he were ever to change his mind and come looking for her, he would have her answer before he stepped through her door.

"Well, Lily? Do you care for me or not?"

"I suppose I might." She pulled her head back, tilted it from one side to the other. "What of you? Do you care for me?"

A corner of his mouth tipped up. He gave a shrug with one shoulder. "I suppose I might, as well."

He leaned closer, keeping her caged, his sweet breath mingling with hers, their gazes locked, his countenance relaxed. "Who was the woman telling me to shove my words up my bum? Could that have been Miss Lily talking? Or could that have been the right and proper Lady Liliana?"

The murmur of her name in that deep voice of his soaked through her skin right to her bones. She couldn't confess that she was Charles's daughter. Not yet anyway. But no matter, she'd still carry the title Lady Liliana. She hiked her chin and let a wave of defiance wash over her. "You tell me."

"Oh, I suspect the culprit was the very proper, play-by-the-snobbish-British-rules-book Lady Liliana."

"Tell me how you reached your conclusion."

"That's easy. It was Miss Lily who dared to ride her horse through town in the dead of night. Proper Lady Liliana would've kept snug in her bed. It was Miss Lily who freely gave her virginity to a no-account Cajun while loving every minute of it. But what do we do with Lady Liliana, seeing as how she has not yet had her night with a wild French Cajun?"

He tugged her night rail. It slipped off her shoulder, exposing one breast. A sultry smile touched his lips. "Perhaps Lady Liliana would like to partake of something a bit racier than what Miss Lily engaged in?"

Lily could barely breathe, felt close to shattering. "And what would that be?"

He bent his head to her ear, his hot breath a whisper across her cheek. Closing his teeth over the lobe of her ear, he gave it a soft nip, shooting arrows through her every nerve and landing in her belly. "Perhaps the right proper Lady Liliana would like—and need—to be well and thoroughly fucked."

Equal parts scandalized and tantalized, she sucked in a breath, her eyes flaring wide. "Oh!"

A soft chuckle left his throat.

She'd heard that naughty word on the London docks, but never knew it could be whispered in her ear in a voice so provocative as to light a firestorm in her blood. "Why, Monsieur Thibodeaux, what colorful language you use."

His gaze dipped down to land on the taut nipple straining against her gown. He gave the thin fabric another tug, baring her to the waist. "I like to enhance my speech with a little color." His voice deepened to a husky rasp in his throat. "I'm creative that way, don'cha know."

She laughed. "I like that word...*creative*. In this case, I've a feeling it holds great promise."

Slowly, he raised his eyes to meet hers. A mischievous smile tipped the corners of his mouth while the banked embers in his sapphire gaze looked ready to ignite. Perhaps the slightest spark might turn those embers into an inferno. And what she wanted most was to light the match.

Her fingers went to work tugging his shirt from his trousers. She ran the flat of her hand over his hard, flat belly, moving downward until she reached the top of his trousers. Freeing the top two buttons, she slid her fingers between skin and fabric. Grasping hold of him, she slid her hand up and down, daring him to make the next move.

He groaned. "Is there really such a thing as naked chess?"

Her breathing grew more labored by the moment, making it hard to speak. "I've heard rumors of Cambridge and Oxford lads using the game as a scandalous way of seducing young innocents. Whoever loses a chess piece is required to remove an article of clothing."

"Well, then." In one move, he divested her of her night rail, swept her up in his arms, and carried her to the bed. "Checkmate."

She landed in the middle of the feather mattress with a squeal of laughter and then settled in to watch him pull his shirt over his head and step out of his trousers, leaving his glorious body on full display.

He wasted no time joining her on the bed, then pulled her full length against him and slid inside her. "Hush," he murmured. "Don't move. Let the energy in our bodies merge. We'll both know when you are ready to step off the cliff and fly with me."

Her sheath pulsed around him. Still, he prevented her from moving until she lost all reason. She cried out his name while a singular thought cascaded like a waterfall over her, through her, around her—she loved him. Wanted him. Needed him.

Forever.

Chapter Twenty-Three

Bastien slipped back into his bedchamber carrying a full breakfast tray. Easing the door shut behind him with a bare foot, he made his way to where Lily lay on her stomach in a tangle of sheets, her flaxen hair fanning out over her pillow—or was it his pillow? His heart kicked up a notch. Christ, even in sleep, she had to be the most beautiful woman alive.

He set the tray next to her and waited for her reaction to the heady scent of fresh-from-the-oven bread slathered with butter and jam. Her nose twitched. Grinning, he lifted the lid off the pot of steaming café au lait, sending another delicious aroma into the air around them. A soft, kitten noise left her throat. Her body shifted.

That didn't take long.

Making his way to the balcony, he set the tray on a table between two chaise lounges, then gave the cuffs of his shirtsleeves a crisp turn and settled into the chaise farthest from the door. With a contented sigh, he stretched out his legs, and clasping his hands behind his head, took in the fresh morning air while he awaited sleepy Lily.

What a night they'd shared. What had occurred between them was better than good—it was life-changing. They'd gone from hot and greedy lovemaking, to a soul-searching emotional journey that would remain with him forever. The serenity flowing through him had been born during the night, coming from deep within his core. Hell, he couldn't explain what had occurred, but it was honest and good for both of them. Finally, he understood the change that had taken place in his brother after Felice came along.

He caught a flash of white out of the corner of his eye, and Lily wandered onto the balcony wearing one of his shirts, her hair a messy golden cloud. His throat tightened, and the air left his lungs. Damn, but she was gorgeous.

Rubbing one eye with the heel of her hand while the other was still half-closed, she stumbled past the empty chaise and, without a word, crawled onto his lap. She curled up on her side against him, her head on his chest.

Heart lifting, he swept his arms around her, brought her in closer to him, her body heat penetrating his clothing. "Are you even awake?"

"Uh-uh," she mumbled. "Gimme a sip of your coffee."

"I brought you a cup as well."

"Too lazy. Want yours."

He chuckled. "Lift your head, or you'll dribble on my shirt." He held his cup to her lips. Yet another emotion he'd never encountered before swept through him. Could life get any better than this?

When Chamberlain returned, Bastien would ask him for her hand. Since the man was her godfather, it seemed the right thing to do. Then he'd tell her he loved her—as if his feelings weren't already apparent after last night. He wanted to save those extraordinary words for when he asked her to spend the rest of her life with him.

"Bastien?"

"Hmm?" His hands moved over her back and along her hip in gentle swirls, caressing her.

"After all this time in New Orleans, I still don't know what it's like to live in your world. Will you show me?"

"*Oui*. Perhaps we should start by taking you to the beautiful parts of the bayou. Erase any bad memories that might linger. The bayou is magnificent at dusk, when fireflies look like dancing lights atop the water and along the banks."

"I would like that. Then take me on a steamboat upriver. Maybe stop and visit Justin Andrews."

Another wave of pleasure washed through him. This wasn't her only indication that she might be open to remaining in New Orleans. She'd mentioned having been born in India and that she hadn't much noticed the heat back then. If she couldn't tolerate summer's oppressive heat here, they could always spend those months someplace cooler.

"Are we cuddling or snuggling?" she asked.

Pulling her even closer, he rested his chin atop her head. "I say we are cuddling. Snuggling should definitely be done in bed, *non*?"

"Mmmm. Let's go snuggle." Her fingers trailed up and down the side of his ribs, sending waves of pleasure through him.

"How about we spend the day upright doing fun things together?" He ran his palm over her hip and flat stomach. What would it be like to see her belly filled with his child? What would it be like to hold their babe in his arms? His heart stuttered in his chest.

She lifted her head and studied him. "What's wrong?"

"Nothing's wrong. Things couldn't be any better. Why do you ask?"

"Because your heart went from a slow beat to a gallop just now."

He laughed and gave her a squeeze. "Merely thinking good thoughts, *chère.*"

"Tell me."

"Soon."

She traced the faint scar leading from his eyebrow to his hairline just above his ear. "How did you come by this?"

A knock at the bedchamber door saved Bastien from responding. He eased her off his lap. "It was a long-ago childhood mishap. Wait here."

She giggled. "I had better remain out of sight since I happen to be wearing your shirt and nothing else."

He strode to the door and pulling it open, found Henri on the other side. "Sorry to disturb you, sir. Monsieur Hardin is here with the two horses you wanted to try out."

"*Merde.* I forgot the time. Give me a few minutes to change." Shutting the door, he headed for his dressing room. "Stay however long you wish, *chère.* I'll only be a couple of hours."

He changed into a pair of tan riding britches, slipped into his tall boots, donned a cravat, waistcoat, and jacket, then stepped into the corridor. He spied Allita exiting Lily's bedchamber. "Collect a frock for Miss Lily, *s'il vous plaît.* She'll be making her toilette in my bathing chamber. *Bonjour.*"

He strode down the corridor with Allita's giggle trailing behind him. *No doubt the entire household is about to learn of Lily's whereabouts last night.* He grinned. What of it? She'd soon become his wife.

He rushed down the stairs and headed for the back door. His mother stepped from the kitchen, blocking his way. Her face a frozen mask, she spoke to him in clipped Cajun French. "Stay away from that woman."

A cold chill ran down his spine. He paused long enough to collect his thoughts. "What brought you here, and why are you standing in my home telling me what I should do with my life?"

"She is British, Bastien. You detest the British."

He lifted a brow. "I got over it. What else do you have to say?"

"Do not forget, she is nobility while you are illegitimate, straight out of the bayou. You are something to toy with, an exotic diversion to someone like her."

He laughed, a low rumbling in his throat that held no relationship to the darkness running through him. "An exotic diversion straight out of the bayou, you say? That is rich, especially coming from you, Maman."

Color rose in her cheeks. "Mark my words. She is bound to grow bored with you. Lady Liliana Stanhope will return to England and wed someone of her ilk. Leave her be. Send her to a hotel until her ship departs. This I can promise you, Bastien—she will break your heart."

Despite the anger heating his blood, ice formed around Bastien's words. "Break my heart, Maman? You shattered it when I was four years old."

The knuckles of Odalie's clasped hands turned white and a muscle in her jaw ticked. "That's enough."

"Oh, I'm only just beginning. How many hours did I sit on our shanty's dock, waiting for René to come home from school? Waiting for him to hide me from that son of a bitch you had in your bed fathering yet another one of his bastards."

Odalie's lips thinned. "I said that's enough. I came to warn you, save you from the trap I fell into."

Bastien pointed to the thin white scar running from eyebrow to hairline. "I would've lost an eye had I not been quick enough to escape his blade. That's what I got for walking in on the two of you in bed together. Yet you failed to step in, said nothing while you stitched me up."

She paled. "Because of my errors, perhaps I am the best person to understand your situation. Your father is a French nobleman. I know all about the ways of their kind. Like him, Lady Liliana Stanhope will not stand by you in the end."

Bastien's certainty was beginning to crumble. He needed to escape. "I understand what you are really saying, Maman."

He swept open his arms, stretched them wide. "Look around," he went on. "You stand in the most opulent home in the Garden District, owned by an executive of one of the largest maritime operations in the world. No longer am I a street thief of little value. Yet you continue to tell me, in every way possible, that I am not good enough. Nor will I ever be."

Odalie's lips thinned even further. "I speak of her, not you. She will surely destroy you. And your reaction to my warning tells me you are already on your way to certain ruin."

"Please take your leave before I become even more disrespectful. You have done things in the past that have caused René and me to shun you for long periods. But we always return. Why? Because you are our mother—our *legitimate* mother. Despite all that has occurred, we have honored you, as the church taught us."

"*Humph.* Until that enraged priest kicked the two of you into the streets for yet another of your misdeeds."

"You know damn well the concoction René and I slipped into the incense burners came from your bag of voodoo potions. We were children, for God's sake. We thought we'd done something good by setting the entire congregation's heads buzzing. And now you want to turn that incident into something terrible?"

He sucked in a deep breath and blew it out. "I've had enough. Leave my home. Do not step through my door until an invitation is issued—if ever." He walked away before she could see the pall descending upon him.

* * * *

After spending a leisurely hour in the bath and another hour lounging on the balcony awaiting Bastien, Lily exited his quarters.

And ran headlong into Charles.

He glanced over her shoulder at Bastien's unmade bed, then back to her, his face the color of ripe plums. "Bloody hell, gel. What have you done?"

She stiffened. "I am a woman, Charles, not a girl. I shall do as I please. However, I should be asking the same question of you—what have *you* done all these years?"

A puzzled frown creased his forehead. "What the devil are you getting at?"

"Come with me." She marched into her bedroom, leaving the door open for him to follow. Without another word, she collected the love letter her mother had written to him about the babe she was expecting—his babe. The letter told of her mother's need to avoid scandal by wedding James in Charles's absence. Lily handed the letter to him and stepped back. She shoved her hands in the pockets of her skirt, hiding her shaky fingers.

He scowled. "What is this?"

She shrugged. "Why don't you tell me?"

He opened the missive. His face, which had moments before been flushed, turned pale. "How did you come by this?"

"You left your box full of letters peeking out from under your bed." Lily began to pace. Her voice sounded calm, completely different from the fury and sadness she felt. "What should I be calling you from here on out, Charles or Father?"

A gurgle left his throat. "Oh, no, Lily. You have things wrong. James is your father, not I."

"Then what is that in your hand if not proof? And do not tell me Mother lied."

He swiped a hand over his eyes as if to wipe away the anguish in them. "No, she didn't…she told the truth. She was indeed expecting when she wrote this. However, you are not that child."

Lily stopped pacing and faced Charles. A chill swept over her. She wrapped her arms about her waist and rubbed at them. "What do you mean?"

"Your mother and I were very much in love. We were planning to announce our engagement following my military assignment in Northern India. A few months later, I received this missive informing me she had wed James to avoid a scandal she would never be able to live down. By the time I returned, she had miscarried our child."

Lily's head swam. "You were still in love with her?"

Charles's eyes filled with liquid and the agony in his face, in the slump of his shoulders, softened Lily. "Indeed. However, it was too late to undo things. James was an honorable man. He had done right by your mother. By me, as well."

Lily stepped to the window and stared out at nothing in particular. "Did you take up with my mother thereafter?"

"God, no. I loved her. Still do, but the die had been cast. She found a sweet kind of love with your father, and his love for her grew in kind, something they both deserved. We remained close friends, so when you came along, they eagerly included me in the family as your godfather."

She glanced over her shoulder and nearly winced at the beseeching look in his eyes. She walked back to the window. "They were willing to share me with you?"

"Indeed. Strange as it may sound. When your mother died in that horrible accident and James was left in a wheelchair, I stepped in to not only care for you, but to look after James as well."

Lily rubbed her forehead against the ache beginning to work itself into a tight band. "I don't know what to say. I do wish you had told me."

"Why? It was all in the past, between your mother, James, and me."

"A lover's triangle," she muttered.

"No…yes…oh, bloody hell. What your mother and I had before she wed James was relegated to the past, but I never stopped loving her, no matter how I tried."

"Is that why you never married?"

"I failed to meet anyone who could live up to her ideal." He cleared his throat. "Let's put this issue to bed for the time being. Now that we are to sail to England next week, I think it best if we remove ourselves to a hotel. Nothing good can come of further associating with Mr. Thibodeaux. You must steer clear of him."

The band around Lily's head tightened. She'd need to take some powders after this. "I do not wish to steer clear of him. Nor will I be joining you in some dreary hotel."

A breath left Charles in a whoosh. "Lily, this is madness. You are a woman of noble blood who is about to come into a vast fortune while he is...he is—"

"He's what, Charles?" She snapped around to face him.

"Oh, my dear, he is so far beneath you. Can you not see he's using you? That he seduced you for his own pleasure? You cannot spend another moment with a...a low-bred bastard who climbed out of life's gutter to dally with you."

The ache in Lily's head streaked down her neck and into her shoulders. "Why, you arrogant fool! Coming from a humble background does not make someone a failure for the rest of their life. In fact, I am in awe of what the man has managed to accomplish."

Charles shook his head. "There are things you do not know about him, Lily. Terrible things I do not want your ears to hear."

"Well, my ears are certainly open to hearing what you have to say," came Bastien's deep and measured voice.

Lily spun around to find Bastien leaning a shoulder against the doorjamb, his booted feet crossed at the ankles. His eyes, shards of blue ice, belied his casual stance.

"Bastien!" She started for him.

A small shake of his head stopped her.

"By all means, enlighten me, Lord Chamberlain. What is it about me you do not wish your goddaughter to know?"

Charles waved a hand in the air as if brushing Bastien aside like a pesky fly. "Be off with you. I'm in no mood for a male whore trying to take the moral high ground."

Shock sent Lily stepping back. "Charles! That's enough!"

Charles's face turned purple again, and his breathing grew labored. "Perhaps you should venture into the Vieux Carré, Lily. Seek out a certain Madame Olympée. Since it is Sunday, you will likely find her at home rather than at her place of business. Thus, you can ask her in private how she employed this bastard in her house of ill repute."

Confusion swept through Lily. *House of ill repute?*

She glanced from Charles to Bastien. Not a flicker of emotion passed over Bastien's countenance. Nor did he deny Charles's accusation. "What are you getting at?"

Charles stomped over to where she stood, so close she could see the veins bulging in his eyes. "I'll bet he thrilled you plenty, seeing as how he's pleasured so many women, he's lost count."

At a loss for words, Lily looked to Bastien. The wall he'd once constructed between them was once again in place.

She opened her mouth to speak, but Charles raised a hand. "I am not finished. In case you fail to understand me, Lily. The man was trained by the madam of a whorehouse in the precise art of pleasuring a woman. For pay. Do I need to make myself any clearer?"

Stunned, she again looked at Bastien. He said nothing, merely leveled his frigid gaze on Charles, leaving her own blood to run cold. She was losing him. "Whatever his past, I do not care. I—"

"Would you hush for one damn minute, Lily?" Charles made his way to where Bastien stood, unmoving. "Did you overhear the earlier conversation between Lily and myself about my relationship with her mother?"

"*Oui,*" Bastien responded.

"Then you heard me telling Lily how much I loved the woman who carried my child and married my best friend?"

"*Oui.*"

"I loved that woman with every inch of my being, but once she wed another, our relationship as we knew it was over. Even though I loved her for the rest of her short life, I did not carry on with her in any form other than friendship. I would not risk the scandal. I would do nothing to sully her name, or the name of my friend. Because I cherished her, I stepped away. I gave her up. And it hurt like the devil had cut my heart out with a spoon."

Bastien's gaze moved across Lily's face as if he were looking for something. "And you would like me to step away from your goddaughter. Have I got the right of it?"

"Think on this, Bastien Thibodeaux from the bayou—she has eight hundred years of noble blood running through her veins. She is all that is left of the Stanhope name. The last thing this lady needs is to get mixed up with some illegitimate nothing who crawled out of a swamp."

Lily burst into tears. "Stop. I don't care about any of that. Get out, Charles. Get out of my life!"

Charles faced her. "Think, Lily. You were the genius behind Cowdrey Imports. You are the one who built the business into a small empire, not

James. There are families depending on you for their sustenance. Your company solicitors cannot continue to act in your stead indefinitely. You have a responsibility to return to England and to wed someone of your standing, not…not this…this…nobody."

Bastien pushed away from the door casing and took a deep breath. "You have managed to insult me in my own home, Lord Chamberlain. I would like you to remove yourself within the hour. I'll arrange for you and your goddaughter to stay in the company townhouse in the Vieux Carré until your ship sails. Or you can choose a hotel."

He looked at Lily. "You should listen to the man, Lady Liliana Stanhope. He makes sense."

"No, Bastien. I won't have it." She started toward him. "You are my world—"

"Stop, Lily." Bastien stepped away from her. "You are only making things worse. Please, do not think to follow me." He turned on his heel and strode down the corridor, then disappeared down the stairs.

Lily swung around to face her godfather. "My God, Charles. What have you done?"

"You still think you are in love with that man? Once you are back home, you'll see things in another light. You'll realize you were only besotted."

"You couldn't be more wrong. Whomever I fall in love with is not your choice. In fact, I doubt it was even my decision. I love you, Charles. I always will, but I don't much like you right now. Nor do I respect you. We need to put some distance between us. Hopefully, one day I will overcome these negative feelings weighing me down. I shall remain here and wait for Bastien. These are my final words, Charles. Do not make me repeat them."

He looked at her through eyes growing damp. Then he nodded and walked away. In an hour he was gone from the house. His belongings were packed in trunks and followed him the next day.

* * * *

Lily waited for Bastien to walk through the door, but night fell and he failed to show. Nor did he appear the next day. Or the next. A hollowness hung in the very air of the home. On the third day of his absence, she wandered into the kitchen.

Bastien's mother sat at the kitchen table. She stood, her spine stiff. "You are still here?"

Lily braced herself against Odalie's frosty tone. "I'm waiting for Bastien."

"He's gone."

"Where?"

"He sailed to Barbados. He won't come back until you are gone from here."

Stunned, Lily lifted her chin. She'd be damned if she'd falter in front of this woman. "Did he tell you this?"

"Believe me, he has no intention of returning until he is certain you are gone. I told him to avoid you, but he wouldn't listen. Although he's made a success of himself, he will never be able to live up to your standards, so he's gone off to lick his wounds. Do you think you should be living in his home while he is not?"

Odalie's last words struck a chord with Lily. If Bastien had left for the purpose of avoiding her, then she had no business remaining.

"Leave this place, Lady Liliana Stanhope. Go back to your own country. Go back to your mansion in the city and your castle in the country. Go back to your rigid British society."

Unable to think, to even respond, Lily started for the door. She nearly fell apart when she spied Régine and Vivienne standing off to the side, saying nothing. She knew then what she had to do.

She walked past them and paused. "Would you mind locating Rubio? Ask him to come to my bedchamber."

Holding back tears lest she fall apart completely, she managed to climb the stairs and stumble into her bedchamber. Reaching under the bed, she removed the large painting she'd done of Bastien and laid it face down.

Rubio entered the room looking downcast.

"Would you be so kind as to create some manner of wooden crate to hold this large canvas? And please ask Allita to come help me pack."

"I don't know what to say, Miss Lily. I'm so sorry things didn't work out."

Lily fought back tears. "Saying nothing would be best. Please, if you'll leave me, I have much to do."

With Rubio gone, she reached into the bottom of her wardrobe and retrieved the small charcoal of Bastien she'd sketched. A tear rolled down her cheek. Making her way into his bedchamber, she slipped the rolled drawing under his pillow, then closed her eyes against the pain that made breathing nearly impossible.

She straightened to make her exit.

Vivienne stood at the threshold, watching her. Lily bent her head and pinched the bridge of her nose. "Please, Vivienne, I do not have an ounce of strength left in me to have any sort of a conversation."

"I mean you no harm, Miss Lily. Except for Bastien's mother, we are all very sad that things took a bad turn. Before you leave, I would like to share something with you."

Lily gave up trying to be strong and let the tears stream down her face. "What is it?"

"As you are aware, life was not easy for René and Bastien, but with Bastien being the younger, he suffered more. By the time he was sixteen, he'd grown into a big, handsome man. Women of all ages adored him, catered to him for all the wrong reasons. They showered him with attention he'd not experienced before. When René left to work on a ship for six months, Bastien got caught breaking into a home to steal food and landed in jail. Madame Olympée bought his release and made him an offer that would save him from the hangman's noose. Once René came back, Bastien quit Madame Olympée's employ and the two brothers left town for a while. He is not in the least proud of what he did. He was only sixteen, Miss Lily. He was going to hang for stealing food. I'm afraid Lord Chamberlain's harsh words are what drove Bastien away."

A sob left Lily's throat. "I never judged him."

She rushed into Vivienne's arms and wept until there were no more tears left.

"Come," Vivienne said. "Let me help you and Allita with your packing."

By morning, the life-size painting of Bastien had been crated and Lily's bags had been sent on ahead. The ship sailed at four in the afternoon with Lily and Charles aboard. She made certain their berths lay at the opposite ends of the ship. He was the last person she wanted to see.

Chapter Twenty-Four

Three weeks later

At the sight of René and Felice standing on the dock watching him guide the *Aria* into port, Bastien growled out a curse. So much for bringing the ship in late and expecting to find the shipping office closed for the night. He wanted nothing more than to be left alone.

Once he'd docked the clipper, and the crew had it safely moored, Bastien strode down the gangplank, grumbled a sullen greeting, and handed the ship's log to René. "We have a new five-year contract with the Gosling Brothers. There's a full supply of rum aboard, ready for sale."

René lifted a brow. "*Merci.* And a warm hello to you as well, *mon frère.*"

Felice laughed and threw her arms around Bastien. "It's so good to see you again. Although you appear a bit gaunt."

"I don't have much of an appetite." Damn it, he wanted to be left alone. Didn't want to so much as think about the reason his stomach rejected food.

"Come inside," Felice urged. "I'll send for some food, and we'll have a chat."

Bastien shook his head. "I'm too tired to do anything but find my bed. Régine will have something at home. I'll see you in the morning."

He turned to Henri. "Run by the boarding house and alert the Kennedys they've a crew coming in. Then let the bathhouse know they'll need to heat water."

"*Oui,*" Henri said and trotted off, shooting René a speaking glance.

"I have some mail for you," Felice said.

"Anything from McGregor up in Canada?" Bastien asked.

"Not that I'm aware. Are you expecting to hear from him?"

"Thought I might." Had Bean, the slave he'd helped to escape, not made it as far as Canada? Not likely or he'd have heard something by now. His low mood sank even lower.

"Come along," Felice insisted. "You have dark circles under your eyes. And your beard needs trimming."

"Are you saying I look like hell?"

"*Oui,*" René replied, and placing a hand at Bastien's back, guided him into the office.

"Doesn't appear I have much choice, but I won't be staying long." He sat in a chair at his desk. Midnight, the shipyard's mouser, wasted no time curling around Bastien's legs, purring and leaving his ever present cat hair on Bastien's pant legs. This time, he didn't bother pushing the pesky feline away.

He glanced under René's work area and spied Miz Sassy, the dog René had saved from drowning. The fluffy little hound thumped her tail but failed to move. "That has to be the laziest damn dog I've ever seen."

Felice laughed, and leaning her elbows on Bastien's desk, reached out and tenderly swept a lock of hair off his brow. "Bastien, she's gone back to London."

His all but dead heart missed a beat. He glanced over Felice's shoulder at René, who silently watched them. "Would you do something about your meddling wife?"

René shrugged. "I happen to be her husband, not her keeper. You should know by now she's like a dog with a bone once she sets her mind on something. Or in this case, someone. I am merely standing by, ready to escort the inquisitive lady home."

Felice ignored René and gave Bastien's beard a little tug. "Go after her or you might die from loneliness."

His gut clenched. *And she wonders why I have no appetite.*

"Why do I have a feeling this is going to be a one-way chat, and you intend to hold me hostage until you've had your say?"

René chuckled. "Sounds about right."

"Hush, husband. Bastien, did you think you could walk away from a woman you love and just like that"—Felice snapped her fingers—"you'd forget all about her? I can see you already have regrets and they will only worsen."

Bastien's veneer was beginning to crack. "Damn it, Felice. I'm no good for her. And I would like to put an end to this conversation."

She ignored his request. "You are grieving the loss of the love of your life, yet you are the one who first did the leaving. Does that make any sense?"

"I departed to give her a chance to leave or stay," he growled. "Obviously, she did her own leaving."

"Perhaps she did not understand your reasoning. It pains me to see you miserable. It also pains me to know Lily is despondent. I'll never forget the abject misery on her face the day she boarded the *Cerise*. She loves you, Bastien. Go after her."

How the hell does Felice know so much? "I'm not some bloody high-ranking British lord. I am not her cup of tea."

"No, you're not. You're more her double shot of rum. Your presence makes her tipsy."

Bastien looked at the ceiling and heaved a tired sigh. "I need to go home."

René pushed his chair back from his desk and faced Felice and Bastien. "Leave him be, Felice. He doesn't want to talk about things just yet."

She waved René off. "I am not finished."

René rolled his eyes. "Of course not. You never are."

She shot him a syrupy smile. "Were I to cease my pursuit of the matter, I wouldn't be the woman you married, would I?"

She focused her attention on Bastien again. "I have one last thing to say to you."

Bastien groaned. "Thank the gods."

"The impact you and Lily had on each other astounded me. Even when the two of you stepped off the boat from Jamaica, I was immediately aware of the sheer energy connecting you."

Bastien's brows furrowed. "Even then? I was treating her illness. A *traiteur* does not become intimate with his patient."

"Pish posh. Of course, your integrity would not allow you to step over professional boundaries. Whatever the invisible force or elusive connection that exists between you two, you'd be a fool to try to pass it off as nothing but shallow attraction. Try not healing a broken heart and see how that works out."

His blood began to thrum at his temples. She was right. No matter where he sailed, for how long, he couldn't escape the truth—he needed to heal instead of continuing to lick his wounds. The devil of it was, he didn't know how to go about it.

She rubbed the small of her back. Then her eyes widened and her hand went to her expanding belly. "Oh. The babe just kicked."

René grunted. "Maybe she or he is trying to tell you something. Such as, it's time to leave well enough alone. *Oui?*"

Bastien took in the scene around him—a pesky cat Felice was attached to, a lazy hound they both spoiled, and two people who made living and working together a harmonious undertaking. Felice's hand circled her expanding belly. A soothing gesture to her unborn babe. One who was already adding another layer to their family. *Family.* His gut clenched and his blood pounded harder in his head.

Christ. He had to get out of there before he fell apart in front of them. Rising from his desk, he managed to casually drop a kiss on each of Felice's cheeks. "As it turns out, *mon frère,* for the first time, I appreciate your wife's interference. Now if you'll excuse me, I shall take myself home. I've some thinking to do."

"Do you need a ride?" René asked. "My buggy's out front."

"*Non.* I can use the walk. Stretch out these wobbly sea legs."

By the time Bastien reached Le Blanc House and greeted everyone, Régine already had a bowl of hot jambalaya and thick slices of bread on the table. "Henri came by here first, did he?"

"*Oui,*" Régine said.

Rubio leaned against the sideboard. Allita kept herself busy folding dish towels, and Vivienne polished spoons. Was it his imagination, or was everyone walking on eggshells?

Armand peeked around the corner and gave him a shy smile.

Bastien grinned. "Come sit by me, son. Did you miss me?"

"*Oui.*" Armand scrambled onto a chair. "You was gone so long, I be thinkin' you won't never be back. Can I have a bowl of jambalaya, too, Miss Régine?"

She set a bowl in front of him before he'd barely finished his sentence. "Thought you'd never ask."

Bastien made note of the improvement in Armand's diction. "Of course, I will always return, seeing as how I live here. Next time I am required to sail somewhere, how about you come along?"

Eyes widening, Armand paused his spoon in midair. "You mean dat?"

Bastien nodded. "*Oui.* Where would you like to go?"

Armand didn't hesitate. "To London to bring back Miss Lily."

Bastien didn't have to turn around to feel Régine stiffen.

Vivienne set aside the spoons and cleaning cloth and took a seat opposite Bastien. "Armand is right. Take him to London. All of us have been feeling low on account of the way you left us. And we've been miserable without Miss Lily."

Bastien slumped in his chair. "I think I might've heard this from Felice, but go ahead."

Vivienne picked up the cleaning cloth, and nervously twisting a corner, switched from English into her native Cajun French. "Miss Lily, she be miserable after you left. And when she sailed back to England, it was like a funeral took place. Your *maman*, she be mean as a snake when things don't go her way. She spoke harsh words to Miss Lily, drove her away. And Miss Lily's godfather, he used hateful words that sent you from your own home. Odalie and Lord Chamberlain, they be two people who never wed those they loved, so their own miserable circumstances colored what you and Miss Lily have together, and that's not right."

Vivienne rose from the table and looked down at him. "You are very dear to me, Cousin. You have given Régine and me a wonderful home, and we are beholden to you. We cannot stand to watch you make a mess of your life. Look me in the eye and tell me you haven't been a miserable wretch, and I will call you a liar. Now take yourself upstairs and shave off that ugly beard."

Rubio stepped forward. "*Sí*. Régine and I will wait to wed until Miss Lily returns so we can be one big family."

Allita stepped forward. "Miss Lily told me nothing you could've done in your past would ever destroy her love for you."

Bastien's stomach clenched, threatening to toss up his dinner. He had to get out of there before he not only fell apart but made a scene. He stood. "Well, I must say, I've never before come home to a reception quite like this. First René and Felice, and now all of you."

He scrubbed a hand over his heavy beard. "You're right, Vivienne. I need to shave."

As he climbed the stairs and passed by the open door leading to what had once been Lily's bedchamber, a great sense of loss descended upon him, leaving him feeling even more bereft. Did he dare go after her? Was it possible she'd have him?

His empty quarters felt unbearably lonely. He shaved his unruly beard, then used the bathing shower instead of taking a long bath, and headed for bed.

Pulling back the covers, he noticed his pillow wasn't quite right. He lifted it to find a rolled sheaf of heavy paper. Curious, he flattened it out on the bed. His whole body gave a jerk. Before him lay the charcoal drawing Lily had done of him, smudged in areas, but still an excellent depiction. He'd all but forgotten about it. He touched the page as if doing so might magically bring her back.

Could everyone be telling the truth? Did Lily love him? Would she let him into her life? Forever? Felice was right, he'd likely wither away from loneliness if he did nothing. The others were right as well—Le Blanc

House was like a funeral parlor without her presence. Hell, even quiet, unassuming Vivienne had taken a stance and lit into him.

He crawled into bed, and for the first time since he'd walked away from Lily, he wept.

* * * *

London

Bastien, Henri, and Armand stepped off the family clipper and into a needle-sharp rain that cut right to the bone. "Are you all right, Armand?"

"*Oui*," he responded, his teeth chattering so hard he could barely speak.

"I'll have you settled in the hotel in no time." Bastien waved down a hackney and squeezed the boy between Henri and himself to provide warmth. "Perhaps it wasn't such a good idea to bring you along. I forgot about the blasted English weather this time of year."

"I'm about to freeze my ass off, but it don' matter, 'cuz I be seein' our Miss Lily again."

Bastien narrowed his eyes at Armand. "Watch your tongue."

Henri chuckled. "Younger than me, yet older in his ways?"

"*Oui*," Bastien replied. "So much to be taught. So much to unlearn."

Armand grinned up at Bastien. "You be shiverin', too. Is it because you be cold? Or scared Miss Lily will turn you away?"

"Probably a little of both." He glanced down at Armand. "Sometimes you have the wisdom of an old sage."

Again, a soft chuckle could be heard from Henri's side of the carriage.

"You got the ring?" Armand asked.

"*Oui*."

"Let me see it again."

"*Non*. It might slip between my cold fingers."

At last, they reached the hotel and, with a promise from Henri never to let Armand out of his sight, Bastien climbed back into the hackney and headed for the Stanhope mansion in Mayfair, less than a mile away.

The carriage passed one grand place after another until finally, the driver halted in front of a massive stone home. Bastien climbed out, ran nervous fingers through his hair, gave a tug to his cravat and climbed the stairs.

A liveried butler answered the door and announced that Lady Liliana Stanhope would not be receiving visitors.

"Tell her Bastien Thibodeaux is here. Tell her if she refuses to see me by way of the front door, I will enter through a window."

Showing no reaction to Bastien's warning, the butler stepped back and before closing the door in Bastien's face, said, "One moment."

Less than five minutes had passed but it felt like five hours when the butler opened the door and invited him in. "If you'll wait in the parlor, Lady Liliana will join you momentarily."

Bastien paced the room, took note of the fine architectural details of the home and the expensive furnishings. Twenty minutes ticked past on the stately floor clock, and suddenly, the room became too confining. He opened the door and strode into the entry with its sweeping staircase. He glanced up and there stood Lily, one hand on the railing.

"I was on my way," she said, her eyes never leaving his as she descended the stairs, her voice like sweet music to his ears.

The very sight of her heated his blood in a way that transcended lust. He had no intention of wasting time with pleasantries. He was here to declare his love and bring her home.

She reached the bottom of the stairs, her pale green gown floating around her like a soft breeze. On closer inspection, he caught the slight flush of her skin, the liquid glow of her eyes. "My God, Lily. You are still the most beautiful woman I have ever seen."

She folded her hands together in front of her and tilted her head. "Is that what you came all this way to tell me, that you think I'm beautiful?"

He itched to touch her. He held back. Suddenly everything he'd rehearsed turned into a jumbled mess in his head. "Well, there's that, but..." He rubbed the back of his neck. "Oh, hell. I had memorized a speech but I cannot remember a damn word. I love you so goddamn much that my feelings rob me of the right words. But none would be enough anyway, so I'll leave it at this...will you marry me?"

Her fingertips covered her mouth, and her beautiful amber eyes glistened with unshed tears. Still, she spoke not a word.

Fear took a bite out of his gut. "Hell, I still can't remember what I meant to say. I'm making a terrible mess of things, aren't I?"

She dropped her hand from her mouth. Her throat moved up and down as she swallowed several times. "What else have you to say?"

"I want to give you the moon, and stars, and fields of fireflies every night..." *Damn, the words looked better on paper.* "Look, Lily. All I have to offer is me, and I am scared to death."

"Why?"

"Because you need a fire-breathing dragon to destroy anyone who tries to harm you. I fear I am not enough, but I adore the hell out of you. If you'll have me, I'll try my best to be enough, *chère*."

"How long have you felt this way?"

"Christ, I don't know. Deep down, I think I already knew something in my life was about to change the moment I laid eyes on you."

"I thought you never wished to marry."

"People can change, Lily. I've come to realize that being married and committed to one person is a beautiful thing indeed."

She could've been a statue. She was going to refuse him. He was beginning to feel sick to his stomach.

Without a word, she walked away and started up the stairs. Then she paused and looked over her shoulder, a smile lighting her face. "Are you coming?"

"What?" Frustration leaked out of him like a dark shadow spilling across the room. "What the hell just happened? Will you marry me or not?"

"Of course. My answer is yes. Not because I want to live with you, but because I've found out I cannot live without you. My answer has always been yes."

"Then why the devil did you let me blather on?"

"Because I dearly wanted to hear you say all those wonderful, silly things that only make me love you more. Are you coming?" she repeated and scampered up the stairs.

Bastien started after her, climbing two stairs at a time. When she saw him gaining on her, she squealed and ran down the corridor into her private quarters.

He strode in after her, gathered her in his arms, and set his lips to hers in a long, tender kiss. Then he touched his lips to the tip of her nose, the corners of her eyes. "You took about ten years off my life back there."

"It sure took you a long time to figure out you missed me. Waiting removed about ten years from my life as well. When did you start missing me?"

"The moment I pulled back. Thought my chest would cave in that day I walked away from you."

"And here I was beginning to think I might have to rescind my recent offer to Justin Andrews."

"What recent offer?"

"To merge Cowdrey Imports with Andrews Shipping Company whilst retaining all of my employees."

Stunned, it took him a moment to realize what such an alliance might mean. "Do you intend for us to work together? Like René and Felice?"

"Something like that."

He trailed his fingers over her lush mouth, as if doing so might capture the smile floating in her words. "I'd like a family, Lily. Perhaps a large one." She laughed. "If Felice can juggle children and running an office, surely I can as well. Remember, I oversee every aspect of my company. Have done so for years. I don't expect life with you to be all butterflies and rainbows, Bastien. Nor would I want it to be. I expect there will be challenges and hard work ahead of us. But I believe as committed partners, we have the capacity to grow through whatever life hands us, and be better people for it."

At a loss for words, he lowered his face to the soft curve of her neck and breathed in her warm, light scent while he grappled with his emotions. "You just gave me yet another glimpse into that magnificent heart of yours."

He kissed her again, then lifted her off her feet and twirled her in a circle. He paused, his gaze sliding to the fireplace and the painting above. A full-length portrait of himself, so lifelike it looked as though he could step right off the canvas. He set her down. "What in blazes is that?"

She laughed. "It's my depiction of the man I deeply love. The man I shall love forever more. Do you like it?"

He studied the portrait for a long moment. "If the summer heat is too much for you, I was thinking we could spend the season here, but that painting has to go."

"Never."

He curled a finger under her chin and lifted it. "You're quite good with a brush, you know. When did you paint this?"

"The month you were gone up north."

He lifted a brow. "That long ago? Seems I got under your skin fairly soon, then?"

"Indeed. And then you reached clear inside me, and touched my soul, else I could not have captured your essence the way I did. Which is why the portrait shall remain where it is—a symbol of the depth of my love for you."

Epilogue

Beyond the wide iron gate and gray stone steps stood St. Anne's Boarding Academy for Young Ladies, a massive three-story brick building. Bastien took a deep breath to relieve the sudden tension gripping him. Tucking Lily's gloved hand into the crook of his elbow, he gave it a squeeze, then reached for his daughter's hand.

Lisette gripped two of his large fingers and gave them a tug. Her expression was somber. "Papa?"

Startled by her trembling fingers, Bastien bent a knee and lowered himself to her level. "What is it, *pischouette?*"

"Are you and Maman going to leave me here?" Her chin quivered, and those blue eyes matching his own filled with tears.

Lily gasped and bent a knee as well. "No, darling. Papa wishes to visit the head mistress, who happens to be a special friend he hasn't seen in many years. We thought you might enjoy the outing with us."

Lisette looked at her father, trepidation still evident in her liquid gaze. "Is this true, Papa?"

"*Oui.*"

"Promise you aren't tricking me, Papa? Promise you won't leave me with strangers?"

"First of all, you know very well I would never play tricks on you or—"

"But you *do* play tricks, Papa. You make cards disappear up your sleeve."

He swallowed a grin and placed a hand over his heart, feigning shock. "Up my sleeve, you say?"

Lisette tutted. "I saw you slip one up there once."

Now he did smile. "Oh, sweetheart. Card tricks are one thing, but leaving my seven-year-old daughter alone in a foreign land wouldn't be playing a trick on you. Doing so would be a dastardly act."

"Then how come you left Etienne back in the hotel with Miss Allita? And who is this person you've come to see? And why have we come to call?"

Bastien blew out a breath as his mind searched for a simple response that wouldn't lead to a barrage of yet more questions from the little chatterbox.

Lily decided it was time to take control of the conversation. "You have the honor of coming with us because you are old enough to act the little lady, while your brother is far too young and rambunctious. Would you care to join us? Or shall we return you to the hotel? The decision is up to you."

Sweeping a rebellious blond curl off her face, Lisette studied her parents through bright blue eyes deepening to sapphire. "*Bien*," she said with a crisp nod that sent the curl flying right back across her cheek.

Bastien tucked the wayward lock behind her ear once again and, rising to his feet, tugged at her hand. "Come along."

Together, the three mounted the first of the wide flights of stairs, passed through the tall wrought-iron gate, climbed several more stairs, then marched to the double doors. Bastien took hold of a heavy golden rope and gave it a tug. The deep, mellow ringing of a large bell could be heard. He leaned to Lily's ear. "Why the devil am I so rattled?"

"You have good reason to be, dear."

Bastien pulled on the rope again.

This time the intricately carved door swung wide. A young woman, her brown hair tucked beneath a white mobcap, greeted them with a slight bow of her head. "May I help you?" she asked in a proper French accent.

Bastien nodded. "*Oui.* We have an appointment with Miss Beatrice McGregor, your head mistress."

"You must be Monsieur Thibodeaux," the girl responded. "Miss McGregor is expecting you."

"*Merci beaucoup.*" A muscle rippled along Bastien's stiff jaw.

He's rattled. Lily's heart thumped so hard she'd not be surprised if it could be heard. She gave his arm a reassuring squeeze.

"What the devil is wrong with me?" he muttered through clenched teeth as they followed the young miss. "We are merely having tea with someone I haven't laid eyes on in nine years."

"Although I've only heard about her, I confess to being a bit nervous myself."

They were ushered down a long corridor and through a set of double doors leading into the head mistress's office.

Miss Beatrice McGregor stood with her back to them before a tall stack of beveled windows overlooking an inner courtyard, her spine ramrod straight. She wore a simple but well-made dark blue gown of fine woolen crepe, its high collar and cuffs trimmed in crisp white. Her raven hair was caught at her nape in a tidy chignon.

Besides Bastien's slow, deep breaths, the ticking of a clock somewhere in the room was the only sound to reach Lily's ears.

Miss MacGregor turned to face them, a picture of refined deportment with her head held at a proud angle, her hands folded in quiet repose before her—a practice she must certainly pass on to the many students who walked these hallowed halls.

Bastien cleared his throat. "Hello, Bean."

Her eyes, black as midnight, suddenly glittered, and her lips twitched, the only sign she was emotionally moved. "Hello, Mister. It's been a long while, but you haven't changed a bit."

His breath left him in a great exhale. "But you have, Bean…may I refer to you so in private or would you prefer Beatrice McGregor?"

A smile touched her lips. "Bean is perfectly fine if I may call you Mister. I rather like your given name, Monsieur Thibodeaux, but I think I shall always think of you as Mister, the kind man of great mystery who rescued me and my babe."

He cleared his throat again. "I cannot tell you how proud I am of you."

Bean motioned to a leather chesterfield flanked on each side by two upholstered chairs. "Please, let us sit. I cannot tell you how thankful I am that you slipped me that note while my babe and I were hunkered down in that wagon."

"You had me deeply concerned when you failed to connect with the McGregors in a timely manner. I didn't know if you'd lost the note I gave you or what had occurred."

A soft smile touched her lips. "I held on to that precious piece of paper for dear life. When we neared the Ohio border, the Underground notified the driver that slave catchers were too thick to risk traveling in that direction. The driver ended up having to navigate the rugged back roads of Pennsylvania and Western New York, which is why we were delayed in reaching Canada by more than a month."

She directed her gaze to Lily. "Not only did the McGregor family take us in, they allowed us to adopt their surname. They educated me right here at St. Anne's, and here I shall remain until my daughter enters medical school in Sweden."

Her voice resonated with strength, kindness, and a slight French accent. She leaned forward and extended her hand to Lily. "Madame Thibodeaux. Or should I call you Lady Liliana?"

"Oh, please, Lily will do. What should I call you since Bastien has always referred to you as Bean?"

This elicited a smile from the woman. "While we are alone in here, why don't you call me Bean as well."

Her eyes glittered with a dampness Lily recognized as tears—tears that were ready to leak from her own eyes if she weren't careful. She glanced at Bastien and her heart caught in her throat. He was blinking fast. Too fast. She'd seen this twice, after the birth of each of his children. The man was also close to tears.

She needed to divert their attention. "Tell me how you came by the name Beatrice."

"I wanted to work Bean into a more dignified appellation, yet still feel as though I hadn't lost the name my mama gave me. Mrs. McGregor and I had a jolly time coming up with Beatrice."

Bastien nodded toward his daughter. "This is Lisette. We left our son, Etienne, in the hotel with his nanny."

Kindness washed through Bean's eyes, and a smile touched her lips. She extended her hand. "It is good to meet you, Miss Lisette. I have a daughter about your age. Her name is Harmony. Would you like to meet her?"

Lisette's eyes lit up. "*Oui!* Does she speak French? I much prefer French to English."

"As do we," Bean responded, laughter filling her eyes. "Some of the people in our little village speak only French."

She moved to her desk and rang a bell. The same young girl who'd opened the door to them entered. "Would you please fetch my daughter from her classroom?"

Lisette grabbed her father's arm, her eyes wide. "She goes to school here?"

Bastien patted her hand. "Have no fear. We are not leaving you behind."

In moments, the door flew open and a beautiful young girl with golden skin and amber eyes stepped into the room. She spoke in French. "You sent for me, Maman?"

Bean introduced the two girls and off they went to play. She looked at Bastien. "I would like to thank you for taking care of Harmony and me."

When he started to interrupt, she raised her hand, and stopped him from speaking. "I've enjoyed a good life since I arrived in Canada. None

of which would have been possible without your carrying me and Harmony
to safety, and then seeing to my education."

Bastien opened his mouth to object.

She shook her head. "I'm no fool, Mister. I know Mr. McGregor was
a bosun on your shipping line who was forced to retire because of a leg
injury. He couldn't possibly have had the means to set up the trust, pay for
my education, and provide Harmony and me with the best life a person
could hope for."

"Is it enough?" he asked. "I understand you live in an apartment here
on the upper floor. You could have your own home, if you wish."

"Heavens, no. We choose to live here where Harmony has friends. I
want the best of everything for her. She is fluent in French, Spanish, and
German. I would like to see her attend university in Sweden now that
ladies are accepted."

"Not in the United States? There are schools that accept—"

"No, Mister. Just because an emancipation took place doesn't mean
certain people have changed. She will attend school in Europe. In the end,
I want her to continue having the freedom she deserves."

There went Bastien's eyelids blinking again. "Gads, but you impress me."

Lily knew her husband…he'd had enough of reining in his emotions.
"We need to be leaving soon, dear. We've one of our ships in the harbor
waiting for us."

"Of course." Bean rang for the secretary to collect the girls. They
returned holding hands, breathless from their time on the swings, and
chattering in French.

"Papa is taking us to our home in New Orleans," Lisette said. "I've
never been there."

"We lived in England during the war between the states," Lily explained.
"After our trip to Niagara Falls, we'll stop in Boston to visit our son
Armand, who is in his first year of law school at Harvard, and then we'll
sail to New Orleans. You are welcome to visit us at any time."

Bean's back straightened and her chin lifted. "Thank you, but I shall
never return to the South. When Harmony is ready to attend university,
I shall retire from this most satisfying career and tag along as family,
wherever she sees fit."

She stood. "Come, Harmony. Let us escort our guests to the door."

Once they'd said their farewells, Lily kissed Bastien on the cheek. "Until
today, I couldn't imagine how I would ever be more impressed by the man
I married. I think I even fell a little deeper in love with you."

"Only a little?" A deep chuckle rumbled in his chest. He swept an arm around her and murmured in her ear. "I needed you with me today, *chère*. Meeting up with Bean and Harmony turned out to be more emotional than I had anticipated."

He pressed his mouth to the lobe of her ear. "However, once the children are asleep tonight, I'm going to need you even more."

The warmth of his lips against her skin, the smoky throatiness in his heated promise rolled through Lily in waves. Filled with a profound sense of contentment, she pulled away and looked up at his heart-stopping smile, at the deep blue ocean of love shining in his eyes. "Could life get any better than this?"

About the Author

Kathleen Bittner Roth creates passionate stories featuring characters faced with difficult choices, who are forced to draw on their strength of spirit to overcome adversity and find unending love.

Her own fairy tale wedding in a Scottish castle led her to her current residence in Budapest, Hungary, considered one of Europe's most romantic cities. However, she still keeps one boot firmly in Texas and the other in her home state of Minnesota.

A member of Romance Writers of America, she was a 2012 Golden Heart finalist. You can find Kathleen on Facebook, and her website at www.kathleenbittnerroth.com.

Read more about the Bayou Bad Boys in…

FELICE

Kathleen Bittner Roth

"An exciting voice in historical romance." —Anna Campbell

When beautiful shipping heiress Felicité Marielle Christiane Andrews finally returns to New Orleans after two years abroad, she does not expect to come face-to-face with the man she cannot forget—or to find him more captivating than ever. Now she must remind herself that she:

Lives a fabulous life in England
Is engaged to marry a fine man of nobility
Cannot allow the wicked Cajun back into her life…

…But indeed, she does.

Charismatic René Thibodeaux, illegitimate son of a voodoo witch, has worked hard to rise above his poverty-stricken bayou youth. He's put his thieving and womanizing days behind him and earned a high-ranking position at Felice's father's company. Seeing her again only intensifies his longing for her—and his deep remorse for his past foolishness. But despite his success, he must remind himself:

He is unworthy of Felice in every way
She is forbidden fruit
He will do anything to win her—even risk his life...

"An extremely promising writer of American historical romance."
—*Booklist* on *Josette*

"Gripped me from the opening page...kept me reading long into the night."
—Jodi Thomas on *Alanna*

"A story to be savored."
—*Publishers Weekly* on *Celine*

Printed in the United States
by Baker & Taylor Publisher Services

Printed in the United States
by Baker & Taylor Publisher Services